RED GLOVE

ALSO BY
HOLLY BLACK

THE CURSE WORKERS
White Cat
Red Glove
Black Heart

MODERN FAERIE TALES
Tithe
Valiant
Ironside

THE SPIDERWICK CHRONICLES
The Field Guide
The Seeing Stone
Lucinda's Secret
The Ironwood Tree
The Wrath of Mulgarath

BEYOND THE SPIDERWICK CHRONICLES
The Nixie's Song
A Giant Problem
The Wyrm King

The Poison Eaters: And Other Stories

THE CURSE WORKERS
book two

RED
GLOVE

HOLLY BLACK

MARGARET K. MCELDERRY BOOKS
NEW YORK   LONDON   TORONTO   SYDNEY   NEW DELHI

MARGARET K. McELDERRY BOOKS

An imprint of Simon & Schuster Children's Publishing Division

1230 Avenue of the Americas, New York, New York 10020

MARGARET K. McELDERRY BOOKS is a trademark
of Simon & Schuster, Inc.

For information about special discounts for bulk purchases,
please contact Simon & Schuster Special Sales at 1-866-506-1949
or business@simonandschuster.com.

The Simon & Schuster Speakers Bureau can bring authors
to your live event. For more information or to book an event,
contact the Simon & Schuster Speakers Bureau at 1-866-248-3049
or visit our website at www.simonspeakers.com.

The text for this book is set in Cambria.

Manufactured in the United States of America

First Margaret K. McElderry Books paperback edition April 2012

10 9 8 7 6 5 4 3 2

The Library of Congress has cataloged the hardcover
edition as follows:

Black, Holly.

Red glove / Holly Black.

p. cm.—(The curse workers ; bk. 2)

Summary: When federal agents learn that
seventeen-year-old Cassel Sharpe, a powerful
transformation worker, may be of use to them,
they offer him a deal to join them rather than
the mobsters for whom his brothers work.

ISBN 978-1-4424-0339-0 (hc)

[1. Science fiction. 2. Swindlers and swindling—Fiction. 3. Criminals—Fiction.
4. Magic—Fiction. 5. Brothers—Fiction.] I. Title.

PZ7.B52878Red 2011

[Fic]—dc22

2010031884

ISBN 978-1-4424-0340-6 (pbk)

ISBN 978-1-4424-0341-3 (eBook)

For the little white cat
that appeared on our doorstep
just after I started this series.
She lived only a short while
and she is much missed.

CHAPTER ONE

I DON'T KNOW WHETHER it's day or night when the girl gets up to leave. Her minnow silver dress swishes against the tops of her thighs like Christmas tinsel as she opens the hotel door.

I struggle to remember her name.

"So you'll tell your father at the consulate about me?" Her lipstick is smeared across her cheek. I should tell her to fix it, but my self-loathing is so great that I hate her along with myself.

"Sure," I say.

My father never worked at any consulate. He's not paying girls a hundred grand a pop to go on a goodwill tour of Europe. I'm not a talent scout for *America's Next Top Model*.

My uncle doesn't manage U2. I haven't inherited a chain of hotels. There are no diamond mines on my family land in Tanzania. I have never been to Tanzania. These are just a few of the stories my mother has spent the summer spinning for a string of blond girls in the hope that they'll make me forget Lila.

They don't.

I look up at the ceiling. I keep on staring at it until I hear my mother start to move in the adjoining room.

Mom got out of jail a couple months back. After school let out she relocated us both to Atlantic City, where we've been grifting rooms and charging up whatever food and drink we want to them. If the staff gets too demanding about payment, we simply move down the strip. Being an emotion worker means that Mom never leaves a credit card at the desk.

As I think that, she opens the door between our rooms.

"Honey," Mom says, as though it's not at all weird to find me lying on the floor in my boxers. Her black hair is up in clips and wrapped in one of her silk scarves, the way she always wears it when she sleeps. She's got on the hotel robe from the last hotel, tied tightly around her ample waist. "You ready for some breakfast?"

"Just coffee, I think. I'll make it." I push myself up and pad over to the complimentary pot. There's a bag of grounds, sugar, and some powdered creamer sitting on a plastic tray.

"Cassel, how many times do I have to tell you that it isn't safe to drink out of those things? Someone could have been brewing meth in it." Mom frowns. She always worries about the weirdest things. Hotel coffeepots. Cell phones. Never normal stuff, like the police. "I'll order us both up coffee from the kitchen."

"They could be brewing meth there, too," I say, but she ignores me.

She goes into her room and I can hear her make the call. Then she comes back to the doorway. "I ordered you some egg whites and toast. And juice. I know you said you weren't hungry, but you need to keep your strength up for today. I found us a new mark." Her smile is big enough that I almost want to smile along with her.

That's my mom.

Believe it or not, there are magazines out there called, like, *Millionaire Living* or *New Jersey Millionaires* or whatever, that feature profiles of old guys in their homes, showing off their stuff. I have no idea who else buys them, but they're perfect for my mother. I think she sees them as gold digger shopping catalogs.

That's where she found Clyde Austin. He's on the page after a feature with curse-worker-hating Governor Patton at his mansion, Drumthwacket. Despite a recent divorce, according to the article, Austin still manages to enjoy a lifestyle that includes a private plane, a heated infinity pool, and two borzois that travel with him everywhere. He has a home in Atlantic City, where he likes to go out to dinner at Morton's and play a little blackjack when he can get away from the office. The picture of him shows a short, squat dude with hair plugs.

"Put on something dirty," Mom says. She's at her desk, altering a new pair of bright blue gloves. She's seeding them with tiny holes at the fingertips: small enough to go unnoticed, big enough for her skin to touch the mark's.

"Dirty?" I say from the couch I'm slumped on in her suite. I'm on my third cup of coffee, all three choked with cream. I ate the toast, too.

"Wrinkled. Something that makes you look homeless and desperate." She begins to take down her curls, one by one. Soon she'll start rubbing gunk into her skin and curling her eyelashes. It takes her hours to get ready.

"What's the plan?" I ask.

"I posed as his secretary and pretended I forgot when his reservation was for," Mom says. "At Morton's. Wasn't it great how the magazine comes right out and says where to find him? It absolutely worked. He's going to eat there at eight o'clock tonight."

"How long have you known that for?" I ask her.

"A couple days." She shrugs, making a careful line of black above her eyes. There's no telling how long she really knew. "Oh—and grab the plastic bag over by my suitcase."

I slug down the last of the coffee and get up. The bag contains panty hose. I put them on her desk.

"They're for you."

"You want me to look homeless, desperate, but also kind of fabulous?" I ask.

"Over your head," she says, turning in her chair and miming the gesture like I'm a moron. "If Clyde works out, I want him to be able to meet you as my son."

"It sounds like you've really got some plan cooked up," I say.

"Oh, come on," she demands. "School starts in less than a week. Don't you want to have a little fun?"

Several hours later Mom clops along the boardwalk behind me in platform heels. Her white dress blows in the late summer wind. The neckline is low enough that I'm worried her boobs are going to actually fall out if she moves too fast. I know it's disturbing that I notice, but I'm not *blind*.

"You know what you're supposed to do, right?" she says.

I wait for her to catch up. She has on gold lamé gloves and is carrying a gold clutch purse. I guess she decided against the blue. Altogether it's quite an outfit. "No, why don't you tell me for the millionth time?"

I see the fury pass over her face like a storm. Her eyes go hard.

"I've got it, Mom," I say in what I hope is a conciliatory way. "Go on ahead. We shouldn't be talking."

She totters off toward the restaurant, and I walk to the railing, looking at the sea. It's the same view I had from Zacharov's Atlantic City penthouse. I think of Lila with her back to me, staring out at black water.

I should have told her I loved her back then. Back when it would have meant something.

Waiting is the hardest thing about any con job. The moments slip by and your hands start to sweat, anticipating what's coming. Your mind wanders. You're all keyed up from adrenaline, but there's nothing to do.

Distraction leads to disaster. Mom's rule.

I turn back toward the restaurant and slip my gloved hand into my pocket, touching the wadded-up piece of panty hose. I hacked off the foot with a room service knife.

I keep focused, eyeing the crowd, watching my mother vamp up her incredibly slow stroll. We could be here awhile. And, honestly, this plan might not even work. That's another thing about cons; you have to go after a bunch of marks before you find the perfect one. The one you can really take for all he's worth.

We wait for twenty minutes, almost a block apart from each other. Mom has done all the innocent things someone does on a nighttime stroll: smoked a cigarette, checked her lipstick, made fake calls on the cell phone she borrowed from me. I, on the other hand, have taken to begging for change. I've made about $3.50 and am about to land another quarter when Clyde Austin lurches out of Morton's.

Mom starts to move.

I jump up and take off toward her, yanking the panty hose down over my face. That slows me down some, because there is no way in hell these things are sheer. I can barely see.

People start yelling. Yeah, because a guy with hose over his head is never the good guy. He is, in fact, the stereotype—maybe even the archetype—of a bad guy.

I keep running, flying past my mother and yanking the gold clutch out of her hand.

She adds her screams to the chorus.

"Thief!" my mother screams. "Help! Heeeeelp!"

Now, this is the tricky part. I have to keep running, but I have to run just slowly enough that a drunk and out-of-shape guy with a couple of martinis rolling around in his belly actually thinks he can catch me.

"Please—someone!" Mom shrieks. "He has all my money!"

It's really hard not to laugh.

I practically run into Clyde, making sure he's got a shot at me. But I've got to give it to Mom. She's right when she says that guys want to be knights in shining armor. He grabs for my arm.

I let myself fall.

It's a bad one. Maybe it's the panty hose over my face, or maybe I'm just off balance, but I go down hard on the asphalt, scraping one hand so roughly, I can feel my glove shred. I'm pretty sure I scrape my knees, too, but all they feel is numb.

I drop the purse.

Clyde clocks me in the back of the head before I can push myself to my feet. It hurts. She better appreciate this. Then I'm up and running. Full out. Pulling that crap off my face and hurling myself through the night as fast as I can.

Leaving Clyde Austin to be a hero, bringing a damsel in distress her golden clutch purse.

Leaving him to notice how charming she is when her eyes well up with gratitude.

Leaving him to check out her rack.

*   *   *

Mom is exultant. She breaks out the bottle of Prosecco from the minibar while I pour frothing hydrogen peroxide over my hand. It stings like crazy.

"He wants to meet for drinks tomorrow night. I told him it was the least I could do to take him out. He said that, after what I'd been through, he was going to pay, and that was that. Now, doesn't that sound promising?"

"Sure," I tell her.

"He's going to pick me up here. At six. Do you think I should be ready when he gets here or do you think I should invite him in for a drink while I do a few last little things? Maybe be in my robe?"

I make a face. "I don't know."

"Stop thinking of it that way. This is a job. We need someone to provide for us. Pay for your fancy school—and Barron's loans. Especially now that Philip can't be sure how long he's going to stay employed." She cuts me a dark look, like I somehow forgot that I'm the one that got him in trouble with the boss of a crime family. Like I am going to start caring. They've done much worse to me.

"So long as you don't work Clyde," I say quietly. "You don't need to. You're plenty charming on your own."

She laughs and pours her Prosecco into a water glass. It fizzes like the peroxide. "Like mother, like son. We're both charming when we want something. Right, Cassel?"

"So I want you to stay out of jail," I say. "So what? Is that supposed to be a secret?"

The doorbell of her room buzzes. "What did you order?" I ask her, and head over to open it.

Mom makes a sound of alarm, but she's too late.

Clyde Austin is standing in the hallway, a bottle of Jack Daniel's swinging from one hand. "Oh," he says, embarrassed. "I must have the wrong room. I thought—"

Then he gets a good look at me—at the blood on my jeans, the scrape on my bare hand. And he sees my mother sitting on the bed. And he knows. His face goes ugly.

"You set me up," he says. "You and her." The way he says "her" tells me everything he's thinking about us.

I start to explain, when he swings the bottle at my head. I see it moving, but I am too clumsy, too slow. It makes a hollow, horrible thunk against my temple.

I hit the carpet, dizzy. Dull pain makes me nauseous. That's what I get for underestimating the guy. I roll onto my back just in time to see him over me, raising the Jack Daniel's to strike again.

With a shriek Mom rakes her nails against his neck.

He whirls around, wild, swinging. His elbow connects. She flies back against the desk. Her magnifying mirror cracks against the wall, the shards falling like glittering confetti.

I reach up my bare hand. I could stop him with a single touch.

I could change him into a cockroach.

I could transform him into a puddle of grease.

I really want to.

Clyde has gone still, though, looking around like he suddenly doesn't know where he is. "Shandra?" he says gently, reaching for my mother. "I'm so sorry. Did I hurt you?"

"That's okay," Mom says in a soothing voice, getting up slowly. She winces. There's blood on her lip. "You just came by to bring me a little liquor, didn't you? And you saw my son. Maybe you mistook him for someone else."

"I guess," he says. "We got along so well that I figured why wait until tomorrow night? And then . . . He does look like the mugger, you have to admit."

Mom's an emotion worker. She can't change his memories; my brother Barron could do that, but he's not here. What Mom can do with a single bare-handed touch is make Clyde Austin like her so much that he's willing to give her the benefit of the doubt. About anything. Everything. Even this.

A wave of dizziness overwhelms me.

"That's true, baby," she says. "He does look a little like the mugger. It was an honest mistake. I'm just going to walk you to the door now." Her fingers go to his neck, which should make anybody flinch—bare fingers, no glove—but it doesn't bother him at all. He lets himself be steered.

"I'm really sorry for what happened," he says. "I don't know what came over me."

"I understand," Mom tells him. "And I forgive you, but I don't think that we can see each other tomorrow night. You get that, right?"

Shame heats his face. "Of course."

My vision blurs. She says something else soothing, but not to me.

*   *   *

We check out in the morning. Sunlight makes my brain feel like it's throbbing inside my skull. Sweat slicks my skin—the kind of unnatural sweat that comes along with injury. Each movement makes me as dizzy as riding a thousand roller coasters all at once. While we wait for the valet to get my car, I fumble through my backpack for sunglasses and try to avoid looking at the dark bruise on Mom's shoulder.

She's been totally silent since she told me we were leaving—all through packing and even the ride down in the elevator. I can tell she's seething.

I feel too sick to know what to do about it.

Finally my ancient and rusted Benz drives up to the front of the hotel. Mom hands something to the driver and gets the keys while I slide in on the other side. The seat is hot on the backs of my legs, even through jeans.

"How could you answer the door like that?" she shouts as soon as we pull away from the curb. "Not looking through the peephole. Not calling out to ask who was there?"

I flinch at her voice.

"Are you stupid, Cassel? Didn't I teach you better than that?"

She's right. It was thoughtless. Stupid. Private school has made me careless. It's exactly the kind of dumb mistake that separates a decent con man from an amateur. Plus the blowback from the emotion work makes her unstable. Not that she isn't normally pretty unstable. But working magnifies it. So does anger. There's nothing for me to do but ride it out.

I was used to her being like this when I was a kid. But she's been in jail long enough for me to forget how bad she can get.

"Are you stupid?" she screeches. "Answer me!"

"Stop," I say, and lean my head against the window, shutting my eyes. "Please stop. I'm sorry, okay?"

"No," she says, her voice vicious and certain. "No one's that pathetic. You did it on purpose! You wanted to ruin things for me."

"Oh, come on," I say. "I wasn't thinking. I said I was sorry. Look, I'm the one with the goose egg to show for it. So we have to leave Atlantic City? We'd have to leave in a week anyway when I went back to school."

"You did this to me because of Lila." Her gaze is on the road, but her eyes glitter with fury. "Because you're still angry."

Lila. My best friend, who I thought I killed.

"I'm not talking about her," I snap. "Not with you."

I think about Lila's wide, expressive mouth turning up at the corners. I think about her spread out on my bed, reaching for me.

With one touch of her hand, Mom made Lila love me. And made sure I could never, ever have her.

"Hit a nerve?" Mom says, gleefully cruel. "It's amazing you actually thought you were good enough for Zacharov's daughter."

"Shut up," I say.

"She was *using* you, you stupid little moron. When everything was said and done, she wouldn't have given you the time of day, Cassel. You would have been a reminder of Barron and misery and nothing more."

"I don't care," I say. My hands are shaking. "It would still have been better than—" Better than having to avoid her until the curse fades. Better than the way she'll look at me once it does.

Lila's desire for me is a perversion of love. A mockery.

And I almost didn't care, I wanted her so much.

"I did you a favor," my mother says. "You should be grateful. You should be thanking me. I got you Lila on a silver platter—something you could have never in your life had otherwise."

I laugh abruptly. "I should be thanking you? How about you hold your breath until I do?"

"Don't talk that way to me," Mom roars, and slaps me, hard.

Hard enough that my battered head hits the window. I see stars. Little explosions of light behind the dark glasses. Behind my eyelids.

"Pull over," I say. Nausea overwhelms me.

"I'm sorry," she says, her voice seesawing back to sweet. "I didn't mean to hurt you. Are you okay?"

The world is starting to tilt. "You have to pull over."

"Maybe right now you'd rather walk than deal with me, but if you're really hurt, then you better—"

"Pull over!" I shout, and something about the urgency of my tone finally convinces her. She steers the car abruptly onto the shoulder of the road and brakes hard. I stumble out while we're still moving.

Just in time to heave my guts up in the grass.

I really hope no one at Wallingford wants me to write an essay on how I spent my summer vacation.

CHAPTER TWO

I PARK MY BENZ IN THE seniors' lot, which is much closer to the dorms than where underclassmen are forced to leave their cars. I feel a little smug until I shut off the engine and it makes an odd metallic cough, like maybe it just gave up the ghost. I get out and kick the front tire halfheartedly. I had a plan to fix up the car, but with Mom home I never quite got around to it.

Leaving my bags in the trunk, I walk across campus toward the Finke Academic Center.

Over the doorway of the large brick building hangs a hand-lettered sign: WELCOME FRESHMEN. The trees rustle with a light wind, and I am overcome with a feeling of nostalgia for something I haven't yet lost.

At a table inside, Ms. Noyes is looking through a box of cards and giving out orientation packets. A few sophomores I don't know too well are shrieking and hugging one another. When they see me, they quiet down and start whispering instead. I overhear "kill himself" and "in his underwear" and "cute." I walk faster.

At the desk a blotchy, trembling girl and her father are picking up dorm keys. She clings to his hand like she'd be lost without it. This is clearly the first time the girl has spent any time away from home. I feel sorry for her and envy her all at once.

"Hey, Ms. Noyes," I say when it's my turn. "How's it going?"

She looks up and smiles. "Cassel Sharpe! I am so pleased you'll be living on campus again." She gets me my manila folder and room assignment. In addition to the exclusive parking lot and, bizarrely, a stretch of grass—no, really, it's called "senior grass"—seniors also get the best dorm rooms. It looks like mine is on the ground level. I guess they're a little leery of me on a high floor after that whole almost-falling-off-a-roof thing.

"Me too." And I am glad to be back. I really, really am. "Has Sam Yu checked in yet?"

She flips through the cards. "No, you beat him."

Sam has been my roommate since we were sophomores, but it wasn't until the end of last year that we got to be friends. I'm still not really good at friendship, but I'm trying.

"Thanks. See you later," I say. There's always an assembly on the first night before classes start. Headmistress Northcutt and Dean Wharton tell us that we're intelligent, capable young men and women, and then proceed to lecture us about how only the school rules keep us safe from ourselves. It's a good time.

"Try to stay out of trouble," she says with a grin. Her voice is teasing, but there's a firmness there that makes me think she doesn't say this to all incoming students.

"Absolutely," I say.

Back in the parking lot I start unloading the car. There's a bunch of stuff. Mom spent Labor Day weekend pretending we'd never had a fight and buying me extravagant presents to make up for that fight we never had. I am now the owner of a new iPod, a leather bomber jacket, and a laptop. I'm pretty sure I saw her paying for the laptop with Clyde Austin's credit card, but I pretended not to notice. Mom packed my bags for me too, on her working theory that no matter what I say I want, she knows what I'll actually need. I repacked them as soon as she was out of the room.

"You know I love you, right, baby?" Mom asked this morning as I was leaving.

The weird thing is, I do know.

When I get to my new dorm room—bigger than the one we had last year, plus the ground floor means I don't have to haul all my crap up a million flights of stairs—I dump everything on the floor and sigh.

I wonder where Lila is right now. I wonder if her father shipped her off to some Swiss Boarding School for worker crime family kids, some place with armed guards and high gates. I wonder if she likes it. Maybe the curse has already worn off and she's just sitting around, sipping hot chocolate and chatting up ski instructors. Maybe it would be safe to call her, just to talk for a few minutes. Just to hear her voice.

I want to, so badly that I force myself to call my brother Barron instead, just to remind me what's real. He told me to call once I settled in, anyway. I figure this is settled enough.

"Hey," he says, picking up after only one ring. "How's my favorite brother?" Every time I hear his voice, I get the same knot in my stomach. He made me into a killer. He used me, but he doesn't remember that. He thinks that we're thick as thieves, hand in glove. All the things I made him think.

Blowback ate away so many of his memories that he believes the fake ones I carefully forged into his notebooks— the ones of us being close. And that makes him the only person I'm sure I can trust.

Pathetic, right?

"I'm worried about Mom. She's getting worse," I say. "Reckless. She can't get caught again, or she's going to jail forever."

I'm not sure what he can do. It's not like I did such a good job of keeping her out of trouble in Atlantic City.

"Oh, come on." He sounds bored and a little drunk. I hear soft music in the background. It's not even noon. "Juries love her."

I'm pretty sure he's missing the point. "Just, please— she's not careful. Maybe she'll listen to you. You were going to be the lawyer—"

"She's an old lady," Barron says. "And she's been locked up for years. Let her have some fun. She needs to blow off steam. Seduce old dudes. Lose money at canasta."

I laugh, despite myself. "Just keep an eye on her before she takes those old dudes for everything they've got."

"Roger dodger. Mission heard and accepted," he says, and I find myself relaxing. Then he sighs. "Have you talked to Philip recently?"

"You know I haven't," I say. "Every time I call, he hangs up on me, and there's nothing I can—"

The doorknob starts to turn.

"Let me call you later," I say quickly. It's too weird to be talking to Barron and pretending everything is normal in front of my roommate, who knows what Barron's done. Who'd wonder *why* I would call Philip. Who doesn't understand what it means to have a family as messed up as mine.

"Peace out, little brother," Barron says, and hangs up.

Sam walks in, duffel bag over his shoulder. "Hey," he says with a shy smile. "Long time, no see. How was Toronto?"

"There was supposed to be an ice castle," I say. "But it melted."

Yeah, I lied to him about where I spent the summer. I didn't have to—there was no really good reason not to tell him I went to Atlantic City, except it didn't seem like a place normal people go with a parent. I told you I'm no good at this friends thing.

"That's too bad." Sam turns to put an aluminum tool-box on the rickety wooden dresser. He's a big guy, tall and round. He always seems to move carefully, like someone who is uncomfortable with taking up too much space. "Hey, I got some new stuff you're going to love."

"Oh, yeah?" I unpack the way I usually do—by shoving everything under my bed until room inspection. That's what happens when you grow up in a garbage house; you feel more comfortable with a little squalor.

"I have a kit to make molds of teeth and craft really perfect fangs. Like, *perfect*. They fit over your teeth as if they were tiny little gloves." He looks happier than I remember him. "Daneca and I went into New York—to this special effects warehouse, and cleaned the place out. Resins. Elastomer. Poly foams. I could probably fake setting someone on fire."

I raise my eyebrows.

"Hey," he says. "After last year I figured I'd better be prepared."

Carter Thompson Memorial Auditorium is the place where, every year, all the students gather to listen while the rules are repeated for anyone too lazy to read the handbook. "Boys must wear the Wallingford jacket and tie, black dress pants, and a white shirt. Girls must wear the Wallingford jacket, a black skirt or black dress pants, and a white shirt. Both boys and girls should wear black dress shoes. No sneakers. No jeans." Fascinating stuff like that.

Sam and I try to grab a seat in the back, but Ms. Logan, the school secretary, spots us and points out an empty row in the front.

"Boys," she says. "We're trying to be an example to all the new students, now that we're seniors, aren't we?"

"Can't we be bad examples?" Sam asks, and I snort.

"Mr. Yu," says Ms. Logan, pressing her lips together. "Senioritis is a serious condition this early in the year. Lethal. Mr. Sharpe, I would appreciate it if you didn't encourage him."

We move to the new seats.

Dean Wharton and Headmistress Northcutt are already up at the lectern. Northcutt starts off with lots of rah-rahing about how we're all one big family here at Wallingford, how we support one another through the hard times, and how we'll look back on our years here as among the best of our lives.

I turn to Sam to make some crack and notice him scanning the auditorium. He looks nervous.

The problem with being a con artist is that it's hard to turn off the part of your brain that's always assessing the situation, looking for a mark, a sucker you can sucker out of stuff. Trying to figure out what that mark wants, what's going to convince him to part with his money.

Not that Sam's a mark. But my brain still supplies me with the answer to what he's looking for, in case it comes in useful.

"Everything okay with you and Daneca?" I ask.

He shrugs his shoulders. "She hates horror movies," he says finally.

"Oh," I say as neutrally as I can.

"I mean, she cares about really important stuff. About

political stuff. About global warming and worker rights and gay rights, and I think she thinks the stuff I care about is for kids."

"Not everyone's like Daneca," I say.

"No one is like Daneca." Sam has that slightly dazed look of a man in love. "I think it's hard for her, you know. Because she cares so much, and most people barely care at all. Including me, I guess."

Daneca used to annoy me with all her bleeding-heart crap. I figured there was no point in changing a world that didn't want to be changed. But I don't think that Sam would appreciate me saying that out loud. And I don't even know if I believe it anymore.

"Maybe you could change her mind about the horror genre," I say instead. "You know, show her some classic stuff. Rent *Frankenstein*. Do a dramatic reading of 'The Raven.' Ladies love 'Get thee back into the tempest and the Night's Plutonian shore! Leave no black plume as a token of that lie thy soul has spoken!' Who can resist that?"

Sam doesn't even smile.

"Okay," I say, holding up my hands in the universal sign of surrender. "I'll stop."

"No, it's funny," he says. "It's not you. I just can't—"

"Mr. Yu! Mr. Sharpe," Ms. Logan says, coming up the center aisle to sit right behind us. She puts her finger to her lips. "Don't make me separate you."

That thought is humiliating enough that we're quiet through Dean Wharton's long list of things we will be punished for—a list that ranges from drinking, drugs, and being caught in the dorm room of someone of the opposite sex, to skipping class, sneaking out after hours, and wearing black lipstick. The sad truth is that there is probably at least one person in each graduating class who's managed to break all the rules in a single wild night. I am really hoping that, this year, that person is not going to be me.

I don't look all that good in lipstick.

Daneca finds us on the way to dinner. She's got her curly brown hair divided into seven thick braids, each one ending in a wooden bead. The collar of her white dress shirt is open, to show seven jade amulets—protection against the seven types of curse work. Luck. Dreams. Physical. Emotion. Memory. Death. Transformation. I gave her the stones for her last birthday, just before the end of junior year.

Amulets are made by curse workers of the type the amulet is supposed to protect against. Only stone seems able to absorb magic, and even then it will work only once. A used stone—one that has kept a curse from its wearer—cracks instantly. Since there are very few transformation workers in the world—perhaps one a decade—real transformation amulets are rare. But Daneca's transformation amulet is the real thing. I know; I made it myself.

She has no idea.

"Hey," she says, bumping her shoulder against Sam's arm. He puts his arm around her.

We walk into the cafeteria like that.

It's our first night back, so there are tablecloths and a rose with some baby's breath in little vases on all the tables. A few parents of new students hang around marveling at the high paneled ceiling, the stern portrait of Colonel Wallingford presiding over us, and our ability to eat food without smearing it all over ourselves.

Tonight's entree is salmon teriyaki with brown rice and carrots. For dessert, cherry crumble. I poke at my carrots. Daneca starts with dessert.

"Not bad," she pronounces. And with absolutely no segue she launches into an explanation of how this year it's going to be really important for HEX to get out the word about proposition two. About some rally happening next week. How prop two augurs a more invasive government, and some other stuff I tune out.

I look over at Sam, ready to exchange a conspiratorial glance, but he is hanging on her every word.

"Cassel," she says. "I know you're not listening. The vote is in November. This November. If proposition two passes, then workers are going to be tested. Everyone will be. And no matter how much the government of New Jersey says it is going to keep that information anonymous, it's not. Soon workers are going to be refused jobs, denied housing, and locked up for the crime of being born with a power they didn't ask for."

"I know," I say. "I know all that. Could you try to be a little less condescending? *I know.*"

She looks, if possible, even more annoyed. "This is your life we're talking about."

I think of my mother and Clyde Austin. I think of Barron. I think of me and all the harm I've done. "Maybe workers *should* all be locked up," I say. "Maybe Governor Patton is right."

Sam frowns.

I shove a big hunk of salmon into my mouth so I can't say anything else.

"That's ridiculous," Daneca says after she recovers from her shocked silence.

I chew.

She's right, of course. Daneca's always right. I think of her mother—a tireless advocate and one of the founders of the worker-rights youth group, HEX—and of Chris, that poor kid staying at her house, with nowhere else to go and maybe no legal reason to be allowed to stay. His parents kicked him out because they thought workers were all like me. There are workers who aren't con artists, workers who don't want anything to do with organized crime. But when Daneca thinks of workers, she thinks of her mother. When I think of workers, I think of mine.

"Anyway," Daneca says, "there's a rally next Thursday, and I want the whole HEX club to go. I got Ms. Ramirez, acting as our adviser, to apply for buses and everything. It's going to be a school trip."

"Really?" Sam says. "That's great."

"Well." She sighs. "It's not *exactly* a go. Ramirez said that Wharton or Northcutt would have to approve her request. And we'd have to get enough HEX members to sign up. So, can I count on you guys?"

"Of course we'll go," says Sam, and I level a glare in his direction.

"Whoa," I say, holding up my hand. "I want more details. Like does this mean we have to make our own signs? How about 'Worker Rights for Everyone Except People Who Don't Need Them' or 'Legalize Death Work Today. Solve Overpopulation Tomorrow!'"

The corner of Sam's mouth lifts. I can't seem to stop myself from being a jerk, but at least I'm amusing someone.

Daneca starts to say something else, when Kevin LaCroix comes up to the table. I look at him with undisguised relief. Kevin drops an envelope into my messenger bag.

"That stoner dude, Jace, says he hooked up with someone over the summer," Kevin whispers. "But I hear all the pictures he's showing around are really pictures of his half sister. Fifty bucks says there's no girlfriend."

"Find someone to bet that he *did* hook up or does have a girlfriend, and I'll give you odds," I say. "The house doesn't bet."

He nods and heads back to his table, looking disappointed.

I started being the school bookie back when Mom was in jail and there was no way I could afford all the little stuff that doesn't come with the price of tuition. A second uniform so that the one you had could get washed more than once a week, pizza with your friends when they wanted to go out, plus sneakers and books and music that didn't fall off a truck somewhere or get shoplifted out of a store. It isn't cheap to live near the rich.

After Kevin LaCroix leaves, Emmanuel Domenech drops

by. I get enough traffic to keep Sam and Daneca from being able to point out how obnoxious I've been. They spend their time writing notes back and forth in Daneca's notebook as other students casually turn over envelope after envelope— each one, a brick rebuilding my tiny criminal empire.

"I bet Sharone Nagel will get stuck wearing the mascot fur suit to football games."

"I bet the Latin club will sacrifice one of its members at the spring formal."

"I bet Chaiyawat Terweil will be the first person to get called into Headmistress Northcutt's office."

"I bet the new girl just got out of a loony bin."

"I bet the new girl just broke out of a prison in Moscow."

"I bet Mr. Lewis will have a nervous breakdown before winter break."

I note down each bet for and against these in a code I created, and tonight Sam and I will calculate the first master list of odds. They'll change as we get more bets, of course, but it gives us something to tell people at breakfast if they want to know where to throw their cash. It's amazing how rich kids get itchy when they can't spend money fast enough.

Just like criminals get itchy when we're not working all the angles.

As we get up to go back to our rooms, Daneca punches my arm. "So," she says. "Are you going to tell us why you're such a moody bastard tonight?"

I shrug. "I'm sorry. I guess I'm just tired. And an idiot."

She reaches up to put her gloved hands around my neck and mock-chokes me. I play along, falling to the floor and pretending to die, until she finally laughs.

I'm forgiven.

"I knew I should have brought a blood packet," Sam says, shaking his head like we're humiliating him.

It is at that moment that Audrey walks by, hand in hand with Greg Harmsford. Audrey, who was once my girlfriend. Who dumped me. Who, when we were dating, made me feel like a normal person. Who I could have, maybe, once, convinced to take me back. Who now doesn't even look at me as she passes.

Greg, however, narrows his eyes and smiles down at me like he's daring me to start something.

I'd love to wipe that smug expression off his face. First, though, I'd have to get up off my knees.

I don't get to spend the rest of the night putting away my stuff or joking around in the common lounge like I planned, because our new hall master, Mr. Pascoli, announces that all seniors have to meet with their guidance counselors.

I have seen Ms. Vanderveer exactly once a year for all the time I have been at Wallingford. She seems nice enough, always prepared with a list of which classes and activities are most likely to get me into a good college, always full of suggestions for volunteer work that admission committees love. I don't really feel the need to see more of her than I already have, but Sam and I, along with a group of other upperclassmen, trudge across the grounds to Lainhart Library.

There, we listen to another speech—this one on how senior year is no time to slack off, and if we think things are hard now, just wait until we get to college. Seriously, this guy—one of the counselors, I guess—makes it sound like in college they make you write all your essays in blood, your lab partners might shank you if you bring down their grade point averages, and evening classes last all night long. He clearly misses it.

Finally they assign us an order for the meetings. I go sit in Vanderveer's section, in front of the screen that's separating her from the rest of us.

"Oh, man," Sam says. He sits at the very edge of his chair, leaning over to whisper to me. "What am I going to do? They're going to want to talk about colleges."

"Probably," I say, scooting closer. "They're guidance counselors. They're into colleges. They probably *dream* of colleges"

"Yeah, well, they think I want to go to MIT and major in chemistry." He says this in a tragic whisper.

"You can just tell them that you don't. If you don't."

He groans. "They'll tell my parents."

"Well, what *is* your plan?" I ask.

"Moving to LA and going to one of the schools that specializes in visual effects. Look, I love doing the special effects makeup, but most stuff today is done on a computer. I need to know how to do that. There's a place that does a three-year program." Sam runs his hand through his short hair, over his damp forehead, like he has just confessed an impossible and possibly shameful dream.

"Cassel Sharpe," Ms. Vanderveer says, and I stand.

"You'll be fine," I say to him, and head behind the screen. His nervousness seems to be contagious, though. I can feel my palms sweat.

Vanderveer has short black hair and wrinkly skin covered in age spots. There are two chairs arranged in front of a little table where my folder is sitting. She plops herself into one. "So, Cassel," she says with false cheerfulness. "What do you want to do with your life?"

"Uh," I say. "Not really sure." The only things I am really good at are the kinds of things colleges don't let you major in. Con artistry. Forgery. Assassination. A little bit of lockpicking.

"Let's consider universities, then. Last year I talked about you choosing some schools you'd really like to try for, and then some safety schools. Have you made that list?"

"Not a formal, written-down one," I say.

She frowns. "Did you manage to visit any of the campuses you are considering?"

I shake my head. She sighs. "Wallingford Preparatory takes great pride in seeing our students placed into the world's top schools. Our students go on to Harvard, Oxford, Yale, Caltech, Johns Hopkins. Now, your grades aren't all we might hope for, but your SAT scores were very promising."

I nod my head. I think of Barron dropping out of Princeton, about Philip dropping out of high school to take his marks and work for the Zacharovs. I don't want to wind up like them. "I'll start that list," I promise her.

"You do that," she says. "I want to see you again in a week. No more excuses. The future's going to be here sooner than you think."

When I walk out from behind the divider, Sam isn't there. I guess that he's having his conference. I wait a few minutes and eat three butterscotch cookies they have put out as refreshments. When Sam still doesn't emerge, I stroll back across campus.

The first night in the dorms is always strange. The cots are uncomfortable. My legs are too long for them and I keep falling asleep curled up, then straightening in the night and waking myself when my feet kick the frame.

One door over, someone is snoring.

Outside our window the grass of the quad shines in the moonlight, like it's made of metal blades. That's the last thing I think before I wake up to my phone shrilling the morning alarm. From a look at the time, it seems like the alarm has been ringing for a while.

I grunt and throw my pillow at my sleeping roommate. He raises his head groggily.

Sam and I shuffle to the shared bathroom, where the rest of the hall are brushing their teeth or finishing their showers. Sam splashes his face with water.

Chaiyawat Terweil wraps a towel around himself and grabs a pair of disposable plastic gloves from the dispenser. Above it, the sign reads: PROTECT YOUR CLASSMATES: COVER YOUR HANDS.

"Another day at Wallingford," Sam announces. "Every

dorm room a palace, every sloppy joe a feast, every morning shower—"

"You enjoy your showers a lot, do you?" Kyle Henderson asks. He's already dressed, smoothing gel into his hair. "Think about me while you're in there?"

"It does make a shower go faster," Sam says, undaunted. "God, I love the Wall!"

I laugh. Someone whips a towel at Sam.

By the time I'm clean and dressed, I don't really have enough time for breakfast. I drink some of the coffee our hall master has brewed for himself in the common room, and eat raw one of the Pop Tarts Sam's mother sent.

Sam gives me a dark look and eats the other.

"We're off to a good start," I say. "Fashionably late."

"Just doing our part to keep their expectations low," says Sam.

Despite having spent the whole summer going to bed around this time in the morning, I feel pretty good.

My schedule says that my first class today is Probability & Statistics. This semester I also have Developing World Ethics (I thought Daneca would be pleased I chose that for my history requirement, which is why I haven't told her), English, Physics, Ceramics 2 (laugh if you must), French 4, and Photoshop.

I am studying the slip of paper as I head out of Smythe House and walk into the Finke Academic Center. Probability & Statistics is on the third floor, so I make for the stairs.

Lila Zacharov is walking through the hallway in the Wallingford girl's uniform: jacket, pleated skirt, and white oxford shirt. Her short blond hair shines like the woven gold of the crest. When she sees me, the expression on her face is some kind of mingled hope and horror.

I can't even imagine my own face. "Lila?" I say.

She turns away, head down.

In a few quick steps I've grabbed hold of her arm, like I'm afraid she's not real. She freezes at the touch of my gloved hand.

"What are you doing here?" I ask, turning her roughly toward me, which is maybe not an okay way to behave, but I'm too astonished to think straight.

She looks like I slapped her.

Good job, me. I'm a real charmer.

"I knew you'd be mad," she says. Her face is pale and drawn, all her usual ruthlessness washed from it.

"It's not about that," I say. But for the life of me, in that moment, I have no idea what it *is* about. I know she's not supposed to be here. And I know I don't want her to leave.

"I can't help—," she says, and her voice breaks. Her face is full of despair. "I tried to stop thinking about you, Cassel. I tried all summer long. I almost came to see you a hundred times. I would sink my nails into my skin until I could stay away."

I remember sitting on the steps in my mother's house last March, begging Lila to believe she'd been worked. I remember the slow way the horror spread over her features. I remember her denials, her final defeated agreement that we shouldn't see each other until the curse ended. I remember everything.

Lila's a dream worker. I hope that means she's sleeping better than I am.

"But if you're here—," I start, not sure how I can finish.

"It hurts not to be near you," she says quietly, carefully, like the words cost her something. "You have no idea how much."

I want to tell her that I have some idea what it feels like to love someone I can't have. But maybe I don't. Maybe being in love with me really is worse than I can imagine.

"I couldn't keep—I wasn't strong enough." Her eyes are wet and her mouth is slightly parted.

"It's been almost six months. Don't you feel any different?" The curse should have begun to fade, surely.

"Worse," she says. "*I feel worse.* What if this never stops?"

"It will. Soon. We have to wait this thing out, and it's better if—," I start, but it's hard to concentrate on the words with her looking at me like that.

"You liked me before," she says. "And I liked you. I *loved* you, Cassel. Before the curse. I always loved you. And I don't mind—"

There is nothing I want more than to believe her. But I can't. I don't.

I knew this conversation would happen, eventually. No matter how much I tried to avoid it. And I know what I have to say. I even planned it out, knowing that otherwise I couldn't say the words. "I didn't love you, though. And I still don't."

The change is immediate and terrible. She pulls back from me. Her face looks pale and shuttered. "But that night in your room. You told me that you missed me and that you—"

"I'm not *crazy*," I say, trying to keep my tells to a minimum. She's known a lot of liars. "I said whatever I thought would make you sleep with me."

She takes a quick, sharp breath of air. "That hurts," she says. "You're just saying it to hurt me."

It's not supposed to hurt. It's supposed to disgust her. "Believe what you want, but it's the truth."

"So why didn't you?" she asks. "Why don't you? If all you wanted was some ass, it's not like I'm going to say no. I can't say no to you."

The bell rings somewhere, distantly.

"I'm sorry," I say, which isn't part of the script. It slips out. I don't know how to deal with this. I know how to be the witness to her grief. I don't know how to be this kind of villain.

"I don't need your pity." Dots of hectic color have appeared on her cheeks, like she's running a fever. "I'm waiting the curse out at Wallingford. If I'd told my dad what your mother did, she'd be dead by now. Don't forget it."

"And me with her," I say.

"Yeah," she says. "And you with her. So get used to the idea that I'm staying."

"I can't stop you," I say quietly as she turns away from me and heads for the stairs. I watch the way the shadows move down her back. Then I slump against the wall.

I'm late for class, of course, but Dr. Kellerman only raises his bushy eyebrows as I slink in. I missed the morning announcements on the television suspended over the blackboard. Members of the AV club would have explained what lunch was going to be and when after-school clubs were meeting. Not exactly thrilling stuff.

Still, I'm glad Kellerman decides not to give me a hard time. I'm not sure I could take it.

He resumes explaining how to calculate odds—something I am pretty good at, being a bookie and all—while I concentrate on trying to stop my hands from shaking.

When the intercom on the wall crackles to life, I barely notice it. That is, until I hear Ms. Logan's voice: "Please send Cassel Sharpe to the headmistress's office. Please send Cassel Sharpe to the headmistress's office."

Dr. Kellerman frowns at me as I stand up and gather my books.

"Oh, *come on*," I say ineffectually to the room.

A girl giggles.

One thing's in my favor, though. Someone just lost the first bet of the year.

CHAPTER THREE

HEADMISTRESS NORTH-cutt's office looks like a library in a baronial hunting lodge. The walls and built-in bookcases are polished dark wood and lit by brass lamps. Her desk is the size of a bed and is made of the same wood as the walls, with green leather chairs resting in front of it, and degrees hanging behind it. The whole thing is designed to be intimidating to students and reassuring to parents.

When I'm shown in, I see Northcutt is the one that looks uncomfortable. Two men in suits are standing beside her, clearly waiting for me. One has dark sunglasses on.

I check for bulges under their arms or against their calves. Doesn't matter how custom the suit is, the fabric pulls a little over most guns. Yeah, they're carrying. Then I look at their shoes.

Black and shiny as fresh-poured tar, with rubbery flexible soles. Made for running after people like me.

Cops. They're cops.

Man, I am so screwed.

"Mr. Sharpe," Northcutt says. "These men would like to have a conversation with you."

"Okay," I say slowly. "About what?"

"Mr. Sharpe," says the white cop, echoing Northcutt. "I'm Agent Jones, and this is Agent Hunt."

The guy in sunglasses nods once in my direction.

Feds, eh? Well, federal agents are still cops to me.

"We understand that we're interrupting your school day, but I'm afraid what we have to talk about is sensitive enough that we can't discuss it here, so—"

"Wait a moment," Northcutt interrupts. "You cannot take this student off campus. He's underage."

"We can," says Agent Hunt. He's got a slight accent. Southern.

Northcutt flushes when she realizes he's not going to say more than that. "If you walk out of here with that boy, I will contact our lawyer immediately."

"Please do," Agent Hunt says. "I'd be happy to talk with him."

"You haven't even told me what this is about," she says in an exasperated tone.

"I'm afraid that's classified," says Agent Jones. "But it has to do with an ongoing investigation."

"I don't suppose *I* have a choice?" I ask.

Neither agent even bothers to answer. With a slight pressure against my back, Agent Jones steers me out of the room, while Agent Hunt gives Northcutt his card, just in case she wants to follow up with that lawyer.

I see her face as we leave. Northcutt's not calling anyone. Someone should warn her never to play poker.

They bundle me into the backseat of a black Buick with dark tinted windows. My mind is running through all the bad things this could be about. Clyde Austin's credit card and my hot laptop come to mind. Plus there's all the hotel employees who let us slide. And God only knows what else Mom has done.

I wonder if the Feds would believe that Austin assaulted me, although the bump on my head is nearly gone. I wonder if there's a way to convince them I'm the one who's responsible for whatever crimes we're talking about. I'm still underage. At seventeen I'd probably get sentenced like a kid. Most of all, I wonder what I can give up that will make them leave my mother alone.

"So," I say experimentally. "Where are we going?"

Agent Hunt turns to me, but with his sunglasses on it's impossible to read his expression. "We have some confidential materials to share with you, so we're taking you to our resident agency in Trenton."

"Am I under arrest?"

He laughs. "No. We're just having a little chat. That's all."

I glance at the doors. It's hard to tell if I could flip the lock myself and jump. Trenton's a big enough city for traffic. Stop and go. Red lights. They can't take the highway straight to the building. If I could get the door open, I could probably run for it. Use my phone. Warn someone. Grandad, probably. He'd know what to do.

I shift closer to the door and snake my fingers toward the lock. I press the window button instead. Nothing happens.

"Do you want the air turned up?" Agent Jones asks, amusement in his voice.

"It's stuffy in here," I say, defeated. If the window controls don't work, there's no way a lock will.

I watch the scrubby landscape slide by until we come to the bridge. TRENTON MAKES, THE WORLD TAKES, it says in big block letters. Then we go over it. We take a couple of turns and park behind an innocuous office building. We go in the back way, one of agents standing on either side of me.

The hallway is tan-carpeted and sterile. All the doors have keypads above the locks. Otherwise it looks like a dentist might rent space here. I don't know what I was expecting, but not this.

We go into an elevator and come out on the fourth floor. The carpet is the same.

Agent Jones punches in a code and twists the doorknob. The con artist part of my brain thinks that I should be memorizing numbers, but I'm not that good. His finger is a blur of movement, and all I get is that he might have hit the number seven once.

We go into a windowless room with a cheap table and

five chairs. There's an empty coffeepot on a sideboard and a mirror—probably two-way—on the wall.

"You've got to be kidding," I say, nodding toward the mirror. "I watch television, you know."

"Hold on," says Agent Hunt. He goes out, and a moment later the lights go on in the other room, turning the mirror to tinted glass. The room beyond the mirror is empty.

Agent Hunt comes back. "See?" he says. "It's just the three of us."

I wonder if he's counting anyone listening to us via whatever recording devices are in the room, but I decide not to push my luck. I want to know what's going on.

"Okay," I say. "You got me out of class. I appreciate that. What can I do in return?"

"You're a character," Agent Jones says, shaking his head.

I study him as best I can, while trying to look bored. Jones is built like a barrel—short and solid, with thinning light brown hair the color of bread. There's a scar at the edge of his narrow upper lip. He smells like aftershave and stale coffee.

Agent Hunt leans in. "You know, most innocent people get upset when they get picked up by the Feds. They demand to see their lawyer, tell us that we're violating their civil liberties. Only criminals are calm like you."

Hunt is longer and leaner than Jones. He's older, too, his short-cropped hair dusted with gray. When he speaks, his voice has the cadences of someone used to speaking to a congregation. I'd bet there's a preacher somewhere in his family.

"Psychologists say that's because subconsciously criminals want to get caught," Agent Jones says. "What do you think about that, Cassel? Do you want to get caught?"

"Sounds like someone's been reading too much Dostoyevsky." I shrug.

Agent Hunt's lip curls a little. "Is that what they teach you at that private school of yours?"

"Yeah," I say. "That's what they teach me." Hunt's contempt is so obvious that I add a mental note about him to my imaginary profile: *He thinks I have it easy, which means he thinks he had it hard.*

"Look, kid," Agent Jones says, clearing his throat. "It's no picnic, leading a double life. We know about your family. And we know you're a worker."

I freeze, my whole body going stiff and still. I feel like my blood just turned to ice.

"I'm not a worker," I say. I have no idea how convincing I sound. I can feel my speeding heartbeat all the way to my skull.

Agent Hunt opens the folder on the table and pulls out a couple of sheets of paper. They look familiar. It takes me a moment to realize they're exactly like the papers I swiped from the sleep clinic, except these have my name across the top. I am looking at my own test results.

"Dr. Churchill sent these to one of our contacts after you ran out of his office," Agent Jones says. "You tested positive. You're hyperbathygammic, kid. But don't tell me you didn't know that already."

"There wasn't enough time," I say numbly. I think of

how I ripped all of the electrodes off my skin after I figured out what the test was for, how I ran out of the office.

"Apparently," says Agent Hunt, understanding me perfectly, "there was."

Mercifully, after that they offer to get me some food. They leave me alone in a locked room with a piece of paper charting my gamma waves. It means nothing to me, except that I am well and truly screwed.

I take out my cell phone and flip it open before I realize that this is probably exactly what they hope I will do. Call someone. Reveal something. The room is definitely wired; it's set up for interrogation, whether they're using the two-way mirror or not.

There are probably hidden cameras, too, now that I think of it.

I flip through the functions on my phone until I get to the one that lets me take pictures. I turn on the flash, aim at the walls and ceiling, and take picture after picture until I get it. A reflection. Pretty invisible when I was just looking at the frame of the mirror, but the tiny lens glows brightly with reflected light, captured in the photo.

I grin and pop a stick of gum into my mouth.

Three chews and it's soft enough to stick over the camera.

Agent Hunt comes in about five seconds later. He's holding two cups of coffee, and he's obviously been rushing. The cuff of his shirt is wet and stained with sloshed liquid. I bet he burned his hand too.

I wonder what he thought I was going to do, once I

was hidden from the camera. Try to escape? I have no idea how to get out of the locked room; I was just showing off. Letting them know I wasn't going to fall for the really obvious stuff.

"Do you think this is a joke, Mr. Sharpe?" he demands.

His panic doesn't make any sense. "Let me out of here," I say. "You said I'm not under arrest, and I'm missing ceramics class."

"You're going to need a parent or guardian to pick you up," he says, placing the coffees on the table. He's no longer flustered, which means they planned for me to ask to be let go. He's back to a script he knows. "We can certainly get your mother to come down and get you, if that's really what you want."

"No," I say, realizing I've been outmaneuvered. "That's okay."

Now Agent Hunt just looks smug, wiping his sleeve with a napkin. "I thought you'd see it my way."

I pick up one of the coffees and take a sip. "And you didn't even have to spell your threat out. Honestly, I must be some kind of model prisoner."

"Listen, smart-ass—"

"What do you want?" I ask. "What is all of this for? Fine, okay, I'm a worker. So what? You've got no proof that I've ever worked anyone. I'm not a criminal until I do, and I'm not gonna." It's a relief to tell a lie this big; I feel like I'm daring them to contradict it.

Agent Hunt doesn't look happy, but he doesn't seem suspicious, either. "We need your help, Cassel."

I laugh so hard that I actually choke on the coffee.

Agent Hunt is about to say something else when the door opens and Agent Jones comes in. I have no idea what he's been doing all this time, but the lunch they promised is nowhere in sight.

"I hear you've been a handful," Agent Jones says. Either he was watching the camera feed or someone told him about my little trick, because he glances over at the gum.

I try to stop coughing. It's hard. I think some of the coffee went down the wrong pipe.

"Listen, Cassel, there's lots of kids like you," Agent Hunt says. "Worker kids who fall in with the wrong element. But your abilities don't have to lead you in that direction. The government has a program to train young workers to control their talents and to use them in the cause of justice. We'd be happy to recommend you."

"You don't even know what my talents are," I say. I really, really hope that's true.

"We employ all different types of workers, Cassel," says Agent Jones.

"Even death workers?" I ask.

Agent Jones regards me closely. "Is that what you are? Because it would be very serious if it were true. That's a dangerous ability."

"I didn't say that," I say, hoping that I sound unconvincing. I don't care if they think I'm a death worker like my grandfather. I don't care if they think I'm a luck worker like Zacharov, a dream worker like Lila, a physical worker like Philip, a memory worker like Barron, or an emotion worker like Mom. So long as they don't guess that I'm a transformation worker. There hasn't been one in the United States since the 1960s, and I am sure that if the government happened to stumble on one now, they wouldn't just let him go back to high school.

"This program," Agent Jones goes on. "It's run by a woman—Agent Yulikova. We'd like you to meet her."

"What does that have to do with you needing my help?" I ask.

This whole setup feels like a con. The way they're acting, the grim glances they share when they think I don't notice. I'm sure their generous offer to let me be part of some secret government training program is part of the shakedown, what I'm not sure about is why they're shaking *me* down.

"I know you have some familiarity with the Zacharov crime family, so there's no point in denying it," Agent Jones begins, holding up his hand when I start to speak. "You don't need to confirm it either. But you should know that over the past three years, Zacharov's been stepping up assassinations both in and out of his organization. Mostly we don't get too worked up about mobsters killing one another, but one of our informants was the most recent target."

A creeping dread chills my skin as he puts a black-and-white photograph down on the table in front of me.

The man in the photo has been shot several times in the chest, and his shirt is a mess of black. He's lying on his side. Blood has soaked into the carpet underneath him, and his loose hair partially obscures his face. Still, it's a face I would know anywhere.

"He was shot sometime last night," says Agent Hunt. "The first bullet penetrated between the seventh and eight ribs and entered his right atrium. He died instantly."

I feel like someone punched me in the gut.

I push the picture back toward Agent Jones. "What are you showing me this for?" My voice shakes. "That's not Philip. That's not my brother."

I'm standing, but I don't even remember getting up.

"Calm down," Agent Hunt says.

There is a roaring in my ears like a tide coming in. "This is some kind of trick," I shout. "Admit it. Admit that this is a trick."

"Cassel, you have to listen to us," Agent Jones says. "The person who did this is still out there. You can help us find your brother's killer."

"You've just been sitting here chatting with me, and my brother's *dead*? You knew my brother was dead and you just let me—you let me . . . ," I stammer. "No. No. Why would you do that?"

"We knew it would be hard to talk with you after you found out," Agent Jones says.

"Hard to talk to me?" I echo, because the words don't make sense. And then something else strikes me, something that doesn't make sense either. "Philip was your informant? He would never do that. He hates snitches."

Hated. Hated snitches.

In my family going to the cops is cowardly, despicable.

Cops already can do whatever they want to workers—
we're criminals, after all—so going to the cops is kissing
the ass of the enemy. If you turn someone in, you're not
just betraying the people around you. You're betraying
what you are. I remember Philip talking about someone in
Carney who'd reported on somebody else for some petty
reason—old guys I didn't know. He spat on the floor whenever he said the man's name.

"Your brother came to us about five months ago,"
Agent Hunt says. "April of this year. Said he wanted to
change his life."

I shake my head, denying what has to be true. Philip
must have gone to the Feds because he had nowhere else
to go. Because of me. Because I thwarted his plan to assas-
sinate Zacharov, a plan that would have resulted in Philip's
closest friend leading the crime family. A plan that would
have gotten my brother riches and glory. Instead I got him
killed; if Philip is dead, Zacharov must be behind it. I can't
think of anyone else with a reason. And what would Zacharov care about his promise to leave my family alone, especially if he was faced with the discovery that Philip made a
deal with the Feds? I was an idiot for believing Zacharov's
word was worth anything.

"Does my mother know Philip's dead?" I finally manage, throwing myself back down into a chair. I feel like I
could suffocate on guilt.

"We've managed to keep it quiet," Agent Jones says. "As
soon as you leave here, she'll get the call. And we won't be
much longer. Try to hang in there."

"There's a kitten poster like that." My voice doesn't sound like my own.

They both look at me oddly.

I feel suddenly so overwhelmingly tired that I want to put my head down right there on the table.

Agent Jones goes on. "Your brother wanted to get out of organized crime. All he needed from us was to get a hold of his wife so he could apologize for what he put her through. We were going to send them into witness protection together. As soon as we got them into the program, he said that he'd give up everything he had on Zacharov's hatchet man. Maybe bring down Zacharov along with him. The guy's real bad news. Philip gave us the names of six workers this sicko killed. We didn't even know for sure they were dead, but Philip was going to lead us to the bodies. Your brother really was trying to turn over a new leaf, and he died for it."

I feel like they're talking about a stranger.

"You find Maura?" I ask.

Maura lit out of town last spring, their kid in tow, once she discovered that Barron had been changing her memories. He'd made her forget every fight she'd had with Philip and remember only some kind of sweet dreamlike relationship. But not remembering their problems didn't stop those problems from cropping up again and again. Plus, being worked that often results in bad side effects, like hearing music that's not there.

Philip was devastated when she left. He blamed me more than Barron, which I don't think is entirely fair, although I guess in the end I gave her the charm that let her realize what was going on. Still, I refuse to feel guilty about breaking up his marriage.

I've got enough to feel guilty about already.

Agent Jones nods. "We talked to her today. She's in Arkansas. We contacted her for the first time about a week ago, and she agreed to hear your brother out; first step was gonna be getting them on the phone together. Now she says she won't come back, not even to claim the body."

"What do you want me to do?" I ask. I just want this to be over.

"Philip told us enough that we think you have access to information. Information we need," says Agent Hunt. "You know some of the same people that he did—and you have connections to the Zacharov family that he never had."

He means Lila. I'm almost sure of it.

"That's not—," I start, but Jones cuts me off.

"We've been hearing about Zacharov making people disappear for years. Just poof! Nothing. No body. No evidence. We still don't know how he—or his wetworks guy—did it. Please, just look at some of the cases. See if there's something familiar. Ask around. Your brother was our first big break. Now he's dead." Jones shakes his head with regret.

I grit my teeth, and after a moment he looks away, like maybe he realizes that was a jackass thing to say. Like maybe, to me, my brother was a human being.

Like maybe if I start looking around, I'll wind up dead too.

"Are you even trying to find who killed Philip?" I ask, since they seem fixated on Zacharov.

"Of course we are," says Agent Jones. "Finding your brother's murderer is our number one priority."

"Any leads on this case are going to point us directly at his killer," Agent Hunt says, standing. "Just to show you we're on the level, I want you to see what we've already got." Reluctantly I follow him out into the hall and then through a door into the observation room behind the mirror. He presses a button on some video equipment.

"This is sensitive material," says Agent Jones, looking at me like he expects me to be impressed. "We're going to need you to be a smart kid and keep this information under wraps."

On a small screen my brother's condo complex comes to life in full color. It's evening, the sun glowing from the edge of the building as it slips below the tops of the trees. I can see the heat shimmer on the asphalt of the driveway. I can't quite see his unit, but I know it's just to the right of the frame.

"The complex put in these surveillance cams recently," Agent Hunt says quietly. "There was a break-in or something. The angle's terrible, but we were able to get this footage from last night."

A figure in a dark coat passes in front of the camera, too close and too fast for the film to register much. The camera is pointed too low to get a glimpse of the face, but a few thin fingers of a leather glove are visible at the hem of a billowing black coat sleeve. The glove is as red as newly spilled blood.

"That's all we have," Agent Hunt says. "Nobody else in or out. It looks like a woman's coat and a woman's glove. If she's Zacharov's regular hatchet guy, shooting isn't her usual method of killing. But lots of death workers turn to nonworker techniques after they lose too many body parts to blowback. That's usually how they trip themselves up. Of course, she could be a new recruit Zacharov sent out blind, just someone to get a job done with no obvious connection to the organization."

"So you've basically got no idea," I say.

"We believe that the person responsible for the murders found out that Philip was going to finger him. Or *her*. When Philip came to us, asking to make a deal, we asked other informants about him. We know he had a falling-out with Zacharov and we know it had something to do with Zacharov's daughter, Lila."

"Lila didn't do this," I say automatically. "Lila's not a death worker."

Jones sits up straighter. "What kind of worker is she?"

"I don't know!" I say, which comes out sounding like the obvious lie that it is. Lila is a dream worker, a really powerful one. Powerful enough to make dreamers sleepwalk out of their own houses. Or dorm rooms.

Hunt shakes his head. "All we know is that the last person to enter Philip's apartment was a woman with red gloves. We need to find her. Let *us* focus on that. You can help by getting us the information that Philip died trying to impart. Don't let your brother's death be in vain. We are certain those disappearances and your brother's death are linked."

It's very moving, the speech. Like I'm really supposed to believe that Philip's last wish was for me to square him with the Feds. But the vision of the woman entering his apartment haunts me.

Agent Jones holds out some folders. "These are the names your brother gave us—the men he swore were killed and disposed of by Zacharov's guy. Just look the pages over and see if anything jumps out at you. Something you might have overheard, someone you might have seen. Anything. And we'd appreciate it if you didn't show these files to anyone else. It serves both our interests if this meeting never happened."

I stare at the tape where he's paused it, like somehow I should recognize the person. But she's just a blur of cloth and leather.

"The school already knows I went for a ride with you," I say. "Northcutt knows."

Agent Hunt smiles. "We don't think that your headmistress will be a problem."

A terrible thought occurs to me, but I quash it before I can even articulate it to myself. I would never hurt Philip.

"Does this mean I'm working for you?" I ask, forcing myself to smirk.

"Something like that," Agent Jones says. "Do a good job, and we'll recommend you to come aboard with Agent Yulikova. You'll like her."

I doubt that. "What if I don't want to go to this training program?"

"We're not like the Mafia," Agent Hunt says. "You can get out any time you want."

I think of the locked door of the room, the locked car doors. "Yeah, sure."

They drive me to Wallingford, but by the time I am back on campus, classes are half over. I don't bother going to lunch. I head to my room, tuck the folders under my mattress, and wait for the inevitable summons from the hall master.

We're so sorry, he's going to say. *We're so sorry.*

But I'm sorriest of all.

CHAPTER FOUR

PHILIP'S FACE LOOKS LIKE it's made of wax. Whatever they did to preserve it for the viewing gives his skin an odd sheen. When I go up to the casket to say my final good-byes, I realize they have painted the visible parts of him with some flesh-colored cosmetic. If I look closely, I can see traces of bloodless skin they missed—behind his ears, and in a stripe above his gloves below the cuff of his sleeves. He's wearing a suit Mom picked out, along with a black silk tie. I don't recall him wearing either one in life, but they must have come from his closet. His hair has been pulled back into a sleek ponytail. The high collar of his shirt mostly obscures the necklace of keloid scars that mark him as a gangster. Not that there's anyone in this room who doesn't know what his job was.

I kneel in front of his body, but I have no words for Philip. I don't want his forgiveness. I don't forgive him.

"Did they take out his eyes?" I ask Sam when I get back to my seat. The room is filling up fast. Men in dark suits, sipping from breast-pocket flasks; women in black dresses, their shoes as pointed as knives.

Sam looks at me, surprised by the question. "Probably, yeah. They probably use glass." He blanches a little. "And fill the body with disinfecting fluid."

"Oh," I say.

"Dude, I'm sorry. I shouldn't have told you that."

I shake my head. "I asked."

Sam is dressed a lot like Philip. I'm wearing my father's suit, the one that had to be dry-cleaned to get rid of Anton's blood. Morbid, I know. It was that or my school uniform.

Daneca comes up to us, looking like she's masquerading as her mother in a navy sheath and pearls.

"Do I know you?" I ask.

"Oh, shut up," she says automatically. Then, "Sorry, I didn't—"

"Everyone has to stop saying they're sorry," I say, maybe a tiny bit too loudly.

Sam looks around the room in a slightly panicked way. "Uh, I don't know how to tell you this, but *all* these people are going to tell you that. That's, like, pretty much the point of funerals."

The corner of my mouth lifts. Having them around makes everything a little better, even this.

The funeral director comes in with another mountain of flowers, Mom trailing him. She's crying, mascara bleeding down her face theatrically as she points to the spot where he's allowed to put the arrangement. Then, seeing Philip's body for about the tenth time, she lets out a small shriek and half-collapses into a chair, sobbing into her handkerchief. A small group of women rushes over to comfort her.

"Is that your *mother*?" Daneca asks, fascinated.

I'm not sure what to say. Mom's putting on a show, but that doesn't mean she's not actually sad. It's just that she isn't letting her grief get in the way of her performance.

"That's our mom over there, all right," a slightly bored voice says from behind me. "It's kind of a miracle we weren't knocking over drugstores in our diapers."

Daneca jumps like she's been caught shoplifting.

I don't have to turn around. "Hello, Barron."

"Dani, right?" he says, giving Daneca a predatory smile as he takes a seat next to me. I find it a hopeful sign that he actually remembers her—maybe he's been staying away from doing much memory work—but I also am suddenly conscious of the danger I have put Daneca and Sam in just by letting them come here. These people are not safe to be around.

"I'm Sam Yu." Sam extends his hand, leaning over so that he's in front of Daneca.

Barron shakes it. His suit is a lot nicer than mine, and

his dark hair is clipped, short and tidy. He looks like the good boy he's never been. "Any friends of my baby brother's are friends of mine."

A minister walks up to the lectern off to one side and then says a couple of words to my mother. I don't recognize him. Mom's not exactly the religious type, but she hugs him like she's ready to be baptized with the next bowl of water she comes across.

A few moments later she yells loudly enough to be heard clearly above the pumped-in elevator music. I have no idea what set her off. "He was murdered! You tell them that! You put that in your sermon. You tell them there's no justice in the world."

On cue, Zacharov sweeps into the room. He's wearing another of his long black coats, this one draped over the shoulders of his suit. His fake Resurrection Diamond glints at his throat, the pin stabbed into the loop of his tie. His eyes are as hard and cold as the chip of glass.

"I can't believe he had the nerve to come here," I say softly, standing. Barron touches my arm in warning.

Beside Zacharov is Lila. It's the first time I've seen her since our disastrous conversation in the hallway at Wallingford. Her hair is damp with rain and she's all in black except for red lipstick so bright that the rest of her fades away. She's all mouth.

She sees me, and then her gaze goes to Barron. Stone-faced, she takes a seat.

"Someone better tell that daughter of mine to pipe down," Grandad says, pointing at my mother as if we might think he had some other daughter here. "I could hear her all the way to the street." I didn't notice him come in, but he's here, shaking out his umbrella and frowning at Mom. I let out my breath all at once, I'm so relieved.

He tousles my hair like I'm a little kid.

The minister clears his throat at the lectern and everyone slowly moves to sit down. Mom is still moaning. As soon as the minister starts speaking, she begins to wail so loudly that I can't hear most of his sermon.

I wonder what Philip would think of his own funeral. He'd be sad that Maura couldn't even bother to bring his son to see him for the last time. He'd be embarrassed by Mom and probably pissed that I'm even here.

"Philip Sharpe was a soldier in God's army," says the minister. "Now he marches with the angels."

The words echo in my head unpleasantly.

"Philip's brother, Barron, will join me at the lectern and say a few words about his beloved departed sibling."

Barron walks to the front and begins telling a story about him and Philip climbing a mountain together and the various meaningful things they learned about each other along the way. It's touching. It's also completely plagiarized from a book we had when we were kids.

I decide it's time I swipe someone's flask and go sit outside.

I find a good spot on the stairs. Across the hall a different viewing is going on. I can just hear the blur of voices in the room, not quite as loud as Barron's voice. I lean back and look up at the ceiling, at the twinkling lights of the crystal chandelier.

This is the same funeral home where we had my dad's viewing. I remember the mothball smell of it, the overly heavy brocade of the curtains, and the flocked wallpaper. I remember the funeral director who looked the other way when envelopes of ill-gotten cash were quietly passed to the grieving widow. The place is outside of the town of Carney—it's the one that a lot of workers use. After we're done here, we'll go over to the Carney cemetery, where Dad and Grandma Singer are already resting. We'll put some of the flowers on their graves. Maybe we'll see who-ever's in the next room there too; curse working has a high mortality rate.

My most vivid memory from Dad's funeral is seeing Aunt Rose for the first time in years. As I stood in front of Dad's casket, I answered her "How are you doing?" with "Good" before I even realized what she meant. It was just what you said to that question, automatic. I remember how her lip curled, though, like I was a terrible son.

I felt like one.

But I was a much better son than I was a brother.

Zacharov walks out of the viewing, carefully closing the door behind him. For a moment Barron's voice swells and I hear the words "we will always remember Philip's unusual balloon animals and his skill with the longbow."

Zacharov has a small smile on his face, and his thick sil-ver eyebrows are raised. "I am learning some very interest-ing things about your brother."

I stand. Maybe I have nothing good to say about Philip, maybe I have no apologies for him, but there is one thing I can do. The least I can do. I can hit the guy who killed him.

Zacharov must notice the look on my face, because he holds up both his gloved hands in a gesture of peace. I don't care. I keep coming.

"We had a deal," I say, lifting my fisted hand.

"I didn't murder your brother," he says, stepping back, out of my range. "I came here to pay my respects to your family and to tell you I had nothing to do with this."

I walk toward him. It gives me dark pleasure to watch him flinch.

"Don't," he says. "I had nothing to do with Philip's death, and you'd realize it if you thought about it for more than a minute. You're much more valuable to me than revenge on some underling. And you're not stupid. You are well aware how valuable you are."

"You sure about that?" I ask.

I hear the echo of Philip's words from months back. *You obviously didn't grow out of stupid.*

"Tell me, how is it that your mother isn't accusing me? Not even Barron. Not even your grandfather. Would they let me walk in here if they really thought I was responsible for Philip's death?" I can see a muscle in his jaw jump, he's clenching his teeth so hard. If I hit him right now, his stiffness would make the blow hurt worse. He obviously hasn't been in a fistfight in a long time.

My hand's shaking with violence. I slam it into a vase sitting near the doorway. The vase shatters; thick chunks of pottery, water, and flowers rain on the carpet.

"You're not sorry Philip's dead," I say finally, breathing heavily with raw fury that's only starting to abate. I don't know what to think.

"Neither are you," Zacharov says, his voice steely. "Don't tell me you're not sleeping better at night with him gone."

In that moment I hate Zacharov more than I ever have. "You're doing a really bad job of convincing me not to punch you."

"I want you to come work for me. Really work for me," says Zacharov.

"No deal," I say, but it makes me realize that by losing Philip, Zacharov has lost half his hold over me. More, even, because if I can't trust him to keep his promises, then all his future threats become hollow. If he tells me I've got to do something "or else" and the "or else" happens even if I go along with him, there's not much motivation for me to do what he says. Philip's death cost him leverage, and as I realize that, I start to believe he's actually not responsible. I'm valuable to him; it's not often that a crime lord gets a transformation worker practically dumped into his lap.

Zacharov inclines his head toward a curtained alcove, one where people are supposed to go to hide their weeping. I follow him uncertainly. He sits down on the long bench. I stay standing.

"You're ruthless, and I don't frighten you," he says quietly. "Both these things I like, though I would like it more if the latter was tempered with a little respect. You are the best kind of killer, Cassel Sharpe, the kind that never has blood on his hands. The kind that never has to sicken at the sight of what he's done, or come to like it too much."

I am chilled to the bone.

"Come work for me, Cassel, and you'll have my protection. For your brother. For your mother. For your grandfather, although I consider him one of mine already. My protection and a very comfortable life."

"So you want me to—," I start, but he cuts me off.

"Philip's death shouldn't have happened. If I'd had people in place, watching over him, it wouldn't have happened. Let me look out for you. Let your enemies become mine."

"Yeah, and vice versa. No, thanks." I shake my head. "I don't want to be a killer."

He smiles. "You may turn our colleagues into living things, if that helps you sleep at night. They will be just as effectively removed."

"That's not going to happen," I say, thinking of the white cat watching me with shining eyes.

"It has happened. Maybe Barron made you forget what you did, but now you remember. You proved that when you undid one of your own curses."

"That was *your daughter* whose curse I undid," I say.

Zacharov takes a sharp breath, and then lets it out slow. "It happened, Cassel. You know how to work. And one of these days, you're going to find yourself in a position where it's going to be tempting. And then more than tempting; there's going to be no other way out. Wake up. You're one of us."

"Not yet," I say. "Not quite." Which is about all I can cling to.

"You will think about my offer," he says. "You'll think about it when you realize there are people close to you that you will have to deal with eventually."

"You mean Barron," I say, amazed. "You're a son of a bitch to imply at one brother's funeral that I would think about killing the other."

Zacharov rises and dusts off his pants. "I'm not the one who thought of him." Then he smiles. "But you're right— I'm a son of a bitch. And someday you're going to need me."

Then he goes back in to the service.

Lila finds me. I'm staring at the fabric of the bench, wondering how many people have wept on it. I'm wondering about whether the inside is crusted with salt, like a blanket that's been soaking in seawater. I'm going a little crazy.

"Hey," she says, holding out a cup of coffee, her mouth still bright as blood. "One of Philip's friends is giving the eulogy now. I think he's telling the story of the first time they held up a liquor store."

I take the cup. I think the only thing I've eaten in the past three days has been coffee. I should be bouncing off the walls. Maybe that explains my nearly attacking her father. "You should go back to the viewing. I'm not—I *can't*—" I shake my head to indicate the enormity of the things I can't do. For one, I can't tell her the truth about my feelings for her. For another, I'm not sure I can keep lying.

I want you so much that I would do almost anything to have you.

Please let me not be willing to do this.

"We used to be friends," she says. "Even if there was nothing else."

"We're still friends," I say automatically, because I really want it to be true.

"Well, good, then." She sits down next to me on the bench. "I don't want you to be mad that I'm here. I'm not going to jump you or anything."

I snort. "My virtue is safe, eh? Well, thank goodness for that."

She rolls her eyes.

"No—I understand why you came. It must be good to see him dead." I think of Zacharov's words about sleeping better at night, even if I steadfastly refuse to apply them to myself. "You must feel safer."

She gapes at me like she can't believe I just said those words. Then she laughs. "It's hard to be a girl again—a human girl with hands and feet and clothes and school. Hard to talk when I'm out of practice. And sometimes I feel—" She stops herself.

"Yeah?"

"Like—I don't know. This is your brother's funeral. We should be talking about *your* feelings."

I take a long, grateful swallow of the coffee. "Honestly, that's the last thing I want to do."

"I can be very comforting," she says with a small, wicked smile.

"Hey—my virtue, remember? Come on, tell me what you were going to say."

She kicks the wall lightly with one of her shiny black pumps. I can see her big toe through the opening in the front. The nail is painted a deep shining blue. "Okay. Do you ever feel so angry that you think you could devour the whole world and still not be satisfied? Like you don't know how to stop feeling that way and it scares you, but that just makes you angry too?"

"I thought we weren't going to talk about my feelings," I say, trying for lightness, because I know exactly what she means. It's like she was speaking my own thoughts aloud.

She looks at the floor, the corner of her lip tilted up. "I'm not."

"Yeah," I say slowly. "Yeah."

"Some days I just hate everything." She looks at me earnestly.

"Me too," I say. "Especially today. I just don't know how to feel. Philip. I mean, we weren't close, obviously. Now that I think back on it, was he ashamed of using me like he did? Was that why he couldn't look me in the face? But then, when it was over, it was him who couldn't forgive me. We could have called it even—okay, not really even, but even enough, but it was like he couldn't face anything he'd done and somehow I was the enemy. Like I wasn't even human to him anymore. Like I wasn't his brother."

I should shut up, but I don't. "And now you. You were the only real friend I had for years. I mean, I had friends at school, but then Mom would mess things up or pull us out of school for some con she was running, or those friends would find out about me being from a family of workers, and that would be that. But you. There was a time when I could tell you anything—and then I thought I killed you, and now when I have you back, I can't—You're—She took—"

Lila leans forward swiftly. Her lips are soft on my cheek.

I close my eyes. Her breath is warm and it would only take the smallest shift of my mouth, just a slight acquiescence, for us to be kissing. Kissing Lila would wash away my grief and pain and guilt. It's all I want in the world.

"You're going to get all the things you think you can't have," she says quietly, reaching out to rub red lipstick from my cheek. "You just don't know it yet."

I sigh at the touch of her glove.

After the eulogies are finished, Grandad steers me toward a black limousine. I slide in, next to my mother, who is already drinking from the minibar. Something brown, out of a heavy-bottomed glass. Barron slides in after me.

We're quiet, riding. I hear the clink of ice cubes, the exhalation of a single ragged breath. I close my eyes.

"I don't know what to do with all of Philip's things," Mom says suddenly. "Maura's not coming to get them. We'll have to put it all in his old room at the house."

Grandad groans. "I just cleaned that place out."

"You two better box everything up after the police are finished," Mom says, ignoring Grandad, her voice threatening hysteria. "His son might want them someday."

"His son's not going to want them," Barron says wearily.

"You don't know that." She goes to pour herself more booze from the bar, but the limo hits a bump and the liquor splashes her dress. She starts to cry, not the loud keening from before but quiet sobs that shake her whole body.

I grab some napkins and try to blot the spill. She pushes my hand away.

"You don't know," she says to Barron through her tears. "Look at Cassel. That's his father's suit."

"Yeah, and it's a million years out of style," says Barron.

I shrug, playing along.

Grandad grins. "It's going to be all right, Shandra," he says.

Mom shakes her head.

"Save the kid from looking like Cassel there," says Barron. "Throw the stuff out. Besides, I got a line on a guy in Princeton looking to buy a painting. I need a roper. We'll buy a dozen silk suits."

Mom sniffs and slugs back the rest of her drink.

The burial takes place in the rain. Barron and I share an umbrella, which means that water constantly streams down the back of my neck. Barron puts his arm over my shoulders and I lean against him for a moment, like he really is my older brother who wants to protect me. The ceremony is subdued, since all the eulogies have been given. Even my mother's tears appear to be wrung out.

Or maybe even she can't compete with the weather.

After it's over, Lila and her father get into the back of a car, and his bodyguards drive them away. She throws me a small wave as she gets in.

The rest of us go to my grandfather's house for the

wake. The old women of Carney are out in force, and Grandad's dining room table is groaning under the weight of casseroles, pies, and cold cuts trays.

A middle-aged woman in a black tweed suit is whispering to her friend. The other woman laughs and says, "Oh, no, Pearl! I've been married three times, and I never let any of them see me without *my* gloves, no less take off theirs."

I head for the kitchen.

Mom stops me on the way out of the room. Her eyes are outlined in the gray remainder of her makeup, making them look sunken. Haunted.

"Baby," she says.

"Mom," I say, trying to slide past. I want her away from me. I already feel too much. I can't bear feeling anything more.

"I know that you always looked up to Philip," she says, as though the last six months never happened. As though the last three years never happened. The smell of liquor is strong on her breath. "But we've both got to be strong."

I say nothing. I don't trust myself to speak.

"Barron says I should move in with him. He says he worries about me being alone."

"That's great," I say, and mean it. Maybe he can distract her.

One of the casserole-makers comes in and wants to console Mom. I get out while the getting's good. Sam follows me, looking a little shaken. I don't think he's used to so many criminals displaying their scarred throats in one place. Daneca stays in the dining room, clearly in awe of being in the center of a worker party in one of the best-known worker towns.

I prepare to get blind drunk in the most efficient way possible. Taking a bottle of vodka out of Grandad's liquor cabinet, I grab three shot glasses from the kitchen and automatically head to the basement.

The basement is just like I remember it from all the summers I spent here. Cool and damp, with a slight smell of mildew. I flop down onto the leather couch in front of the television.

I set up the glasses on the coffee table, pour a shot into each one, and grimly down the whole line.

I feel better, but also worse here. Better because the memories are so close. Worse because of the memories themselves.

"Oh," I say, looking over at Sam. "I should have gotten another glass for you."

He lifts his eyebrow and picks up one of mine. "How about I just take this one at the end."

"Lila and I used to come down here a lot. Watch movies," I say, waving vaguely toward the set.

Philip and Barron and I spent a lot of time in this room too. I remember lying on the floor and playing Battleship with Philip, laughing so hard I was afraid I was going to piss my pants. I remember a teenage Anton and Philip forbidding us to come into the room while they had on a horror movie. Barron and I sat on the stairs instead, not technically in the room, watching from the dark so we wouldn't get in trouble, utterly terrified.

I pour myself two more shots. Grudgingly I pour one for Sam, too.

"What's going on with you and Lila?" he asks. "I thought you liked her—you know, last year, when we pulled the thing. But you've been avoiding her since she started at Wallingford."

Self-revulsion lets me gulp down the booze without wincing.

"I don't want to talk about that," I say, shaking my head. "Not here. Not tonight."

"Okay," says Sam, with a false reasonableness in his voice. "What do you want to talk about?"

"My new career," I say. "I am going to help the Feds catch my brother's killer. It's going to be just like *Band of the Banned*."

"No one watches that show," Sam says. "No one under fifty."

Someone is coming down the stairs. I pour another round of drinks in case the newcomer is planning on stealing my booze. In this crowd one can't be too safe.

"A wonderful piece of cinema verité," I declare. "It is going to be my new life. And I am going to get a badge and a gun and hunt down evildoers." I am flooded with a sense of well-being. Everything sounds perfect. Like a dream I don't want to wake from.

"Did you just say 'evildoers'?" Daneca asks, flopping onto the couch next to us. "Did you know Betty the Butcher is upstairs? And she's wearing a gold mask. That means it's got to be true! Killing her last husband must have rotted her nose off."

I point to the shots I have lined up. She takes one. I feel quite magnanimous. Also kind of light-headed. "That's what I plan on calling them when I apprehend them. Evil-doers, that is, not Betty. I would call only Betty by the name Betty. Well, I call her Aunt Betty, but still."

"I'm not really sure," Sam tells Daneca, "but I believe our drunk friend here is claiming that he was approached by federal agents."

"They gave me files," I say delightedly.

"You really do have all the luck," says Daneca.

We sit in the basement, drinking steadily until I pass out on the old leather couch in front of the television. The last thing I remember is blurrily noticing Sam and Daneca kissing on the floor. I want to get a glass of water, but I don't want to disturb them, so I stay where I am and close my eyes as tightly as they will go.

When I wake up, Sam and Daneca are curled up together on the rug under an afghan. I go to the kitchen, sticking my head under the sink and guzzling as much water as I can get down.

Out the window I can see by the light cast from the kitchen that it has stopped raining. I can also see Grandad sitting on a lawn chair, a beer in hand, looking at the dark expanse of his muddy backyard and ramshackle shed. I still feel a little tipsy.

I let the screen door slam behind me as I join him. He barely even looks up.

"Hey," I say as I fumble to unfold another chair.

"You look a little worse for wear," Grandad says, pulling out a pipe from his pocket and packing it with tobacco. "Better sit down before you fall down."

I sit unsteadily. The chair creaks. "Since when do you smoke a pipe?"

"I don't," he says, lighting a match and touching it to the tobacco. "Quit years ago, after Shandra was born."

"Right," I say. "Silly me."

"We couldn't have kids, me and your grandmother. Mary kept having miscarriages. She really took it hard—went on bed rest as soon as she thought she might be pregnant. The doctors said we had the Rh factor, but I kept thinking that it was really because of my death work. I thought maybe the blowback made it so I couldn't make healthy babies. Could be superstition, but when I stopped killing people with curses, your mother got born."

"I didn't think you were allowed to quit that kind of job," I say.

"The Zacharovs wouldn't have let me stop being a killer, but no one gets to tell me how to kill." Sweet smoke rises from his pipe. "A man's got to be an expert at his own trade."

"Ah," I say. Even though I saw him kill Anton, it's still hard to think of my grandfather as really dangerous. But I have to remember that he was already an assassin when Lila's scary dad was still a boy.

"Magic gives you a lot of choices," Grandad says. "Most of them are bad."

He takes another sip of his beer.

I wonder if that's my future. Bad choices. It certainly feels a lot like my present.

"If I'd done things different," Grandad goes on, "maybe your brother would be alive right now. Me and Mary spoiled your mother rotten, but I didn't keep her out of the life the way I should've. We thought that because she never officially joined up with one of the families, that meant you kids would have a chance at another kind of life, but then I let you all come down here in the summers. I wanted to see my grandkids."

"We wanted to see you, too," I say. My voice sounds a little slurred. For a moment, I miss being a kid with a painful intensity. I miss my dad being alive. I miss running around on Grandad's lawn under the sprinkler.

"I know." He claps his hand against my shoulder. "But I didn't keep you three out of the life either. I guess I thought that even though I was leading the horse directly to the water, it didn't mean I was making it drink."

I shake my head. "We were *born* into the life. Just like every other curse worker kid in the world. You couldn't have kept us out if you tried."

"Philip's dead at twenty-three. And I'm still around. That's not right." He shakes his head.

I have nothing to say to that, except that if I had to pick him or Philip, the choice would be easy. I'd take him any day. Since I know he doesn't want to hear that, I take a sip of Grandad's beer and join him in contemplating the muddy lawn and fading stars.

CHAPTER FIVE

I WAKE UP SUNDAY MORN-
ing with a pounding headache and a mouth that tastes of
death. I get up out of the lawn chair in the chill sunlight.
Grandad's not there. When I head to the basement, I see that
Daneca and Sam are gone too, but at least they've left a note:

SEE YOU BACK AT WALLINGFORD.
—S & D

I stumble back upstairs and realize that for some people
the wake is still going on. The dining table is in bad shape,
hunks of macaroni and cheese oozing onto the tablecloth,
mingling hideously with blueberry pie filling. Bottles and

cans litter all surfaces. I see Barron in the living room, his arm around an elderly lady I don't know. She's telling him about how back in her day, if you really wanted to make money, you went into opium. Clearly she doesn't know that today all you need for meth is a hotel coffeepot, but I'm not going to be the one to tell her.

Grandad is asleep in his recliner, the steady rise and fall of his chest an indicator that he's okay.

A few other people are sitting around, mostly young mobsters still in their rumpled suits, collars loose enough to show their neck scars. When I pass, I hear them talking about a big job involving a bank, thirty feet of rope, and a lot of WD-40. They are red-eyed and laughing.

I go into the guest bedroom and find my mother sitting in front of a television, watching the soap opera channel. "Oh, honey," she says when she sees me. "I never met those friends of yours. They seemed really nice."

"Yeah," I say.

She studies me for a long moment. "You look terrible. When's the last time you ate?"

I lean my head against the wall, arching my neck. "I have a hangover."

"There's aspirin in the bathroom, but it'll tear up your stomach if there's nothing in it. You should eat."

"I know," I say. She's right.

I get into my car and drive to a diner I remember from the summers when Philip, Barron, and I lived with Grandad. The waitress doesn't seem to be bothered by my wrinkled day-old suit or by the fact that I eat two breakfasts, one right after the other. I cut the eggs and watch the yolk run across my plate in a yellow tide. Then I pepper the mess and sop it up with rye toast. By the time I get through a pot of coffee, my head stops hurting.

I leave some bills on the table and head for school. The steering wheel of my car has been warmed by the sun, and as I cruise along the highway, I roll down my windows to drink in the last rain-soaked breath of summer.

The last thing I expect when I walk into my dorm is to find Daneca and Sam with a two-liter bottle of Mountain Dew and all of the files the Feds gave me spread out across various surfaces of my room. I freeze with my hand on the door frame.

For a moment all I can feel is blind, unreasoning rage. Those papers are *mine*.

"Oh, hey," Daneca says, looking up from the floor, where she's sitting with her back braced against my bed. She's looking pretty casual for someone who is courting a demerit just for being in here. She grins. "Nice look. I can't believe you were telling the truth about the Feds."

"That's because after Barron's eulogy, you have all new trust issues regarding my family," I say, as casually as I can manage. I take off my jacket and throw it onto the bed. Then I roll up my shirtsleeves. That's about as together as I can get myself without a shower and a change of clothes. "And now I have all new trust issues with you. What exactly do you think you're doing?"

"Wait, you're saying that thing Barron told us about

the Himalayas and saving that goat wasn't true?" Sam asks. He's got on a black T-shirt and jeans. His hair's still wet.

I am almost one hundred percent sure he's messing with me.

I roll my eyes. "Anyway, just because I said I had files— during a period, I will remind you, when I was severely compromised by drink and grief—doesn't mean I gave you permission to read them."

"Evildoers don't care about rules," Daneca says, and then has to snicker for a while.

"Oh, come on," Sam says. "You hid them under the mattress. That's like *begging* for someone to find them."

I have a bad feeling that Sam is quoting something I said back at me. I groan and slump into my desk chair, then realize I am sitting on a stack of papers. I pull them out from under me.

"So, what are we looking at?" I ask them, peering at what I'm holding. There are pictures clipped to the files, a bunch of tough-looking guys clearly getting their picture taken because they were busted for something. And then, candid shots of those same guys drinking coffee in cafés or reading the paper on the balcony of a hotel, a woman in a bathing suit beside them. Surveillance shots.

"There are six victims here," Daneca says. "All workers."

"All dudes," puts in Sam.

Daneca stretches, grabbing one of the pages. "Giovanni 'Scars' Basso. He's in the real—and fake—amulet trade. Was apparently shorting some people money. As far as the Feds know, he didn't work directly for Zacharov. Probably did deals with a bunch of the families. No body. No nothing. One night he was just gone."

"So we don't even know that he didn't just skip town," says Sam.

"Yeah," I say. "Maybe they *all* skipped town."

"Together?" Daneca asks Sam. "Like now all six of them are living in a villa in the south of France like in a wacky TV sitcom?"

Sam shakes his head sadly. "Okay. Admittedly, probably not."

Daneca shuffles. "Guy number two—James 'Jimmy' Greco. He ran an illegal gambling operation—Hey, kind of like you, Cassel."

I make a rude gesture halfheartedly. I am sure the federal agents don't want me sharing these files with civilians, especially ones they have no legal reason to harass. Even though I am still annoyed with Daneca and Sam, that knowledge gives me some measure of satisfaction. Anything that pisses off the Feds can't be all bad.

Daneca smiles. "Greco was a luck worker, so no surprises there on his choice of profession. No idea how he crossed Zacharov, since he was a big earner. Then, bam. Taken out. Last seen passed out in a bar in Philadelphia."

It seems easy to imagine that hit. Greco stumbling, carried out on the shoulder of someone claiming to be a friend. Maybe someone who *was* a friend. Tip to the bartender. Killed in the car.

Or the killer was a woman, pretending to be his girlfriend, his wife. Even better. Maybe even a last drink, with a little something to make him sleep. Flash of her red gloves.

Nothing the Feds haven't already considered, I'm sure.

"That brings us to Antanas Kalvis. Ran a pretty high-end call girl service out of Newark along with his wife." Daneca likes playing detective. It's just a game to both of them, a murder mystery with fancy props. At the end you guess it was the butler with the candlestick and turn over a card to find out if you're right.

"They ran it together?" Sam asks.

"When I picture pimps, I picture fur coats, wide lapels, and no fixed address," I say.

"Yeah, because all criminals are like in the movies," Daneca snaps. Maybe she's taking it more seriously than I thought. "Kalvis was an emotion worker. Ugh. That's just so gross. Anyway—"

"You said he was married, right?" I say, interrupting her. "How did he go missing without his wife knowing anything about it?"

She flips over a couple of pages. "Actually, it's really creepy. He disappeared from bed. Like, right next to her. So either that's true or Mrs. Kalvis was in on the hit."

I'm warming to the idea of a murderess. I imagine her posing as one of the call girls—maybe in distress—and arranging an emergency meeting with Kalvis. He slips out of bed without waking his wife.

Or maybe he was sleepwalking. Right into Philip and Anton's waiting arms. Then someone like me makes the body disappear.

Or maybe I did. Maybe it was me.

"It sounds like the wife was covering up," Daneca says speculatively. "We could start with her. Maybe you know someone who knows someone who could ask—!"

"Cassel? Is something wrong?" Sam scoots to the edge of his bed.

"No," I say, shaking my head. "Let's hear the rest."

"Okay," Daneca says slowly. "Henry 'Trigger' Janssen. Physical worker. Soldier in the Zacharov family. Apparently worked closely with an Anton Abramov. Anton? Is that the Anton who died—"

I nod. "His mother's maiden name was Zacharov."

"Could he have been the killer?" Sam asks. "I mean, not of your brother, obviously."

"So that we're talking about two different people? Yeah, I'm wondering about that too. The Feds think—" I pause, because I don't know if I should tell them that the Feds are looking for a woman with red gloves. And I am sure I shouldn't tell them the Feds probably should be looking for me. "They think the person got sloppy, but I don't know. These other people just disappeared."

"Maybe the FBI have evidence they're not telling you about," Daneca says.

Sam shrugs. "Or maybe they want you to help solve this case and they think if they tell you it had something to do with your brother, you will."

"That's really paranoid," I say admiringly. "I'm going with that."

"You can't seriously think that federal agents would lie in a way that would put you in danger." Daneca seems exasperated with both of us, which seems just as ridiculous to me.

"Yeah, because they are tireless advocates of worker rights," I say with plenty of sarcasm.

"Next up," she says, ignoring my point because she'd have to concede it. "Sean Gowen."

I hold up a hand. "Wait, how did Janssen die?"

"Going home from his mistress's house, apparently. She says he left in the middle of the night and she figured he went home to his wife, which pissed her off, until she found out he was dead. Or, well, *gone*. No body."

An involuntary shudder runs through me, like someone's walking over my grave.

Middle of the night again. No body.

Lila told me how Barron and Philip sent her into houses as a cat. She could make anyone she'd given the touch to sleepwalk right out into my waiting arms. Then, although I can't remember it, I transformed them. We must have been a hell of a team.

No bodies.

"Back to Sean Gowen," Daneca says. "Gowen was a loan shark and a luck worker. That's weird. He disappeared in the early afternoon. All the others—"

"He worked nights," I say.

"What?" Sam says. "Did you know him or something?"

I shake my head. "It's just a guess. Did he?" I want very badly to be wrong.

That prompts a hunt through the strewn files. Finally Sam holds one up. "Yeah, I guess so. Or at least he usually got home around four in the morning, which is pretty much the same thing."

He was asleep. The one thing they all had in common.

"Do you have a theory or something?" Daneca asks.

I shake my head. "Not yet," I say, lying through my teeth. I've told Daneca and Sam more about me than I've ever told anyone else, but I can't tell them this. I think I did it. I'm the killer. I grip my knees to keep my hands from shaking.

Zacharov's job offer makes a whole lot more sense right now. All those people, gone. Just gone.

Daneca flips pages relentlessly. "Well, let's look at the last one. Then we can hear your not-a-theory. This guy is Arthur Lee. Another luck worker and an informant for the FBI. Died out on a job for Zacharov."

A cold sweat breaks out at my temples. Now that I think I did it, every piece of paper seems damning. Every detail, obvious.

Anton and Barron in the front of the car, me and Philip in the back with Lee. No sleep magic needed. Just a touch from my bare hand.

"The thing I don't understand is—," Daneca begins.

Our new hall master, Mr. Pascoli, clears his throat outside the open door. Daneca's busted. At least it's a new year and we're all starting from zero demerits. I open my mouth and try to come up with some excuse for why she's in a guy's room, no matter how flimsy.

"I think this project of yours has taken long enough, don't you?" he asks, before I can speak.

"Sorry," Daneca says, gathering up some of the papers.

Pascoli smiles benevolently and walks away, like nothing happened.

"What was that?" I ask.

"I just told him that Sam and I had a project to do together and that the common room was too noisy. He said as long as we kept the door open and actually studied, he didn't mind."

"Nerds get away with everything," Sam says.

Daneca grins. "Don't we just."

I smile back, but if there's one thing I know, it's that eventually we all get caught.

Even though I'm exhausted, I can't sleep. I pored over the files once Daneca left, and I run through the details again and again in my mind, trying to remember some part of what happened. I keep twisting on my bed, making the springs squeak. My body feels wrong, hot and uncomfortable.

Finally I grab my phone and text Lila.

U awake? I type.

Then I actually look at the screen and realize it's three thirty in the morning. I punch my pillow and flop down onto it, face forward.

My phone chirrups. I roll over and snatch it up.

Bad dreams, it says. *Always awake.*

Sneak out, I text back, and pull on a pair of jeans.

The great thing about a room on the ground floor is that you can just push open your window and hop right into the bushes. Sam moans at the creak of the wooden frame, kicks at his blankets, and goes back to snoring.

I'm not sure which dorm is hers, so I stand in the middle of the quad.

The night air is still and heavy. Nothing feels real. I wonder if this was what it was like when we waited outside someone's house for the victim to walk right into our arms. The whole world seems dead already.

After a few moments I see a rope dangle from a low window in Gilbert House. I pad over and realize Lila has somehow managed to jam a grappling hook into the sill. Which means she thought to bring a grappling hook to school and managed to hide it in her room. I am all admiration.

She spiders down and then drops, barefoot, still in her pajamas. She's grinning, but when she sees my face, her smile fades.

"What's wrong?" Lila asks.

"Come on," I say softly. "We have to get away from the dorms."

She nods and follows me without saying anything else. This, the language of deception, we both understand. We were born to it, along with the curses.

I go out to the track. Nearby are only tennis courts and the patch of woods that separates the Wallingford campus from a stretch of suburban homes.

"So, what do you think of it here?" I ask her.

"School's school," she says with a shrug. "A girl on my hall wanted me to go shopping with her and her friends. I didn't go. Now she's always on my case about being stuck up."

"How come you didn't—?"

Lila is looking at me·uncertainly. I can see the hope

in her face, along with the dread. "Who cares?" she asks finally. "Well, *what*? Why are we here?" Her pajamas are blue, covered in stars.

"Okay. I want to ask you about what we did—about what I did. The murders or whatever you want to call them." I don't look at her, so instead I look back at Wallingford. Just some old brick buildings. I have no idea how I thought they were going to shelter me from my own life.

"That's what you brought me all the way out here to talk about?" she says, her voice hard.

"This is definitely not where I would take someone for a romantic rendezvous." When she flinches, I keep going. "I saw some files. Some names. I want you to tell me if they're the ones."

"Fine," she says. "But it's not going to help you to know."

"Antanas Kalvis?"

"Yeah," she says. "You changed him."

"Jimmy Greco?"

"Yeah," she says again, softly. "Him, too."

"Arthur Lee."

"I don't know. If you did, I wasn't there. But since you knew the names of the first two, you're probably right about the third."

My hands are shaking again.

"Cassel, what's the difference? You knew about all of this before. They're just names."

I sink down to the grass. It's damp with dew. I feel sick, but self-loathing has become a familiar sickness. I was a monster before. A monster with the excuse that he didn't know details so he didn't really have to think about it. "I don't know. I guess there's no difference."

She sits next to me and pulls up a handful of weeds. She tries to throw it, but most of the blades stick to her bare fingers. Neither of us is wearing gloves.

"It's just—why? Why did I do it? Barron could make me remember anything, but what did I remember that let me change these people into *objects*?"

"I don't know," Lila says in a monotone.

I reach out for her shoulder without thinking, rubbing my fingers over the cotton. I no longer know how to say aloud what I feel. Sorry my brothers kept her in a cage, sorry that it took me so long to save her, sorry I changed her in the first place. Sorry I'm bringing up those memories now.

"Don't," she says.

My bare fingers still. "Right. I wasn't thinking."

"My father wants you to work for him, doesn't he?" she asks, scooting away from me. Her eyes are bright in the moonlight.

I nod. "He offered me a job at Philip's funeral."

Lila groans. "He's got some conflict going with the Brennan family. He does a lot of his business at funeral parlors these days." She pauses. "Are you going to do it?"

"You mean am I going to keep on murdering people? I don't know. I guess I'm good at it. It's good to be good at something, right?" There's bitterness in my voice, but not as much as there should be. The horror I felt earlier is fading, being replaced by a kind of resignation.

"Maybe they don't die when you change them into objects," Lila says. "Maybe they're just in suspended animation."

I shudder. "That sounds even worse."

She flops back in the grass, looking up at the night sky. "I like how you can see stars out here in the country."

"This isn't the country," I say, turning toward her. "We're close to two cities and—"

She smiles up at me, and all of a sudden we're in dangerous territory. I'm above her, looking down at the fall of her silvery hair on the grass, at the way her neck moves when she swallows nervously, at the way her fingers curl in the dirt.

I try to say something, but I can't remember what we were talking about. All my thoughts melt away as her lips part and her bare hand slides through my hair, pulling me down to her.

She makes a soft sound as my mouth presses against hers, hungry, desperate. Only a monster would do this, but I already know I'm a monster.

I roll toward her, not breaking the kiss, crushing her body against mine. My eyes close, so I don't have to see what I'm doing, but my hands find her easily enough. She moans into my mouth.

Her fingers are still knotted in my hair, gripping it hard, like she's afraid I am going to pull away.

"Please," I say breathlessly, but then we're kissing again and it's hard to concentrate on anything but the feel of her body arching under mine, and I never get the rest of the words out.

Please stop me.

I drag my mouth away from hers, moving to kiss the hollow of her throat, my teeth gliding over her skin, my tongue tasting sweat and dirt.

"Cassel," she whispers. She's said my name a hundred times before, a thousand times, but never like this.

I pull back, abruptly, panting. Never like this.

She rises with me, but now at least we're both sitting up. That helps. She's breathing hard, her eyes black with pupil.

"I don't—," I start. "It's not—not real."

The words make no sense. I shake my head to clear it.

She looks at me with an expression I cannot name. Her lips are slightly apart and swollen.

"We have to go back," I say finally.

"Okay." I can barely hear the word. Her voice is all breath.

I nod, pushing myself to my feet. I reach out my hand, and she lets me pull her up. For a moment her hand is in mine, warm and bare.

At the window to my room, I catch my reflection in the glass. Shaggy black hair. Sneer. I look like a hungry ghost, glowering in at a world I am no longer fit to be part of.

The dream takes me by surprise. I'm standing at the edge of a lawn. Barron's beside me. I know, without any reason to know, that we're waiting for someone to come out of the big pillared white house in front of us.

"Join me in a cup of tea?" he asks, holding out a paper cup with a smirk. The amber liquid inside is boiling, bubbles rising along with steam. It's going to scald us both.

"Oh," I say. "Do you think we'll fit?"

CHAPTER SIX

I'M USELESS IN CLASSES
the next day. I fail a quiz in physics and conjugate my verbs
completely weirdly in French. Luckily, I probably won't
need French in my future assassination career, unless I'm
one of those fancy movie assassins who travel the world
and also steal jewels. Physics I might need—got to calculate the trajectory of bullets somehow.

I call Barron on my lunch break to avoid the cafeteria.
I don't know how to say anything to Sam and Daneca that
isn't all lies. And I don't know how to say anything to Lila
that isn't the truth.

"Hey," he says. "We still on for Tuesday pizza?" His voice

is casual. Normal. It makes me almost believe that I can relax.

"I need to ask you something. In person. Where are you?" A teacher walks by and gives me a look. We're not supposed to be calling people during the school day, even between classes. I'm a senior, though, so she doesn't give me a hard time.

"Mom and I are having fun. We're staying at the Nassau Inn. It's pretty swank."

"That's in Princeton," I say. It's right downtown, minutes away from Daneca's house. I experience a frisson of horror at the thought of my mother and hers in the same pharmacy line.

Barron laughs. "Yeah. And? Mom says you two basically tore up Atlantic City, so we're looking for a fresh start."

I have no idea why I thought that Barron would do anything but amplify all of Mom's problems. A memory of him saying something about a painting nags at me; I should have seen this coming.

"Look, whatever," I say. "Can you meet me somewhere at six? I can skip dinner and some of study hall."

"We'll come over now. Mom can sign you out, remember? We'll get sushi."

"Sure, okay," I say.

It takes them an hour and a half to make the twenty-minute trip from Princeton to Wallingford. By the time they get there, I am in the "extra help" period, where I have to suffer through realizing that almost all my physics mistakes were dumb and obvious.

It's a relief to be called to the office.

Barron is lounging against the secretary desk in a sharkskin suit. Mom is next to him, her hair pulled back into a Hermès scarf with a massive black-and-white hat over it, black gloves, and a low-cut black dress. They're both wearing sunglasses. She's bent over, signing a sheet.

I think she's supposed to look like she's in mourning.

"Mom," I say.

"Oh, honey," she says. "The doctor wants to see you to make sure you don't have the same thing that killed your brother." She turns to Ms. Logan, who looks scandalized by the whole encounter. "These things can run in families," she confides.

"You're afraid I'm going to come down with a bad case of getting two in the chest?" I say. "'Cause you might be right about that running in families."

Mom purses her lips in disapproval.

Barron claps me on the back hard. "Come on, funnyman."

We walk toward the parking lot. I shove my gloved hands deep into the pockets of my uniform. Barron is keeping pace with me. He has left the top couple buttons of his crisp white shirt undone, enough so that I can see a new gold chain slide against his tan skin. I wonder if he's wearing charms against being worked.

"I thought you *wanted* us to come get you," Mom says as she lights a cigarette with a gilt lighter and takes a deep drag. "What's the matter?"

"All I want is for Barron to tell me where the bodies are," I say, keeping my voice down as I walk across the lawn.

...ving them here is surreal. They don't belong at Wallingford, with its manicured lawns and low voices. They're
both larger than life.

They exchange a look brimming with discomfort.

"The people I transformed. Where are they? What did I
turn them into?"

I don't know exactly what Barron remembers about
the disappearances of Greco and Kalvis and all the rest. I
have no idea how many of Barron's memories are missing,
how extensively he's damaged himself with blowback, but
if there's a record in his journals, then maybe he knows
something. Yeah, sure, I changed his journals so that he forgot that he wanted to use me to kill Zacharov, forgot that he
wasn't on my side against Philip and Philip's buddy, Anton.
But I didn't change anything else.

"There's no reason why you need to know that," Barron
says slowly. Which sounds promising.

"Let's just say that I do." I stop walking, forcing them to
either stop too or go on without me. They stop.

"Don't argue, boys," Mom says, blowing out a cloud of
smoke that hangs in the air. "Cassel, come on, baby. Let it go."

"One," I say. "Give me one body."

"Fine." Barron shrugs nonchalantly. "Remember that
chair you hated?"

I open my mouth and then close it, like a fish. "What?"
I say, but I know which chair he means. The one I almost
threw out when Grandad and I cleaned the house, because
the thing always creeped me out. It was a too-exact replica
of one I'd seen on television.

He laughs and tilts up his sunglasses, so I can see him raise his eyebrows at me. "Yep."

I root my keys out of my bag. "Thanks for signing me out, Mom," I say, kissing her on her powdered cheek.

"I thought we were going to have lunch," she says. "Whatever you're thinking of doing—"

"I've got to go," I say. "I'm sorry."

"Sorry nothing," Mom says in a syrupy voice, grabbing hold of my upper arm. "You can come to lunch with us or I can call that nice lady at the desk and tell her that your appointment got canceled, I brought you back to school, and won't she be a dear and make sure you're where you're supposed to be?"

"Don't threaten me," I say, which makes Barron look at me like I've gone crazy. Telling Mom what to do is never a great idea.

Her hand clenches tighter around my arm, nails biting into my skin through the white dress shirt. I look down; somehow she got her glove off without my noticing. If she slides her fingers lower, she could touch my bare wrist. Or she could go higher and grab for my neck. "A mother shouldn't have to threaten her son into wanting to spend time together."

She's got me there.

Mom slides into the booth at Toriyama's and plunks down her purse next to her, leaving Barron and me to use the chairs. Her gloves are back in place. When I study them to figure out how she rigged things to remove one so fast, she gives me a pointed look. I study the framed kimonos hanging above us and the pale bamboo table instead.

The waitress comes, dressed all in black, and pours us tea. She's pretty, with supershort bangs and a nose ring that glitters like a single drop of absinthe. Her name tag says Jin-Sook.

Barron orders one of the big platters of sushi. "It comes on one of the boats, right?" he asks, pointing toward a shelf of lacquered wooden ships, some of them with two masts, that rests above where the chef carves fish. "Because one time I ordered it and it just came on a plate. But on the menu it says boat, so I just want to be sure."

"It comes on a boat," Jin-Sook says.

I take a sip of the tea. It's a jasmine, so hot it nearly scalds my throat.

"So," Barron says. "We've got a new mark we're looking at. Someone big. We could use a hand. And you could use the money. Besides, we're family."

"Family looks out for family," says Mom, a line I've heard her recite more times than I can count.

It's tempting to say yes, even after everything. I used to long to be asked to grift alongside my brother. To prove that even though I wasn't a worker, I could con along with the best of them. And my brother and mother are up there with the best of them.

But now I know I'm a worker and a con artist and maybe a murderer, too. And if there is one thing I want to prove to myself, it's that I can be different.

"Thanks, but no thanks," I say.

Barron shrugs philosophically.

Mom reaches for her teacup, and I see the flash of a fat blue topaz circled in diamonds sitting on her first finger, over her leather glove. The ring's new. I shudder to think where it came from. Then I spot the ring on the other hand. The stone is reddish, like a single droplet of blood spilled into water.

"Mom," I say hesitantly.

Something in my expression makes her look down at her hands.

"Oh," she gushes, clearly pleased. "I met the most fantastic man! He's absolutely perfect." She waggles the finger wearing the topaz. "And such good taste."

"He's the one I was telling you about," Barron says. At my blank look he lowers his voice and raises his eyebrows. "The *mark*."

"Oh," I say. "But what about that other ring?"

"This old thing?" Mom says, holding out her other hand. The pale red diamond flashes in the fluorescent restaurant lights. "Also a gift. One I haven't worn in years."

I think of the pictures I found when I was cleaning out the house. Photos of Mom in vintage lingerie, posing for a person I couldn't see. Someone with an expensive wedding ring. Someone who wasn't my dad. I wonder if the man from the photograph had something to do with the diamond.

"Who gave *that* to *you*?" I ask.

She gives me a look across the table like she's daring me to contradict her. "Your father, sweetheart. He had the best taste of any man."

"Well, I don't think you should wear it in public. That's all." I smile to let her know I'm not fooled. It feels like we're alone in the restaurant. "Someone might *steal* it."

That makes her laugh. Barron looks at us both like we're speaking a language he doesn't understand. For a change, I am the person with the insider information.

The food comes. I mix plenty of wasabi into my soy sauce and drag a piece of sashimi through it. The fish is salty on my tongue, and the green horseradish flares all the way up my nose.

"I'm glad you came to lunch," Barron says, leaning in to me. "You seemed a little freaked-out back at school."

I don't mention that by the time they picked me up it was way past time for lunch. We're surrounded by an early dinner crowd.

"What you're feeling is part of the grieving process," he goes on, with the total sincerity that makes him so convincing. "There's no making sense out of what happened to Philip, so you're trying to make sense out of something else instead."

"Maybe that's it," I say.

He ruffles my hair with a gloved hand. "Sure it is. You'll see."

Jin-Sook brings our check in a narrow black folder. Mom pays for it with one of a dozen stolen credit cards.

Unfortunately for her, the credit card is declined. The waitress brings it back with apologies.

"Your machine must be broken," my mother says, her voice rising.

"It's fine," I say, reaching for my wallet. "I've got it."

Barron turns to our waitress. "Thanks for such great service." His bare hand is on her wrist.

For a moment she looks disoriented. Then she smiles back, a big grin. "Thank *you*! Come back again."

Mom and Barron get up and start toward the door, leaving me there staring after Jin-Sook, trying to figure out how to tell her that her memories just got rearranged.

"What's done is done," Mom says from the front of the restaurant. The look she gives me is a warning.

Family looks after family.

The girl's memories are gone. I could get Barron in trouble, but I can't undo what's already done.

I push back my chair and follow my mother and brother out. Once we're on the street, though, I shove Barron's shoulder. "Are you crazy?"

"Come on!" he says, grinning like it's all a great joke. "Paying is for suckers."

"I get that you don't care about other people. But you're messing up your own head," I say. "You'll use up all your memories. There won't be anything of you left."

"Don't worry," Barron says. "If I forget anything important, you can just remind me."

Mom looks over at me, eyes glittering.

Yeah. Right. What's done is done.

They drop me off back at Wallingford, in front of my own car. I start to get out.

"Wait," Mom says and takes out a pen from her handbag. "I got a cute little phone! I want to give you the number."

Barron rolls his eyes.

"You hate cell phones," I say.

She ignores me as she scribbles. "Here, baby," she says. "You call me whenever. I'll call you back from the nearest pay phone or landline."

I take the slip of paper with a smile. After her three years in jail, I don't think she realizes just how rare pay phones are these days. "Thanks, Mom."

She leans in and kisses my cheek. I can smell her perfume, sweet and heavy, long after they pull away.

My car makes a horrible noise when I try to start it up. For a moment I think I am going to have to chase down Mom and Barron for a ride. Finally I put it in second gear and get it rolling. Somehow the engine turns over and the motor roars to life. I have no idea how long my car is going to stay running or whether I'm going to be able to get it started again when I want to return to Wallingford.

I drive to the big old house I grew up in. From the outside the unpainted shingles and off-kilter shutters give it the look of a building long abandoned. Grandad and I cleaned out most of the garbage, but inside I can smell the faint odor of mold under the Lysol. The place still looks tidy, but I can tell Mom's been here. There are a couple of shopping bags on the dining room table and there's a mug of tea rotting in the kitchen sink.

Good thing Grandad's down in Carney; he'd be annoyed.

I walk straight to the chair. It's covered in a kind of a mustardy cloth and is perfectly normal-looking for a club chair, except for the feet, which, now that I really look at them, are awful. I thought they were claw feet holding on to painted balls, and at a glance that's what they look like. But now that I am inspecting the chair closely, those claws are actually human hands, the knuckles bent under.

A shudder runs through me.

I sit down on the floor beside it, despite wanting nothing more than to get as far away from it as I can. I reach out a hand and concentrate. The power still feels strange, and my whole body is braced for what comes after, for the pain and helplessness of the blowback.

As my palm comes down on the chair, everything goes fluid. I can feel the curse here, feel the threads of it, and even feel the man underneath. I rip the magic with a push that's almost physical.

After a moment I open my eyes, not even realizing I had closed them.

A man stands before me, his skin pink with life, his eyes open. He's wearing a white sleeveless undershirt and underwear. I feel a wild hope.

"Henry Janssen," I say, my voice trembling. He looks just like the picture paper-clipped to his file.

Then he falls, his skin turning ashen. I remember how we tried to fake Zacharov's death. Seeing Janssen fall, I realize how wrong we had it. You can see the moment it happens, like a light burning out in a lamp.

"No," I yell, crawling over to him.

And the blowback hits me. My body cramps all over, limbs elongating like a spider, reaching toward the ceiling.

Then it's like I'm made of glass and each twist of my body creates cracks that turn to fissures until I am lying in pieces. I try to scream, but my mouth has turned to crumbling earth. My body is turning itself inside out. As agony grips me, I turn my head and stare into the glassy eyes of a dead man.

I wake up, drenched in sweat, next to Henry Janssen.

Every muscle in my body is sore, and when I look at the corpse, I feel nothing except a growing sense that I have to get rid of it. I no longer understand the urgency that sent me here. I no longer understand why I thought there could be any other outcome but this. What did I think was going to happen? I know nothing about transformation or its limits. I don't even know if it's possible to turn an inanimate object back into something alive.

I don't care, either. I'm tired of caring.

It's like the part of me that feels all that guilt has finally overloaded. I feel nothing.

Even though the most practical solution is to curse him back into being a chair, I can't face another round of blowback. I think of burying him, but I'm pretty sure the hole has to be deeper than I have time to dig.

I could dump him in deep water, but since I'm not even sure my car is going to start, that seems problematic too. Finally I remember the freezer in the basement.

It's harder to carry a dead person than someone who's alive. It's not that they're heavier; it's that they don't help you. They don't bend their body into your arms or hold on to your neck. They just lie there. On the plus side, you no longer have to worry about hurting them.

I drag Janssen down the stairs by his shoulders. His body makes a sickening thud with each step.

There's nothing in the freezer except half a pint of Cherry Garcia ice cream, rimed with frost. I take it out and set it on my father's old workbench. Then I put one hand under the dead man's clammy neck and hook the other around his knee. I lift and half-roll, half-toss him into the freezer. He sort of fits, but I have to bend his limbs so that I will be able to close the lid. It's pretty bad.

I'll come back, I tell myself. *In a day or two I'll come back and change him.*

Looking down at a freezer full of Henry Janssen, I think about Philip's corpse laid out in the funeral home. Someone—a woman—was caught on video walking into Philip's condo. And since I know I killed the rest of the people in the files, the FBI are on the entirely wrong track. They're looking to connect the killers. But whoever murdered Philip had nothing to do with all this, probably didn't know anything about it.

Maybe I should get back to thinking about suspects other than myself.

My car starts without a problem; the first good thing that's happened to me in a while. I drive back to Wallingford eating the Cherry Garcia ice cream and thinking about red gloves, gunshots, and guilt.

CHAPTER SEVEN

IT'S IMPOSSIBLE TO
avoid the cafeteria forever.

When I walk in to dinner, I see Daneca and Sam sitting with Jill Pearson-White and a bunch of Sam's chess club friends. I start over to them, until I see Lila, her head bent toward Daneca's. I can only imagine the speech Lila is being given about worker rights and HEX meetings.

I veer abruptly toward another table and spot the flame of Audrey's red hair.

"Hi," I say as I sit down.

Greg Harmsford is there, along with Rahul Pathak and Jeremy Fletcher-Fiske. They all look surprised to see me. Greg's hand clenches around his fork in a way that suggests I better say something clever, fast. He might be dating Audrey now, but I dated her once, and clearly Greg worries there might still be something there. Probably because once, at a party, she arrived with him but made out with me.

Here's the thing about influencing a group to do what you want. It's a lot easier if what you want and what they want line up. Getting marks interested in easy money only works on the greedy. I hope I can interest Greg in the promise of easy revenge while I distract the rest of the table. I'm counting on his being threatened enough that he'll want to make me look like a fool. I just hope that he's not so threatened that he decides to punch me in the face.

"Get out of here," Greg says.

"I wanted to talk with you all about the senior prank," I improvise wildly.

Rahul frowns. "The school year just started."

I nod. "Look, last year the class left it until the end and they got the kind of lame prank that you'd expect. I want ours to make our graduating class infamous."

"You're totally taking bets on it," says Jeremy. "You just want an inside line."

"I want to get a horse into Northcutt's bedroom," I say. "Wearing an enormous thong. Now, please tell me how admitting that to you is going to make me any money."

Rahul and Jeremy laugh, Jeremy spitting a piece of salad out onto his plate. Now Greg can't just boot me from the table. He won't let me leave with Rahul and Jeremy well-disposed toward me.

"Can you picture her face?" Rahul says gleefully.

"Whatever," says Greg. "We can come up with something better than that."

"Like what?" asks Audrey. She doesn't sound like she's challenging him. She sounds like she's sure he's going to come up with an absolutely brilliant suggestion in just a moment and she's patiently waiting. She sounds kind. I'm sure she wouldn't mind if her new boyfriend made her old boyfriend look like a fool either.

By this point I'm sure I have somewhere to sit for dinner. I get my food and eat it, listening to them trade prank ideas back and forth. The more we talk about it, the more I warm to the idea of deciding the scheme early so we can focus for the rest of the year on the perfect execution. I let Greg get in a few digs.

And if I sometimes flash to the image of the body in the freezer, to the waxen face of my brother, or to the wide-eyed way Lila looked when I pulled away from her last night, well, then, I have had a lifetime of experience keeping what I'm thinking off my face.

"Hey, look at the new kid. Isn't she supposed to be some crime boss's daughter?" Jeremy says.

I swivel my head to see Lila standing. A junior girl I don't know is talking to her, gesturing grandly with blue-gloved hands. I can't hear what they're saying over the general dining hall noise, but the junior's expression is alight with malicious glee.

"Girl fight," Rahul says, grinning.

But when Lila takes a step toward the sophomore,

it's not to punch or pull hair. She starts removing a single black glove.

I see a flash of bare fingers and hear Greg's indrawn breath beside me. The junior girl stumbles back.

"She's crazy," says Jeremy. "That's *nuts*. She's going to —"

People are getting up, conversations are pausing. In that lull of sound I hear Lila's voice distinctly.

"You sure you want to cross me?" she says. In that moment she's her father's daughter.

The junior runs off toward the teacher's table, and Lila sits down, pulling her glove back on. I see Daneca gaping at her. After a few moments Dean Wharton comes over and escorts Lila out of the building.

I push around the Salisbury steak in front of me. After a while of doing that, I get up.

"Greg," Audrey says, rising with me. "Can you give me a minute with Cassel?"

"Whatever." He shrugs, but the look he shoots me is anything but casual. It's hard to picture a guy like Greg Harmsford loving anyone, but the way he watches Audrey is at least possessive.

"What's going on with you?" Audrey asks as we walk toward the dorms. The sun is just going down and the sky is dim. The leaves are turned over on their backs, waiting for rain. "You don't care about the senior prank. I know that because you never, ever say what you actually mean."

Six months ago we almost got back together. I'd thought that being with her would, through some power of alchemy, transmute me into being a normal guy with normal problems. When she looks at me, I see the reflection of a different self in her eyes. Someone I long to be.

I lean toward her. She puts a hand on my chest and pushes me back, hard.

"What are you doing?" she says.

"I don't know. I thought—" I thought I was supposed to kiss her.

"*Cassel*," she says, exasperated. "You're always like this. Hot or cold. Do you even know what you want?"

I look at the concrete path beneath me, at the desiccated bodies of earthworms who crawled out of the ground in the rain, only to get scorched by the sun.

"You're the one who wanted to talk," I say defensively.

"Do you even remember last year? I cried my eyes out after you came back to school and acted like nothing we'd said to each other while you were kicked out mattered."

I nod, not looking at her, because she's right. After my mother worked Lila, the only reason I didn't flunk out was because Sam did half of my homework for me. Everything felt hollow and unreal. I blew off Audrey without even making up excuses.

"Why? And why talk to me now like *that* never happened?" Her voice has a funny quality to it. I know that if I look up at her, her neck will be all blotchy, like it always gets when she's upset.

"I'm sorry," I say. "You're right. I'm not really good at relationships."

"No, you're not!" Audrey says, seeming relieved that I

have finally said something she can totally endorse. "You're not, and I don't know how to deal with you."

I consider and dismiss many variations of the suggestion that we be friends. Finally I look at her.

"I'm sorry," I say.

"Lila's not your cousin either, is she?" Audrey asks.

"No," I say. "I told you that because—"

She holds up her hand, and I gratefully stop talking. "You didn't tell me that. She did."

At that I just stare. I honestly don't remember who started that whole line of lies. We did it just to borrow her shower. Now it seems like the height of callousness.

"I've seen the way you look at her," Audrey says. "I know you, Cassel. So that brings me to asking you again—what are you *doing*?"

"Screwing up," I say.

"Good answer." She smiles a little, almost despite herself, and leans in to pat me on the cheek. "Stop it."

Then she walks off. I turn to go back to my dorm, but my gaze is caught by Lila, standing across the quad. She sees me and enters the Gilbert Hall dorms, leaving me to wonder how long she was standing there. Leaving me to wonder how in the world she talked her way out of all the trouble.

Sam is tapping away on his laptop when I come in. He looks up and goes back to what he's doing, for which I'm thankful. I get through my Probability & Statistics homework (possibly my favorite class *ever*), and start a proposal paper for the semester-long project in physics. Then I settle on my bed to do some of my *Madame Bovary* reading.

I don't get too far before Sam closes his computer. "Everything okay? Daneca said you got called to the office."

"Family stuff," I say. "My mom."

He nods sagely. "Get anywhere with those files?"

I shake my head. "There goes my career in law enforcement, I guess."

Sam snorts and starts hooking up his PlayStation to the tiny portable television he got for his birthday. "When you're done with that, you want to shoot some bad guys?"

"Evildoers," I say. "Yeah. Definitely."

It should bother me to point my controller at the screen and watch pixelated guys fall over. It should remind me of Janssen or Philip and my hand should hesitate or something. I get the high score instead. After all, it's just a game.

After dinner we have study hall in our rooms. This is the time of night when we're supposed to do homework. If we actually finish it in the two hours allotted, then we can spend half an hour in the common room. But it also means that once we're checked on by our hall master to make sure we're studying, we have almost three hours before we're likely to be checked on again.

"I think I am going to go out," I say to Sam.

He frowns at me. "Where?"

"There's someplace I've got to see." I push open the window. "For the investigation."

"Okay," says Sam. "I'll come too. Let's go."

"You know we're sneaking out of here. We could get busted." I hold up my hands. "It's your senior year. You don't have to do this."

"Well, you're our expert on getting away with things. It's your job to make sure we *don't* get caught, right?"

"No pressure. Thanks," I say. I open iTunes on my laptop and set a file to play. Then I turn up the volume a couple of notches.

"What's that?" he asks.

"I recorded this last year. Study hall. So things won't be too quiet. It's mostly just clicking on laptops and us joking around. I thought it might come in handy someday."

"That's creepy, dude," he says.

I point to my head with both hands. "Expert, remember?"

Then we go out the window and close it behind us. I think of the night before and Lila, her back pressed against the lawn. The smell of crushed grass underfoot is as heady as any perfume.

"Walk casually," I say.

We get into my car, which stalls twice before it starts, causing Sam to give me the wide-eyed expression of a man who's looking down the barrel of explaining a suspension to his parents. A moment later, though, we're pulling out of the lot with the headlights off. I click them on as we turn onto the highway.

Then I head toward the address in the file, the one where Janssen was last seen. Quarter of an hour later we're parking near Cyprus View apartment complex. I get out.

It's one of those modern places with a doorman in the lobby and probably a gym up near the penthouse. There are bright lamps burning on the manicured lawn, bushes cut into round balls near the stretch of concrete walkways, and a park across the street. A block over is a supermarket, and a block from that is a gas station, but when you look at it from the right angle, the place is nice. Expensive. Sprinkler system, but no cameras that I can see, and I walk twice around one of the lights to be sure.

"What are we looking at?" Sam asks, leaning against the side of the car. In his uniform jacket, with his tie loose, he could almost be a gangster. So long as you don't notice the Wallingford logo over his breast pocket.

"Janssen's mistress's condo. I wanted to see if it felt—I don't know—familiar."

Sam frowns. "Why would it be familiar? You didn't even know Janssen. Did you?"

I'm slipping up. I shake my head. "I don't know. I just wanted to see it. Look for clues."

"Okay," Sam says skeptically, glancing down at his watch. "But if this is a stakeout, I vote for us getting snacks."

"Yeah," I reply, distracted. "Just give me a second."

I walk across the grass and past the groomed bushes. I don't remember any of this. I must have stood on this grass and waited for Janssen, but I don't recall a single thing.

A woman in jogging clothes runs in the direction of the apartment building. She's got two of those big black standard poodles on a leash. Staring at her, I get a flash of memory, but it feels so distant that I can barely catch it. She looks in my direction, then turns abruptly, jerking the leashes. I get a really good look at her face just before she takes off down the street.

She must be an actress, because the memory I have of her is a scene from a movie. I'm sure it was the jogger, but she was wearing a short black dress, with her hair up, and a necklace with a single sparkling amulet dangling in the valley between her breasts. She had a bruise on her face and she'd been crying. A faceless actor in my brother's leather jacket took her by the shoulders. A man was lying on the grass, facedown.

I can't remember anything else. No plot. Not even whether I saw the film in a theater or on television late one night. The memory makes no sense.

If she's some actress, how come she started running when she saw me?

And how come one of the actors was wearing my brother's leather jacket?

Only one way to find out. I chase after her, my Wallingford dress shoes clacking like beetles on the pavement.

She veers off across the street, and I follow. A car's high beams catch me, and the grill of a Toyota nearly slams into me. I hit my hand against his hood and keep going.

She's almost made it to a small park. There are a couple of other people, walking under flickering streetlights, but she doesn't call out to them and they don't seem to want to involve themselves.

I pump my legs faster, pounding my feet against the

dirt. I'm gaining on her now. One of the dogs barks as I reach out and catch the hood of the woman's pink velour top.

She stumbles, and the dogs go crazy. I had no idea enormous poodles were so protective, but these things look like they want to rip my arms off.

"Wait," I say. "Please. I'm not going to hurt you."

She turns back toward me, the barking dogs between us. I hold up my hands in surrender. The park is quiet and dim, but if she starts running again, she could make it to the buildings beyond it, businesses that would probably not see my chasing her in a favorable light.

"What do you want?" she says, studying my face. "Our business is over. Done. I told Philip I didn't want to see any of you."

The creeping realization that there was no movie comes over me. *Of course.* Barron must have taken my memory and changed one small detail—the part where it happened in real life. That must have been easier for him than erasing the memory completely. And I'd forget it the same way I forget every other late-night cop show.

"I already paid you," she's saying, and I focus on memorizing her, shaking off all other thoughts. Her dark hair is pulled back into a ponytail, and her artificially plumped lips are painted a bubble-gum pink. Her eyes are tilted up at the corners, her eyebrows high enough to give her a perpetual expression of mild surprise. Between that and her wrinkled neck, I guess she's had some work done. She's beautiful and unreal; I can see why Barron changed her into a movie star in my head. "I'm not giving you anything else. You can't blackmail me."

I have no idea what she's talking about.

"He strung me along, you know. Told me he was going to marry me. Then, *bam,* starts knocking me around when I find out he's *already* married. But what do you care about that? Nothing. You probably have a girl back home that you treat no better. Get out of here, you piece of trash."

When I look at her, I still see the woman I mistook her for. I wonder what she sees when she looks at me. A drip of sweat runs over the curve of her cheek. Her breathing is rapid and shallow. She's scared.

An assassin, that's what she sees.

"You're the one who wanted the hit," I say, untangling what she's saying. "You paid Anton to take out Janssen."

"What are you, wearing a wire?" she asks, raising her voice and talking into my chest. "I never killed nobody. I never had nobody killed." She looks back toward her apartment building, like she's thinking about bolting.

"Okay," I say, holding up my hands again. "Okay. That was stupid."

"Yeah," she says. "Are we done?"

I nod my head, and then suddenly think of another question. "Where were you on Tuesday night?"

"Home with the dogs," she says. "I had a headache. Why?"

"My brother got shot."

She frowns. "Do I look like a killer?"

I don't point out that she hired a team of hit men to kill

her lover. My silence must make her feel like she scored a point, because with a final triumphant glare she takes off, dogs sprinting alongside her.

I walk back to my car, feeling each step. A blister has risen on my big toe. These shoes were never made for chase scenes.

The door of the Benz opens. "Cassel?" Sam calls from the driver's side. "She tell you anything good?"

"Yeah," I say. "That she was going to mace me."

"I was ready to fire up the getaway car." Sam grins. "Doesn't she know that muggers don't wear ties?"

I straighten my collar. "I'm a better class of criminal. A gentleman thief, if you will."

I let Sam drive. We head back to Wallingford, stopping for drive-through coffee and fries along the way. When we hop back through the dorm window, the smell of take-out clings to our clothes so strongly that it takes half a bottle of air freshener to disguise it.

"Stop smoking in your room," the hall master says at lights-out. "Don't think I can't tell what you've been doing in here."

We laugh so hard that, for a moment, it seems like we're never going to be able to stop.

The next morning I am walking to Developing World Ethics when Kevin Ford runs up to me. He stuffs an envelope into my hand.

"What are the odds that Greg Harmsford nailed Lila Zacharov?" he asks, breathless.

"What?" I say.

"Am I the first one to put down money? Dude!"

"Kevin, what are you talking about?" I resist grabbing his shoulders and shaking him, but I don't think I manage to keep the edge out of my voice. "I can't calculate odds on something when I have no idea what you're talking about."

"Last night I heard that they went into the sitting room and did it. Greg was bragging about it. His roommate, Kyle, had to totally distract their hall master."

"Okay," I say, nodding. My mouth feels dry. "I'll keep the money, but if no one else bets or no one bets against, I'm going to have to give it back." That's my standard line for things like this and I say it automatically.

He nods and races off. I stagger into class.

Greg Harmsford is sitting in his usual desk by the windows. I take a seat on the other side, staring at the back of his head, flexing my gloved hands.

While Mr. Lewis rattles on and on about trade agreements, I think about what it would be like to shove a sharpened pencil into Greg's ear. This is the kind of rumor that people start about new girls, I remind myself. They're never based on anything but wishful thinking.

Once we're dismissed, I head toward the door, passing Greg. He smirks, raising his eyebrows like he's daring me to start something.

Okay, that's weird.

"Hey, Cassel," he says, his smile getting wider.

I bite the inside of my cheek and continue into the

hallway. The copper taste of blood fills my mouth. I keep walking.

As I stalk toward Probability & Statistics, I see Daneca, her arms full of books.

"Hey, have you seen Lila?" I ask her, my voice strained.

"Not since yesterday," she says with a shrug.

I clamp my gloved hand on her shoulder. "Do you have any classes with her?"

Daneca stops and looks at me oddly. "She does a lot of remedial stuff."

Of course. Being a cat for three years might leave you a little behind on your schoolwork. But I've been too much in my own head to notice.

I get passed three more envelopes in statistics. Two of them are betting on Lila and Greg. I hand both of those back with such a dark look that no one asks me for an explanation.

She's not at lunch, either. Finally I walk into her building and head up the stairs, figuring that if I get caught, I'll come up with some explanation. I count over the number of doors, assuming that, like in my dorm, everyone gets one window to a room.

Then I knock. Nothing.

The locks are simple. I've been breaking into my own room for so long that I don't even carry my keys half the time. Just a quick pin twist and I'm inside.

She's got a single, which means her father must have made a pretty hefty donation. Her bed is jammed up against the window and there's a tangle of light green sheets dragging on the floor. An overstuffed bookcase that she must have brought with her sits against one wall. A totally forbidden electric kettle, and a tiny scarab green iPod glittering in an expensive-looking speaker system, wires connecting it to headphones, all rest on top of a low trunk. She's also brought in a vanity with a mirror that sits against the wall where a roommate's desk usually goes. The walls are covered in black-and-white photos of old movie stars: Bette Davis, Greta Garbo, Katharine Hepburn, Marlene Dietrich, and Ingrid Bergman. And Lila's pasted-up quotes near them.

I walk up to the picture of Garbo, smoldering behind a Vaselined lens. The paper near her says, "I'm afraid of nothing except being bored."

It makes me smile.

I relock the door and turn to go down the steps, when I realize that the dull hum in the background—a sound I barely even registered—is a shower running in the hall bathroom.

I head toward it.

The bathroom is tiled in pink and smells like girls' shampoos, tropical and sugary. As I push open the door, I realize that there is no excuse that can explain my being in here.

"Lila?" I call.

I hear a soft sob. I stop caring about getting caught.

She's sitting in the middle shower stall, still in her uniform. Her hair is plastered to her head and her clothes are soaked through. The water is pounding down so relentlessly that I'm surprised she can breathe. It runs in rivulets over her closed eyes and half-open mouth. Her lips look blue with cold.

"Lila?" I say again, and her eyes open wide.

I did this to her. She was always the fearless one, the dangerous one.

Now she looks at me like she doesn't believe I'm really here. "Cassel? How did you know—" She bites off the question.

"What did he do to you?" I say. I am trembling with fury and powerlessness and sick jealousy.

"Nothing," she says, and I can see that familiar, cruel smile of hers, but all of its mockery is turned inward. "I mean, I wanted him to. I thought maybe it would break the curse. I've never really—I was just a kid when I changed— and I figured that maybe if I slept with someone, it would help. Obviously it didn't."

I swallow carefully. "Why don't you come out of there and dry off? It's cold." I put on a fake voice, like I'm one of the old ladies from Carney. *You'll catch your death.*

She looks a little less dire, her smile a little less like a rictus. "The water was hot before."

I hold out a towel that's lying on a bench nearby. It's a sickly shade of magenta, covered with purple fish. I'm pretty sure it's not hers.

She gets up slowly, stiffly, and comes out of the shower. I wrap her in the towel. For a moment my arms close around her. She leans into me and sighs.

We walk together across the hallway to her room. There

she pulls away to sit on the bed, dripping onto her sheets. She looks curled in on herself, arms crossed over her chest.

"Okay," I say. "I'm going to go stand in the stairway and you're going to get dressed, and then we're going to get out of here. I've got lots of untried schemes for walking out of Wallingford in the middle of the day; let's try one. We can get some hot chocolate. Or tequila. And then we can come back and kill Greg Harmsford, something I personally have wanted to do for a while."

Her fingers pull the towel tighter. She doesn't smile. Instead she says, "I'm sorry I haven't been handling this— the curse—very well."

"No," I rasp. Guilt is closing up my throat. "Don't. You shouldn't have to apologize. Not to me."

"At first I thought I could just ignore it, and now— well—it's like ignoring made the wound go septic. And then I said that if I came here and at least could see you, it would help. But it didn't. Everything that I think will help just makes it worse.

"So I want to ask you to do something," she says, looking at the floor, at a collection of textbooks that I'm pretty sure she's not actually seeing. "And I understand it's not fair, but it won't cost you much, and it would mean everything to me. I want you to be my boyfriend."

I start to say something, but she talks over me, already sure I'm going to say no.

"You don't have to really like me. And it will just be for a little while." She's looking up at me now, her eyes hard. "You can pretend. I know you're a good liar."

I don't even know how to protest. I'm scrambling. "You said that everything you think will help actually makes it worse. What if *this* makes it worse?"

"I don't know," she says, so low I can barely hear it.

It's not real or right or fair, but I no longer have any idea what is. "Okay," I say. "Okay. We can date. But we can't—I mean, that's all that can happen. I can't live with you sitting on the floor of a shower in six months, regretting being with me."

I am rewarded with her coming into my arms, her clothes damp and cold, her skin feverishly hot. I can see the relief in the sag of her shoulders, and when I put my arm around her, she leans against my chest, tucking her head under my chin.

"Hopefully . . . ," she says, a hitch in her voice like a swallowed sob. "Hopefully by then I won't be thinking about you at all."

She smiles up at me, and I am, for a long moment, unable to speak.

Boyfriends, even fake boyfriends, sit with their girlfriends at dinner. So I'm not surprised when Lila sets her tray down next to mine and touches me briefly on the shoulder. Daneca, however, bristles with curiosity. It's clearly costing her something not to speak.

When the first person walks over and tosses an envelope into my bag, Lila smiles into her paper napkin.

"You're a bookie? I thought you were the good brother," she says.

"I'm good at what I do," I say. "Virtue is its own revenge."

"Its own *reward*," says Daneca, rolling her eyes. "Virtue is its own reward."

I grin. "That's not the version I've heard."

Sam plunks down his tray and grabs for the apple about to roll off it. "You know how Mr. Knight is getting a little bit on the senile side? Like walking past the classroom and having to double back, or putting on his sweater over a winter coat?"

I nod, although I haven't had Mr. Knight for anything. I've just seen him in the halls. He looks like a typical ancient English professor—tweedy, with leather elbow pads and white nose hair.

"Well, today he came into class, and not only had he forgotten to zip up after a trip to the bathroom, he forgot to *tuck his junk back in*."

"No way," I say.

Lila starts to laugh.

"That's the thing, right? It should be funny," Sam says. "It's funny now. But right then it was so awful that all we could do was sit there in shock. I was so embarrassed for him! And he just lectured the class on Hamlet like nothing was happening. I mean, he's quoting Shakespeare while we're all just trying not to look down."

"Didn't anyone say anything?" Daneca asks. "All those jokers?"

"Finally," says Sam, "Kim Hwangbo raises her hand."

I shake my head. Kim is quiet, nice, and will probably go to a better college than anyone else at Wallingford.

Even Daneca is laughing now. "What did she say?"

"'Mr. Knight, your pants are unzipped!'" says Sam. He laughs. "So Mr. Knight looks down, barely has a reaction, says 'Uneasy lies the head that wears a crown,' tucks himself in, and zips up. The end!"

"Are you going to tell anyone?" Daneca asks.

Sam shakes his head as he opens his milk. "No, and don't you, either. Mr. Knight is harmless—it's not like he did it on purpose—and he'd get in a lot of trouble if Northcutt found out. Or parents."

"They're going to find out," I say. I wonder how long it will take before bets start flooding in about him getting fired. "No one can hide anything for long around here."

Daneca frowns in my direction. "Oh, I don't know about that."

"What do you mean?" Lila asks, not entirely friendly.

Daneca ignores her question. "We're going to the movies this weekend," she says instead. "Do you guys want to come? We could double-date."

A flush creeps up Sam's neck.

Lila turns to me uncertainly. I smile.

"Sure," she says. "If you want to, Cassel?"

"What's the movie?" I ask. With Daneca, we could wind up going to some kind of documentary on the evils of baby seal clubbing.

"We're going to see *The Giant Spider Invasion*," Sam says. "They're playing it at the Friday Rewind. It's a classic Bill Rebane film—the special effects crew created the giant spider by covering a Volkswagen Beetle in fake fur and using the taillights as its red glowing eyes."

"What's better than that?" I ask.

No one can think of a thing.

That night I dream I'm in a room of corpses, all of them wearing dresses and lipstick, sitting stiffly on couches. It takes me a moment to realize they're all my ex-girlfriends, their dead eyes glittering, their mouths barely moving as they whisper a list of my flaws.

He kisses like a fish, says my kindergarten girlfriend, Michiko Ishii. We'd meet behind a fat oak tree on the playground, until we got caught by another girl who ratted us out. Her corpse is that of a very little girl; glassy eyes make her look like a doll.

He flirted with my friend, says the girl who ratted us out, Sofia Spiegel, who was technically also my girlfriend at the time.

He's a liar, says a girl from Atlantic City. The one in the silver dress.

Such a liar, says my eighth-grade girlfriend. I didn't tell her that I was going to Wallingford until after I left. I don't blame her for still being mad.

After the party he pretended not to know me, says Emily Rogers, who, to be fair, pretended just as hard that *I* didn't exist after we'd spent the night rolling around on a pile of coats at Harvey Silverman's freshman-year house party.

He borrowed my car and totaled it, says Stephanie Douglas, a worker girl I met in Carney over the summer after I was sure I'd killed Lila. She was two years older than me and could knot the stem of a cherry with her tongue.

He never really loved me, says Audrey. *He doesn't even know what love is.*

I wake up while it's still dark outside. Rather than go back to sleep, I start on some homework. I'm tired of the dead ganging up on me. There's got to be a problem somewhere that wants solving.

CHAPTER EIGHT

WALLINGFORD PREP-
aratory prides itself on getting its young men and women
ready not just for college but for their place in society. To
that end, students not only have to attend all their classes—
they also have to participate in two enriching after-school
activities. This year mine are track in the fall and debate
club in the spring. I like the feeling of running, the rush of
adrenaline and the pounding of my feet on the pavement. I
like that it's just me deciding how far to push myself.

I also like thinking up ways to trick people into agree-
ing with me, but debate club doesn't start for many months.

I'm just finishing my last lap when I see two dark-suited
men talking to Coach Marlin. He waves me over.

Agent Jones and Agent Hunt are wearing mirrored sunglasses along with their dark suits and darker gloves, even though the weather is still unseasonably warm. I'm not sure they could be more unsubtle if they tried.

"Hello, Officers," I say with a fake grin.

"Haven't heard from you in a while," Agent Jones says. "We got concerned."

"Well, I had this funeral to go to, and then I had all this extra grieving to do. Really filled up my social calendar." Although I think I'm managing to smirk like an innocent man, knowing that I'm the murderer they're looking for really adds an uncomfortable layer of terror to the whole interaction. "There's been loads going on since last Wednesday."

"Why don't you take a ride with us?" says Agent Hunt. "You can tell us all about it."

"I don't think so," I say. "I've got to take a shower and get changed. Like I said, really busy. But thanks for stopping by."

Coach Marlin has already started over toward other runners. He's shouting their times off his stopwatch. He's either forgotten about me or is trying to forget.

Agent Jones lowers his glasses. "Heard your mother was skipping out on some hotel bills in Princeton."

"You should probably just ask her about that," I say. "I'm sure it's a big misunderstanding."

"I don't think you really want us asking her about it, do you?" Agent Hunt asks.

"That's true, I don't, but I can't control what you decide

to do. I'm just an underage minor and you're big strong federal agents." I start walking away.

Agent Hunt grabs my arm. "Stop messing around. Come
with us. Right now, Cassel. You don't want us making things
hard on you."

I look over at my team, jogging toward the locker room,
Coach Marlin in the lead. Some of them are jogging backward to see what's going to happen to me.

"The only way I am getting in a car with you is if you
handcuff me," I say with resolve. There are some things a
boy like me can't live down, and being too friendly with
the law is definitely one of them. No one wants to make an
illicit bet with someone unless they're sure that someone is
actually a criminal.

They take the bait. I am pretty sure Agent Hunt has been
wanting to do this since the moment we met. He catches
my wrist, pulls it behind me and smacks a cuff down onto
it. Then he grabs for my other wrist. I only struggle a little,
but apparently it's enough to annoy him, since when he
gets the other cuff on me, he gives me a little shove. I wind
up on my stomach in the dirt.

I turn my head toward the locker room and see a couple
of guys and the coach still watching the show. Enough people
to pass on the rumor.

Agent Jones pulls me back to my feet. Not too gently
either.

I don't say anything as they march me to the car and
shove me into the back.

"Now," Agent Jones says from the front seat, "what do

you have for us?" He doesn't start the car but I hear the locks of all four doors engage.

"Nothing," I say.

"We heard Zacharov came to the memorial service," says Agent Hunt. "And he brought his daughter with him. A girl that no one has seen in public in a long time. Now she's back. Here at Wallingford, even."

"So what?" I say.

"We hear that you and her were pretty close. If that's even his daughter."

"What do you want?" I ask, giving an experimental tug on the cuffs. They're double-lock and plenty tight. "You want me to tell you whether that's really Lila Zacharov? It is. I used to play marbles with her down in Carney. She's got nothing to do with this."

"So what's she been doing all this time? If you know her so well, how about you tell me that."

"I don't know," I lie. I have no idea where this line of questioning is going, but I don't like it.

"You could have a life outside of all this," Agent Jones says. "You could be on the right side of the law. You don't have to protect these people, Cassel."

I am these people, I think, but his words make me fantasize for a moment about what it would be like to be a good guy, with a badge and a stainless reputation.

"We talked to your brother," Agent Hunt says. "He was very cooperative."

"Barron?" I say, and burst out laughing. I let myself flop down onto the leather seat with relief. "My brother is a *compulsive liar*. I'm sure he was cooperative. There is nothing he likes better than an audience."

Agent Jones looks embarrassed. Agent Hunt just seems pissed. "Your brother said that we might start looking at Lila Zacharov. And he said that you'd protect her."

"Did he?" I say, but I'm in control of this conversation now, and they both know it. "I looked over those files you gave me. Are you saying that Lila is a death worker who started killing people at the age of fourteen? Because that's how old she was when Basso disappeared. And not only that, but she would have to have hidden the death rot really well. Really well, because I can tell you that I've see her with not even a stitch of—"

"We're not saying anything." Agent Jones puts his hand down hard on the seat, interrupting my little speech. "We're coming to you for information. And if you don't give us something, then we're going to have to listen to other sources. Maybe even sources you don't consider to be as reliable. You understand me?"

"Yeah," I say.

"So what are you going to have next time we come to talk?" Agent Jones asks in a kind voice. He takes out a business card, reaches back, and tosses it into my lap.

I take a deep breath, let it out. "Information."

"Good," says Agent Hunt.

They exchange a look I can't interpret, and Agent Hunt gets out of the car. He opens my door. "Turn around so I can take those off."

I do. A twist, two clicks, and I'm rubbing my wrists, free.

"In case you get some idea that we can't pick you up whenever we want," Hunt says. "You're a worker. You know what that means?"

I shake my head. Finding the business card Jones tossed at me, I shove it into my pocket. Jones watches me from where he's standing.

Hunt grins. "It means you've already done something illegal. All workers have. Otherwise, how would you know what you are?"

I get out of the car and look him in the face. Then I spit on the hot black asphalt of the parking lot.

He starts toward me, but Agent Jones clears his throat, and Hunt stops.

"We'll be seeing you around," Agent Jones says, and they both get back into the car.

I walk back to Wallingford, hating both of them so much that I'm jittery with rage. The thing I hate most is that they're right about me.

I am called into Headmistress Northcutt's office almost immediately. She opens the door and waves me inside.

"Welcome, Mr. Sharpe. Please have a seat."

I sit in the green leather chair opposite her wide expanse of a desk. Several tidy folders are corralled in a wooden box on one side, and a well-used planner sits beside a golden pen in a stand. Everything is organized, elegant.

Except for the cheap glass bowl of mints. I take one and unwrap it slowly.

"I understand you had some visitors today?" Northcutt

asks. Her eyebrows lift, like having any visitors at all is suspect.

"Yeah," I say.

She sighs deeply at my forcing her to ask the question directly. "Would you like to explain what two federal agents wanted with you this time?"

I lean back in the chair. "They offered to make me a narc, but I said that the workload here at Wallingford was too intensive for me to take on an after-school job."

"Excuse me?" I didn't think it was possible for her eyebrows to rise even higher on her forehead, but they do. It isn't a nice thing I'm doing—selling a story that's less ridiculous than my presentation of it. Worst thing she can do is give me a couple of detentions or a demerit for my smart mouth, though.

"A narc," I say excessively politely. "An informant who reports on observed narcotic violations. But don't worry, there is no way I would ever agree to rat out my fellow students. Even if they made the poor decision to use drugs, which I am sure no one here ever would."

She leans forward and picks up her golden pen, points it at me. "Do you seriously expect me to believe that, Mr. Sharpe?"

I widen my eyes. "Well, I guess there are some people here who do look like they're stoned all the time, I'll give you that. But I always figured they were just—"

"Mr. Sharpe!" She looks like she's ready to actually stab me with the pen. "It is my understanding that the agents handcuffed you. Would you like to change your story?"

I think of sitting in this same office last year, begging to be allowed to stay. Maybe I'm still angry about that.

"No, ma'am. They just wanted to give me a little demonstration of how safe I would be working with them, although I can see how someone observing it might have come to a different conclusion. You can call the agents yourself," I say, reaching into my pocket. I pull out the card Agent Jones gave me and set it down on Northcutt's desk.

"I will do that," she says. "You may go. For now."

The agents will back me up. They have to. They're not done with me yet. And Agent Hunt doesn't really want to explain why he was slamming around a seventeen-year-old with no criminal record. So I get the satisfaction of their having to agree to a silly story. And I get Northcutt's annoyance at having to accept a story she's pretty sure isn't true.

Everyone wants to get out of a situation with dignity.

The HEX meeting has already started by the time I get there. The desks in Ms. Ramirez's music room have been rearranged into an impromptu circle, and I see Lila and Daneca are sitting together. I pull up a seat next to Lila.

She smiles and reaches over to squeeze my hand. I wonder if this is her first meeting. I haven't attended enough to know.

On the blackboard, there's the address for the worker rights protest Sam promised we'd attend way back when school started. Turns out it's tomorrow. I guess that's what they were talking about before I got here. Rules are written below the protest information: stick together, no talking to strangers, stay in the park.

"I'm sure that many of you didn't see yesterday's speech, since it ran during study hall," Ramirez says. "I thought we could watch it together and discuss."

"I really hate Governor Patton," says one of the sophomore girls. "Do we have to see his face spewing more crap?"

"Like it or not," says Ms. Ramirez, "this is what America sees. And this is what New Jersey will be thinking about in November when we vote on proposition two. This or a speech very like it."

"He's ahead in the polls," Daneca says, biting the end of one of her braids. "People actually approve of his performance."

The sophomore gives Daneca a horrible look, like Daneca was suggesting people *should* approve of Patton.

"It's a stunt," says one of the boys. "He just acts like he cares about this because it's a popular issue. Back in 2001 he voted with worker rights. He goes where his bread is buttered."

They talk some back and forth, but I lose the thread of it. I'm just happy to be here, not getting yelled at or handcuffed. Lila's watching the discussion, gaze flashing to each of the speaker's faces, but her hand rests in mine and she seems more relaxed than I've seen her in a long time.

Everything seems possible.

If I just think hard enough, plan carefully enough, maybe I can solve my problems—even the ones I was considering unsolvable. First off, I need to actually figure out who killed

Philip. Once I know that, I can engineer the steps to get the Feds off my back. Then maybe I can figure out what to do about Lila.

Ms. Ramirez pushes a television in front of a chair on one side of the circle. "Enough! Let's leave some discussing until after watching, okay?"

She presses a button, and the screen flickers to life. She points the controller at it, and Governor Patton's pasty face fills the screen. He's at a lectern, with a blue stage curtain hanging behind him. The few white hairs he still has are slicked back, and he looks through the screen like he wants to eat us all up.

The camera pulls back so that we can see the press pit in front of him. Lots of people in suits raising their hands like it's high school all over again, just waiting for the teacher to call on them. And at one side there's an aide standing on the narrow steps to the stage, like he's guarding them. Beside the aide is a woman in a severe black dress, her hair pulled into a chignon. There is something about her that makes me look again.

"You're hurting my hand," Lila whispers.

I let go of her, ashamed. My glove was pulled tight over my knuckles, like I was trying to make a fist.

"What?" she asks me.

"It's just hard to listen to," I say, which seems to be true, since I wasn't actually listening at all.

She nods her head, but there is a pin scratch line between her brows. I wait interminable minutes until I think I can safely turn to her and say, "Be right back.

"Bathroom," I say to her frown of inquiry.

I head down the hallway the opposite way from the bathroom, lean against the wall, and take out my phone. As it rings, I think over and over about *Millionaires at Home* or whatever that stupid magazine was.

"Hello, sweetheart," my mother says. "Let me call you back on a landline."

I clear my throat. "First, would you explain what you were doing on television?"

She laughs girlishly. "You saw that? How did I look?"

"Like you were wearing a costume," I say. "What were you doing with Governor Patton? He hates workers, and you're a worker *ex-convict*."

"He's a nice man once you get to know him," she says sweetly. "And he doesn't hate workers. He wants mandatory testing to save worker lives. Didn't you listen to the speech? Besides, I'm not an ex-convict. My case was overturned on appeal. That's different."

At that moment I hear shouting back where the HEX meeting is being held.

"I got you freaks," someone yells.

"I'll call you back," I say, folding the phone closed against my chest as I head back down the hall. Greg is watching as Jeremy holds a video camera in front of the doorway, swinging it back and forth, like he's trying to get everyone. Jeremy's laughing so hard that I wonder if he's holding it steady enough for it to record anything but streaks of color.

Ms. Ramirez steps into the hall, and the boys stumble

back, but they keep filming. Now they're just filming her.

"I am giving you both two demerits," she says. Her voice sounds odd, shaky. "And for every second that you don't turn off the camera, I am giving you another one."

Jeremy swings it down, right away, fumbling with the controls.

"You are both going to have detention with me for the rest of this week, and you are going to erase the recording, do you understand me? That was an invasion of privacy."

"Yes, Ms. Ramirez," Jeremy says.

"Good. Now you can go." She watches them lope off. I watch her watching them, a cold dread settling into my bones.

The website goes up that night. On Thursday morning I hear the rumor that Ramirez goes ballistic, but Northcutt doesn't know who to blame. Jeremy claims he was intending to delete the footage, that someone snuck into his room and stole his camera. He says he didn't upload the stills; Greg says that he never touched any of it.

The bets start flooding in. Are they or aren't they? It seems like everyone in the school wants to put down money on which of the people at that meeting were workers. A room that I would have been in too, if it wasn't for the barest coincidence.

"Do we take the money?" Sam asks me in the hallway between classes. He looks miserable. He's a clever guy and he's thought through this far enough to know that there are no easy answers.

"Yeah," I say. "We have to. If we don't, we won't be able to have any control."

We take their money.

On Thursday afternoon the website goes down without a trace.

CHAPTER NINE

BACK AT THE DORMS SAM is stripping off his uniform and putting on a T-shirt with I'M THE HONOR STUDENT YOU READ ABOUT across the front. He sprays some cologne at his neck while I dump my books onto the bed.

"Where are you going?" I ask.

"The protest." He rolls his eyes. "Don't try to weasel out of it. Daneca will kill you. She will *skin* you."

"Oh, right," I say, combing my fingers through my hair. It's getting shaggy again. "I guess I thought, with all the craziness . . ."

He lets me trail off vaguely but doesn't say anything helpful. He is probably used to me being an idiot. I sigh and kick off my dress shoes and black dress pants, pulling on jeans. After unknotting my tie and tossing it onto my rickety desk, I'm pretty much ready to go. I'm not even bothering to change out of my white button-down.

We cross the quad together and find Daneca with Ramirez outside of Rawlings Fine Arts Center, home to Ramirez's music room, and the location of most HEX meetings. The day is warm for September. Daneca's dressed up in a long batik skirt with bells dangling from the hem. She's even dyed the tips of her braids a muddy purple.

"It's canceled," Daneca says, turning to us. She's practically shouting. "Can you believe it? All Northcutt cares about is placating alumni donors! This isn't fair! She already said okay."

"It's not just the administration," Ms. Ramirez says. "*Students* dropped out of the trip too. No one wants to be seen getting on the bus."

"That's ridiculous," Daneca mutters, then louder she says, "We could have done something. Met somewhere other than here."

"Some of them are actually workers, you know," I say. "It's not just a cause for them. It's their actual lives. So maybe they're worried about the actual consequences of people guessing their secret."

Daneca gives me a look of loathing. "How do *they* think anything's going to get better with that attitude?" She clearly thinks *they* means *me*.

"Maybe *they* don't," I say.

"I'm sorry," Ramirez says with a heavy sigh. "I know you had your heart set on this."

"What's going on?" a soft voice asks from behind us. I turn to see Lila, backpack over one shoulder. She's wearing a yellow sundress and big, clunky boots. I feel that same odd shock that I always feel when I see her, like an electric current passing through my body.

"Trip's canceled due to administrative cowardice," Sam says.

"Oh." Lila looks down at her boots and kicks a clump of dirt. Then she looks up. "Well, can the four of us still go?"

Daneca stares at her for a long moment, then turns to Ramirez. "Yes! She's right. We already turned in our permission slips, so our parents have already agreed to letting us out."

"On a school-supervised trip," Ramirez protests.

"We're *seniors*," Daneca says. "We've got our parents' permission. Northcutt can't stop us."

"I don't recall Mr. Sharpe turning in a permission slip."

"Oops," I say. "Left it in my room. Let me just run back and get it."

Ramirez sighs. "Fine. Give me that form, Cassel, and the four of you can sign out and go to the protest. But I want your word that you will be back in time for study hall."

"We will," Lila promises.

After a little bit of forgery on my part, we're heading to Sam's 1978 vintage Cadillac Superior side-loading hearse. Lila stops to read the bumper sticker.

"This thing really runs on vegetable oil?" she asks.

The afternoon sun bakes the asphalt of the parking lot, making heat radiate off it. I wipe my brow and try not to consider the sweat beading at Lila's collarbone.

Sam grins proudly and slaps the hood. "It wasn't easy to find a diesel hearse to convert, but I did."

"Smells like french fries," says Daneca, climbing in. "But you get used to it."

"French fries are delicious," says Sam.

Lila scrambles into the backseat, which is custom—scavenged from a regular Cadillac and installed by Sam—and I slide in after her.

"Thank you guys for coming," Daneca says. She looks in my direction. "I know you don't really want to go, so let me just say—I appreciate it."

"It's not that I don't want to," I say, and take a deep breath. I think of my mother at that other rally with Patton. "I'm just not that into politics."

Daneca turns around in her seat to look at me incredulously. "Oh?" She doesn't seem mad, more amused.

"Deathwërk's playing later," Sam says, steering the hearse out of the parking lot as he steers the conversation away from me. "We'll probably get there in time for Bare Knuckles."

"*Bands?* Really? I was imagining less fun, more marching with placards," I say.

Daneca grins. "Don't worry, there'll be plenty of placards. The march goes past city hall to Lincoln Park—that's where the bands are supposed to perform. There are going to be speeches, too."

"Well, good," I say. "I would hate to think we're giving

up valuable studying time for anything less than a—"

Lila laughs, leaning back against her headrest.

"What?" I say.

"I don't know," Lila says. "You have nice friends." She touches my shoulder lightly with the tips of her gloved fingers.

A shiver starts low on my spine. For a moment I remember the feel of her bare hands on my skin.

It's just the four of us in the car, and even though the plan is to go to the movies tomorrow, I have to try really hard to convince myself this isn't anything like a double date.

"That's *right*," says Sam. "You knew our man Cassel back when. Got the dirt for us?"

She looks at me slyly. "When he was a kid, he was a total shrimp. Then around thirteen, he shot up like a beanpole."

I grin. "And you stayed a shrimp."

"He loved cheap horror novels, and when he started one, he'd read it straight through until the end, no matter what. Sometimes his grandfather would come into his bedroom and switch off the lamp when it got really late, so Cassel would climb out the window and read by the streetlight. I'd come over in the morning and find him asleep on the lawn."

"Awwww," Daneca says.

I make a rude sound, accompanied by an equally rude gesture.

"One time, at a fair in Ocean City, he ate so much cotton candy that he threw up."

"Who hasn't?" I say.

"He had a black-and-white film marathon, after which

he wore a fedora." She raises her brows, daring me to contradict her. "For a *month*. In the middle of summer."

I laugh.

"A fedora?" Sam says.

I remember sitting in the basement for hours, watching movie after movie of rough-voiced women and men in dapper suits with drinks in their gloved hands. When Lila's parents got divorced, she went to Paris with her father and came back smoking Gitanes and outlining her eyes in smudgy black kohl. It was like she'd stepped out of the movie I wanted to be in.

I see her now, the stiffness of her body as she leans deliberately away from me, pressing her cheek against the window. She looks tired.

In Carney, back then, I didn't care about blending in. I wasn't constantly trying to bluff my way into seeming like a better guy. I had no secrets I was desperate to keep. And Lila was brave and sure and totally unstoppable.

I wonder what the kid I was then would think of the people we are now.

Cops are standing by blockades far from where the march is supposed to be. Traffic cones are set up, flares sparking with sizzling orange flames. There are people, too, more than I expected, and a distant roar that promises even more than that.

"There's no place to park," Sam complains, slowly circling the same block for the third time.

Daneca pokes at her phone as we inch along behind a

line of cars. "Turn left when you can," she says after a few minutes. "I have an app that says there's a garage a couple blocks from here."

The first two we pass are full, but then we find cars just parking on top of the median and along the sidewalks. Sam pulls the hearse onto a patch of green grass and kills the engine.

"Rebel," I say.

Daneca grins hugely and opens the door. "Look at all these people!"

Lila and I get out, and the four of us head in the direction most are going.

"It makes you feel like everything could change, you know?" Daneca says.

"Everything *is* going to change," says Sam, surprising me.

Daneca turns and gives him a look. I can tell he surprised her, too.

"Well, it is," he says. "One way or another."

I guess he's right. Either proposition two will get voted down and workers will start to rise up, or proposition two will pass and other states will fall all over themselves to try the same trick.

"Changing is what people do when they have no options left," Lila says cryptically.

I try to catch her eye, but she's too busy watching the crowd.

We walk like that for a few more blocks and start to see signs.

WE ARE NOT A CURSE, one reads.

I wonder what kind of slogans they had at the press conference Mom attended.

A group of kids are sitting on the steps of a Fidelity bank. One throws a beer in the direction of the protesters. It shatters, glass and foam making everyone near its impact start shouting.

A man whose huge beard is long enough to overlap his T-shirt jumps up onto the hood of a car and yells louder than the others, "Down with proposition two! Flatten Patton!"

A policeman standing in front of a bodega picks up his radio and starts speaking rapidly into it. He looks flustered.

"I think the park is this way," Daneca says, pointing from the screen of her phone to a side street. I'm not sure she noticed anything else.

A couple more blocks and the crowd becomes so thick that it's more like a tide we have been swept up in. We're a vein rushing blood toward the heart, a furnace of sun-warmed body heat, a herd barreling toward a cliff.

I see more and more signs.

HANDS OFF OUR RIGHTS.

TESTING EVERYONE/TRUSTING NO ONE.

THIS ISN'T WORKING.

"How many people are they estimating will come out for this?" Lila shouts.

"Twenty, maybe fifty thousand maximum," Daneca shouts back.

Lila looks toward where our street intersects with Broad, where the main protest is. We can't see too far, but

HOLLY BLACK

the wall of noise—of slogans being screamed through bull-horns, of drums, of sirens—is almost deafening. "I think that number was off—way off."

As we get closer, it's easy to see why. I no longer have to imagine what signs Patton's supporters might have been waving around. They are out in force, lining the street on either side of the march.

MURDERERS AND MANIPULATORS OUT OF MY STATE, says one sign.

NO MORE HEEBEEGEEBIES.

WHAT DO YOU HAVE TO HIDE?

And finally, simply, GOTCHA, with a circle drawn to look like the crosshairs of a gun. That one is held up by an old woman with frizzy red hair and bright pink lipstick.

She's standing on the steps of city hall, the golden dome glowing above her.

As I scan the crowd of proposition two supporters, I see a familiar face far in the back. Janssen's mistress. She's got her dark hair pulled into a ponytail, sunglasses on top of her head. No poodles with her today.

I slow down, trying to make sure I'm seeing what I think I'm seeing.

She's taking bills from someone, both of them standing close to the glass window of a restaurant.

The crowd keeps moving around me, pushing me along with it. Someone's shoulder bangs into my arm. A guy a little older than me, snapping pictures.

"Who are you looking at?" Lila asks me, craning her neck.

"See that woman by the window?" I say, trying to shove

my way sideways through the crowd. "Ponytail. She hired the hit on Janssen."

"I know her. She used to work for him," Lila says, following me.

"What?" I stop so suddenly that the man behind me slams into my back. He grunts.

"Sorry," I tell him, but he just gives me a dirty look.

Daneca and Sam are ahead of us in the crowd. I want to call out to them to slow down, but there's no way they'd hear.

The woman is walking away from the march. As slowly as I'm moving, I am never going to get to her.

"I thought she was his girlfriend," I tell Lila.

"Maybe, but she was also his underling," she says. "She lines up buyers. High rollers. People who can afford to buy regular doses of ecstatic emotion—the kind of blissed-out happiness that'll send you spiraling into depression if you stop. Or they buy luck from half a dozen curse workers at a time. Use enough luck at once and it can change big things."

"Did she know Philip?" I ask.

"You said she ordered the hit."

Janssen's mistress disappears into the throng. We're not moving fast enough to follow. Daneca and Sam are gone too—somewhere ahead of us on Broad Street, I'm sure, but I can't spot them anymore.

I mop my brow with the tail of my white shirt. "This sucks."

Lila laughs and gestures to the large sign flapping in the wind above us. It's covered in glitter and reads BARE

HANDS; PURE HEARTS. "Before Wallingford, I'd never met many people who weren't workers—I never know what to make of them."

"Just me," I say. "I was the nonworker you knew."

She gives me a quick look, and I realize, of course, that she left out the most critical thing when she summarized my past in the car.

Back then I was beneath her.

Even if she never said it to me, even if she didn't act like what she could do mattered, everyone else said it enough that there was no chance I'd forget. She was a worker; I was part of the world of marks who existed to be manipulated.

I see another sign in the crowd, POWER CORRUPTS EVERYONE.

"Lila—," I start.

Then a girl walking just ahead of us takes off her gloves. She holds up her hands. They look pale and wrinkled from being inside leather in this heat.

I blink. In my life I haven't seen many bare female hands. It's hard not to stare.

"Bare hands, pure heart!" the girl yells.

Beside her I see a few other people pulling off gloves with wicked smiles. One throws a pair up into the sky.

My fingers itch for release. I imagine what it would be like to feel the breeze against my palms.

The combination of heat and rebellion spreads like a ripple through the crowd, and suddenly bare fingers are waving in the air. We are stepping over discarded gloves.

"Cassel!" someone calls, and I see Sam. He's managed to wedge himself and Daneca between two parked cars and out of foot traffic. He's red-faced from the heat. She's glove-less and beckoning us over.

Her hands are pale, with long fingers.

We push our way through the crowd to them. We're almost there when we hear the sound of a bullhorn from somewhere in front of us.

"Everyone must cover their hands immediately," a tinny voice booms. A siren wails. "This is the police. Cover your hands immediately."

Daneca looks as horrified as if they were talking personally to her.

There is technically nothing illegal about bare hands. Just like there is technically nothing illegal about a sharp kitchen knife. But when you wave one around, the police don't like it. And when you point it at something, that's when the cuffs really come out.

"Lift me up," Lila says.

"What?"

All around us people are jeering. But there is another sound, farther away, a roar of engines and cries that no longer contain words.

A news helicopter buzzes overhead.

"Up," she says with a smile, pointing in the air. "I want to see what's happening."

I put my arms around her waist and lift her. She's light. Her skin is soft against me, and she smells like sweat and crushed grass.

I set her down on the hood of the car, next to where Sam's standing.

"There's a bunch of cops," she says, hopping down. "Riot gear. We've got to get out of here."

I nod once. Criminals like us are good at running.

"We're not doing anything illegal," Daneca says, but she doesn't sound sure. Around us the crowd feels it too. They aren't moving in the same direction anymore. They're scattering.

"Inside," I say. "If we can get to one of the buildings, we can wait out whatever happens."

But as we move toward the doorway nearest to us, cops start streaming across the sidewalk, their faces covered by helmets.

"Get down on the ground!" comes the command. They spread out, shoving protestors if they hesitate. One girl tries to argue, and a cop swings a baton at her leg. Another girl gets sprayed in the face with some chemical. She falls to the ground, clawing at her skin.

Lila and I drop down onto the asphalt immediately.

"What's going on?" Sam says, kneeling down too. Daneca squats beside him.

"Under the car," Lila says, crawling forward on her elbows.

It's a pretty good plan. We still get arrested, but at least it takes a little longer.

The last time I was in a prison was to visit Mom. Prisons are places where people live. They're dehumanizing, but they have things like tables and cafeterias and exercise rooms.

This is different. This is a jail.

They take our wallets, cell phones, and bags. They don't even bother fingerprinting us. They just ask us our names and march us down to a holding cell. Girls in one, guys in the one next door. And so on, down a long noisy hallway.

There's a couple of benches, a sink, and a single disgusting toilet. All occupied.

Daneca tries to tell them that we're underage, but the cops don't pay any attention to her. They just lock us up.

Sam is standing near me, his head leaning against the bars and his eyes closed. Daneca found a spot on one of the benches and is sitting, her face streaked with tears. They made her cover her hands before they hauled us into their armored van—and when she couldn't find one of her gloves, they taped a bag all the way to her elbow. It's cradled against her body now.

Lila paces back and forth.

"Lila," I say, and she whirls, teeth bared, hand striking at me through the bars.

"Hey," I say, catching her wrist.

She looks so surprised that I wonder if, for a moment, she forgot she was human.

"We're going to be okay," I say. "We're going to get out of here."

She nods, embarrassed now, but her breaths are still coming too fast. "What time do you think it is?"

We got to the protest at about four thirty and we never even made it to the park. "Maybe around seven," I say.

"Still early. God, I am such a mess." She pulls away from me, rubbing her gloved hand through her hair.

"You're fine," I say.

She snorts.

I look around the room at all the desperate faces. I bet none of them have ever seen the inside of a jail before. I bet none of them have family who've been in prison.

"Ever think about the future?" I ask, trying to distract her.

"Like, the future in which we're not locked up?"

"After graduation. After Wallingford." It is much in my thoughts lately.

She shrugs, leaning her face against a metal bar. "I don't know. Dad took me to Vieques this past summer. We'd just lie on the beach or swim. Everything's brighter and bluer there, you know? I'd like to go back. Soak it all up. I'm tired of being shut in dark places."

I think of her trapped in that horrible wire cage by Barron for months at a time. During one of my bleaker moments the past summer, I looked up the effects of solitary confinement on prisoners. Depression, despair, crippling anxiety, hallucinations.

I can't imagine what it must be like to be in a cage again.

"Never been out of the country," I say. Who am I kidding? I've never even been on an airplane.

"You could come," she says.

"If you still want me with you after we graduate, I'm yours," I say, trying to make my vow sound a little more casual.

"So that's it? You're just going to lie around on a beach."

"Until Dad needs me," she says. Her breaths are more

even now, her eyes less wide and wild. "I've always known what I was going to be when I grew up."

"The family business," I say. "You ever think of doing something else?"

"No," she says, but there's something in her voice that makes me wonder. "It's all I'm good at. Besides, I'm a Zacharov."

I think about the things I'm good at. And I think about Ms. Vanderveer, my guidance counselor. *The future's going to be here sooner than you think.*

We're in the cells for what I estimate to be another hour before a cop walks in, one we haven't seen before. He's got a clipboard.

Everyone starts shouting at once. Demands to see lawyers. Protestations of innocence. Threats of lawsuits.

The policeman waits for the furor to die down, then speaks. "I need the following people to come to the front of your cell and press your hands together in front of you with your fingers laced. Samuel Yu, Daneca Wasserman, and Lila Zacharov."

The cells again erupt in shouts. Daneca gets up off the bench. Sam follows her to the front of the cell, turning back toward me and widening his eyes in an expression of bafflement. After a few moments, the shouting dies down.

I wait for him to call me next, but there appear to be no more names on the clipboard.

Lila steps forward, then hesitates.

"Go," I tell her.

"We have a friend with us," Lila tells the officer, looking back in my direction.

"Cassel Sharpe," Sam supplies. "That's his name. Maybe you missed it?"

"This is all my fault—," Daneca starts.

"Be quiet, look straight ahead, hands clasped in front," the cop yells. "Everyone else take three steps away from the door. Now!"

They're cuffed and marched away, all of them turning their heads back toward me as I try to come up with explanations for why they're gone and I'm not. Maybe their parents were called and mine couldn't be reached. Maybe it was just random groups of three that were being taken for fingerprinting. I'm still trying to convince myself when Agent Jones saunters up to the cell door.

"Oh," I say.

"Cassel Sharpe." A small smile lifts a corner of his mouth. "Please step to the front of the cell, hands clasped together in front of you."

I do.

Jones leads me grimly into another hallway, one he has to swipe a card to enter. One without cells, just white walls and windowless doors. "We put an alert on your name, Cassel. Imagine my surprise when it turned up that you were in custody in Newark."

I swallow nervously. My throat feels dry.

"You got that information for me yet?" His breath smells like sour coffee and cigarettes.

"Not quite yet," I say.

"Have a good march?" he asks. "Get lots of exercise running from the law? Growing boy has got to get his exercise."

"Ha, ha," I say.

He grins like we really did just share a joke. "Let me tell you how this is going to go. I'm going to give you two choices, and you're going to make the right one."

I nod my head to show I'm listening, although I'm sure I'm not going to like what comes next.

"A couple doors down I've got Lila Zacharov and the other two you were brought in with. You and I can go there, and I'll explain that any friend of Cassel's is free to go. Then I'll let them out. Maybe I'll even apologize."

My shoulders tense. "They'll think I'm working for you."

"Oh, yeah," he says. "Definitely."

"If Lila thinks I'm working for the Feds and tells her father, I'm not going to be able to find out anything for you. I'll be useless." I'm talking too fast. He can tell he's getting to me. If the rumor gets around that I'm working for the Feds, my own mother won't want to be seen with me.

"Maybe I don't consider you all that useful anymore." Jones shrugs. "Maybe if we're all the friends you've got, you'll see things a little differently."

I take a deep breath. "What's my second choice?"

"Tell me that by the end of next week you'll have that lead for me. You're going to find out something on this mysterious assassin. Something I can use. No more excuses."

I nod. "I will."

He claps my shoulder heavily with his gloved hand. "I told you you'd make the right choice."

Then he lets me into the room with the others.

Daneca scrambles up from where she's sitting on the floor and hugs me. She smells like patchouli. Her eyes look bloodshot.

"I'm sorry," she says. "You must be so mad at me. But we're not going to do it. Don't worry. We would never—"

"Nobody's mad," I say, then look over at Sam and Lila to see if they can explain the rest of what she was saying.

"They told us we could walk out of here," Sam starts, then pauses, "if we volunteered to be tested."

"Tested?" I want to kill Jones right then. Of course he's got some stupid extra angle going.

"The hyperbathygammic test," Lila says quietly. She looks tired.

I punch the concrete wall. It just hurts my hand.

"We're not going to take the test, Cassel," Daneca says.

"No," I say. "No. You should. Both of you. Then you can call someone for Lila and me when you get out."

I have no doubt that Zacharov's lawyers will have Lila out of jail within moments. Me? Well, it'll take Grandad a little longer, but if the Feds want me to hunt for their lead, they're going to have to help out.

"But they're going to know that you're both—," Sam starts.

"That's the beauty of the test," Lila says. "The only people afraid to take it are people with something to hide."

"It's not legal to force us," Daneca says, shaking her head. "We're being held unlawfully. We weren't properly booked or Mirandized. We didn't commit any crime. This is a clear case of the government exploiting its power for its own anti-worker agenda."

"You think?" I sit down next to Lila on the floor. But despite my flippant answer, it's impossible not to be impressed with Daneca. She's never been in trouble before, and even in *jail*, she cares about what's right.

"You're shaking," Lila says softly, putting her gloved hand on my arm.

I'm surprised. I look down at my hands like I no longer remember to whom they belong. The knuckles of my left glove are scuffed from throwing that punch. Scuffed and trembling.

"Sam," I say, trying to steady myself. "You, at least, don't have to stay."

Sam looks at me and turns to Daneca. "I know you want to do the right thing, but if we don't agree to get tested, what happens next?" He lowers his voice. "What if they stop asking?"

"What if they don't let us out, even after they test us?" Daneca says. "I'm not doing it. It's against absolutely everything I believe in."

"You think I don't know it's wrong?" Sam snaps. "You don't think I get that this is unfair? That it sucks?"

I don't want them to fight. Not over this.

"Forget it," I say loudly, trying to sound like I know what I'm talking about. "Let's just wait. They're going to let us out soon. They've got to. Like Daneca said, they didn't really book us. We're going to be fine."

We lapse into an uneasy silence.

An hour later, just as panic begins to gnaw my gut, just when I'm ready to admit that I'm wrong and they're going to let us rot in here, just as I'm about to bang on the door and beg to see Agent Jones, a cop comes in and tells us we're free to go. No explanation. We're just shown the door.

The car's as we left it, except for the driver-side mirror, which is cracked.

We get back to Wallingford by ten. As we cross the quad, I have the strange feeling that we've been gone for days instead of just a couple of hours. We're too late for study hall, but in time for in-room check.

"I heard Ramirez let you boys go to that protest," Mr. Pascoli says, giving me a suspicious look. "How was it?"

"We decided to drive down to the beach instead," says Sam. "Good thing too. I hear the march got really out of control." His cheeks color a little as he speaks, like he's ashamed of lying.

He doesn't say anything else about it.

By lights-out it's as if the whole thing never happened.

Friday afternoon I'm sitting in the back of physics class, staring at the quiz in front of me. I am concentrating on the problem of a girl increasing the amplitude of a swing's oscillations by moving her legs along with the motion. I am not sure if this is an example of resonance, wave transmission, or something else that I've forgotten. The only thing that I am sure of is that I am going to fail this quiz.

I'm filling in one of those multiple-choice bubbles, my pencil going around and around in a circle, when Megan

Tilman screams. My pencil streaks across the paper, making a line of graphite.

"Ms. Tilman," Dr. Jonahdab says, looking up from her desk. "What is the matter?"

Megan is clutching her chest and staring at Daneca, who's one desk over from her. "My luck amulet broke. It snapped in half."

Gasps run through the class.

"You worked me, didn't you?" Megan says.

"Me?" Daneca asks, blinking at her like she's gone crazy.

"When did you feel your amulet break?" Dr. Jonahdab asks. "Are you sure that it broke right at this moment?"

Megan shakes her head. "I don't know. I just—I grabbed for it and there was only half still on the chain. Then when I moved, the other piece fell onto my desk. It must have been stuck in my blouse."

Yes, she really says "blouse," like she's someone's grandmother.

"Sometimes stones just break," says Dr. Jonahdab. "They're fragile. No one *touched* you, Megan. Everyone here is wearing gloves."

"She's on the video at that worker meeting," Megan says, pointing to Daneca. "She sits right next to me. It must have been her."

I expect Daneca to lecture her. I really do. I figure Daneca's been waiting all the time I've known her for a chance to really let some idiot have it, especially after yesterday. Instead she sinks down in her chair, her face going bright red. Tears glisten in her eyes. "I'm not a worker," she says quietly.

"Then why do you go to those meetings?" one of the other girls asks.

"Heebeegeebies." Someone fake coughs.

I stare at Daneca, willing her to speak. To tell Megan that a decent person cares about people other than herself. To explain about the plight of workers and put everyone in their place. All the righteous stuff she says to me and Sam. All the stuff she said, even in jail. I open my mouth, but even in my mind the lecture gets garbled. I can't remember the slogans. I don't know how to talk about worker rights.

Besides, for some reason, that seems like the last thing Daneca wants me to do.

I turn to Dr. Jonahdab, but she's glancing between Daneca and Megan, like somehow she's going to be able to sense the truth if she just watches them a little longer. Something's got to wake her up. Leaning toward the guy at the desk next to mine—Harvey Silverman—I say, "Hey, what did you get for problem three?" I say it loud enough that my voice carries even to the front of the class.

Daneca turns toward me. She shakes her head narrowly in warning.

Harvey looks down at his paper, and Dr. Jonahdab finally seems to snap out of her trance. "All right, everyone, that is enough talking! We are in the middle of a quiz. Megan, you may bring up your paper and take the rest of the test at my desk. After that we will go to the office together."

"I can't concentrate," Megan says, standing up. "Not while she's here."

"Then you can go down to the office now." Dr. Jonahdab writes something on a piece of paper and rips it off a legal pad. Megan takes her bag and the paper, leaving all her books behind as she walks out.

As soon as the bell rings, Daneca races toward the door, but Dr. Jonahdab calls her back. "Ms. Wasserman, I know they'll want to talk to you."

Daneca reaches into her bag. "I'm calling my mother. I'm not—"

"Look, we know that you didn't do anything wrong—" She cuts herself off when she notices me loitering by the door. "Can I help you, Mr. Sharpe?"

"No," I say. "I was just—no."

Daneca gives me a tremulous smile as I go.

On my way to French class, I walk by one of the announcement boards. It's plastered with a bunch of those public service posters you see in magazines—the kind that say I'D RATHER GO NAKED THAN BE WITHOUT MY GLOVES. Or JUST BECAUSE EVERYONE ELSE IS DOING IT, DOESN'T MAKE IT OKAY. HIRING CURSE WORKERS IS A CRIME. Or simply NO GLOVE, NO LOVE—except that the faces of models have been replaced with grainy stills of students from the video. Photos that the school secretary is frantically trying to rip down.

By the time I get to my French class, the news of what happened to Megan is all over the school.

"Daneca cursed her with bad luck, so she'd fail the test," someone says as I pass. "That's how she keeps up her GPA. She's probably been doing it to all of us for years."

"And Ramirez knew about it. That's why she's leaving."

I spin around. "What?"

It turns out the speaker is Courtney Ramos. Her eyes go wide. She was in the middle of applying lip gloss, and the wand hovers in the air, like she's frozen.

"What did you say?" I shout. People in the hallway turn toward us.

"Ms. Ramirez resigned," Courtney says. "I heard it when I was in the office waiting for my guidance counselor."

Ramirez, who let us go to the protest. Who was the only one willing to sponsor HEX, so Daneca could organize the club on campus two years ago. Who doesn't deserve to get taken down for us. Mr. Knight flashes his class, but he stays. Ramirez goes.

I grab Courtney's shoulder. "That can't be true. Why would that be true?"

She pulls out of my grip. "Get off of me. There's something really wrong with you, man. You know that?"

I turn away from her and walk off toward Ramirez's music room. I get halfway across campus before I see her in the faculty parking lot, shoving a cardboard box into the trunk of her car. Ms. Carter is with her, a milk crate under her arm.

Ramirez looks over at me and then shuts the trunk with a finality that keeps me from walking toward her.

Everyone knows "resigned" is a fancy word for "fired".

It feels totally surreal to take Lila to the movies. We both have notes from our parents on file that let us leave on

Fridays for the weekend, so we can just get into my car and meet Daneca and Sam at the theater.

She slides into the passenger side. She's got on long silver earrings that dangle like daggers, and a white dress that rides up her thighs when she sits down. I try not to notice. Okay, I try not to *stare*, because that would make me crash the car and kill us both.

"So is this what kids at Wallingford do when they're going out?" Lila asks me.

"Oh, come on," I say, laughing. "You've been gone for three years; you're not a time traveler. You know what a date is."

She smacks my arm. It stings, and I smile. "No, I'm serious," she says. "It's just all very proper. Like maybe we're going to go parking later or you're going to give me your pin."

"How was it at your old school? Straight-up Roman orgies?"

I wonder if she's seen any of her friends from that fancy Manhattan school. I remember them from her fourteenth birthday, full of glittering superiority. Rich worker kids, about to rule the world.

"There were a lot of parties. People just hooked up sometimes. No one was exclusive." She shrugs her shoulders, and then looks up at me through her pale lashes. "But worry not. I am amused by your quaint customs."

"Thank goodness for that," I say, touching my heart in mock earnestness.

Sam and Daneca are waiting for us at the concessions

stand, having an argument about whether red licorice is or is not more disgusting than black licorice. Sam's cradling an enormous glistening tub of popcorn.

"So, uh, you want anything?" I ask Lila.

"Are you offering to buy me my movie snacks?" she asks delightedly.

Sam laughs, and I give him the filthiest look I can summon up.

"Cherry slushy," Lila says quickly, maybe feeling she's taken teasing me too far, and comes with me to the counter.

We watch as they color the ice red. Lila leans against my shoulder.

"I'm sorry if I'm horrible," she says, her mouth moving against my sleeve. "I'm really nervous."

"I thought we already established that I like it when you're horrible," I say under my breath, picking up the slushies.

Her smile is as bright as the marquee lights.

Then the four of us get our tickets ripped and go into a room that's already playing the opening credits. The theater isn't crowded or anything, so we get to sit in the back.

Through some unspoken decision, none of us mentions the previous day's events, not the protest or the jail. The cool of the movie theater seems solid and real, making everything else feel very far away.

The Giant Spider Invasion is awesome. Sam talks through the whole thing, explaining which spiders are puppets and what the webbing is constructed from. I have no idea what the plot is except that the giant spider crisis seems to be powered by some kind of outer space energy. Scientists make out. The spiders die.

Even Daneca has a good time.

Afterward we go to a diner and eat club sandwiches and fries, accompanied by endless cups of black coffee. Sam shows us how to use ketchup, sugar, and Worcestershire sauce to make pretty decent-looking fake blood. The waitress is not amused.

Lila tells me I can just drop her off at the train station, but I drive her into Manhattan instead. And as we stop in front of her father's Park Avenue apartment, surrounded by city lights, she leans over to kiss me good night.

Her lips and tongue are still stained cherry red.

CHAPTER TEN

I STAY AT THE GARBAGE
house, in my old room, tossing and turning on the bed. Try
as I might to not think about the dead guy chilling in the
freezer two floors below me, all I can imagine is Janssen's
dead eyes staring up through the floorboards, begging
silently to be discovered.

He deserves a better burial than being shut in an ice
chest, no matter what he did in life. And God knows what I
deserve for putting him there.

Since I can't sleep anyway, I open up the file the Feds
gave me and spread the pages across my mattress. It gives
me Janssen's girlfriend's name—Bethenny Thomas—and
some sketchy details about her statement that night. Noth-

ing all that interesting. I picture her, pressing an envelope of cash against Anton's chest. And then I picture myself, leaning over Janssen, my bare hand reaching for him, fingers curling.

I wonder if I'm the last thing he saw, a gawky kid with a bad haircut, fifteen years old at the time.

I flop onto my back, scattering papers. None of them matter. They don't add up to Philip's murderer. No wonder the Feds are confused. All they want to know is what this big secret is Philip had, but it isn't here. It must be maddening to get so close to solving something and then have a new mystery on top of the old one. What was Philip's big secret, and who killed him to protect it?

The first part is easy. I'm the secret.

Who would kill to protect me?

I think of the figure in the oversize coat and the red gloves. Then I think about her some more.

The next morning I pad downstairs and make coffee, never having managed more than a little fitful sleep. Somewhere in the night I determined that the only way I am going to be able to figure out anything is if I start looking.

I figure the best place to start is Philip's house. The cops might have already gone through it, and so might the Feds, but they don't know what they're looking for. Of course, I don't know what I'm looking for either, but I know Philip.

And I'm on a deadline.

I drink the coffee, take a shower, put on a black T-shirt

and dark gray jeans, and go out to my car. It doesn't start. I pop the hood and stare at the engine for a while, but diesel cars aren't really my area of expertise.

I kick the tires. Then I call Sam.

His hearse pulls into my driveway not long after.

"What did you do to her?" Sam asks, petting the hood of my car and looking at me accusingly. He's wearing his weekend attire: a shirt with Eddie Munster on it, a pair of black jeans, and mirrored aviator sunglasses. How his parents don't see that he wants to work on special effects for movies, I don't know.

I shrug.

He pokes around for a couple of minutes and tells me I need to replace one of the fuses and probably the battery, too.

"Great," I say, "but there's something else I need to do today."

"What's that?" Sam asks.

"Solve a crime," I say.

He tilts his head, like he's considering whether or not to believe me. "Really?"

I shrug. "Probably not. How about committing a crime instead?"

"Now, that sounds more like you," he says. "Any particular one you had in mind?"

I laugh. "Breaking and entering. But it's my brother's house. So it's not that bad, right?"

"Which brother?" he asks, pulling the sunglasses down his nose so he can peer over them and raise a single eyebrow. He looks like a cop in a bad TV show, which I think is what he's going for.

"The dead one."

He groans. "Oh, come on! Why don't we just get the key from your mother or something? Doesn't his apartment belong to you guys anyway? Next of kin and all that."

I get in on the passenger side. The fact that he's trying to think of an easier way to get in is close enough to assent for me. "I think it belongs to his wife, but I really doubt she's going to come back to claim it."

I give him directions. He drives, shaking his head the whole time.

Unlike Bethenny's fancy apartment building with the doorman, Philip lived in a condo complex that looks like it might have been built in the 1970s. When we pull up, I hear the distant sounds of jazz on a radio, and I smell frying garlic. Inside, I know, the condos are huge.

"I'm going to wait in the car," Sam says, looking around nervously. "Crime scenes creep me out."

"Fine. I won't be long." I can't really blame him.

I know there's a security camera, since I saw the pictures it took of the red-gloved woman. It's easy to disconnect on my way to the door.

Then, as I pull out a stiff piece of metal from my backpack and squat in front of the knob, my nerves get the best of me. I'm not sure I'm ready to confront my brother's empty home. I take a couple of deep breaths and concentrate on the lock. It's a Yale, which means I have to turn it clockwise and the pins will have beveled edges. The familiar work is a welcome distraction from my thoughts.

Picking locks isn't hard, although it can be annoying. Normally you stick a key in the keyway, it turns the pins, and bingo, the door opens. When you're picking a lock, the easiest thing to do is scrub over the pins until they set. There are more sophisticated techniques, but I'm not the expert my dad was.

A few minutes later, I'm inside.

Philip's apartment has a stale rotten-food smell when I open the door. There's still police tape up, but it comes away easily. Other than that, the place just looks messy. Take-out boxes, beer bottles. Stuff a depressed guy leaves out when he has no wife and kid around to object.

When Philip was alive, I was afraid of him. I resented him. I wanted him to suffer like he'd made me suffer. Looking around the living room, I realize for the first time how honestly miserable he must have been. He lost everything. Maura ran off with his son; his best friend, Anton, was killed by our grandfather; and the only reason a crime boss he'd worked for since he was a teenager didn't kill him was because of me.

I thought of how proud he was when he took the marks—cutting the skin of his throat in a long slash and then packing it with ashes until keloid scars rose up. He called it his second smile. It was a brand, marking Philip as belonging to the Zacharovs, marking him as an insider, a killer. He would walk around with his collar open, a swagger in his step, grinning when people crossed to the other side of the street. But I also remember him in the bathroom of the old house, tears in his eyes as he took a sharp razor to the swollen, infected skin so he could darken his scars with fresh ash.

It hurt. He felt pain, even if it's easier for me to pretend he didn't.

There's a chalk outline of his body on the carpet and deep brown stains around a chunk of rug that's been removed—I assume for forensics.

I walk through the familiar rooms, trying to see what's out of place. Everything and nothing. I have no idea what Philip moved around before he died—I was in the house enough to know where things were in general, but not enough to memorize details. I go up the stairs and into his office—basically a spare room with a bed and a desk. The computer is missing, but I figure the Feds took it. I open a few drawers, but there's nothing more interesting than a bunch of pens and a switchblade.

Philip's bedroom is strewn with clothes that he obviously just dropped onto the floor when he took them off, and maybe occasionally kicked into piles. There's broken glass chunks near the baseboard, including the jagged bottom of a highball glass with some brown fluid dried inside.

His closet is full of his remaining clean clothes and not much else. In one of his shoe boxes I find foam cut to accommodate a gun, but the gun's gone. There's a rattling assortment of bullets in another.

I try to think back to when we were kids, when Dad was

alive. I can't remember any of Philip's hiding spots. All I remember is Dad coming into my room to get—

Oh.

I walk into Philip's son's room. His bed is still pushed against one wall, covered in stuffed animals. The drawers of the dressers are open, although some of them still have clothes in them. I can't tell if Maura left the room like this or if this is the result of cops pawing through everything.

The closet door is standing ajar. I carry over a mushroom-shaped stool and hop up onto it, reaching up to where I keep my bookmaking operation in my own dorm room, up to the shadowy recesses of the closet above the door. My hand connects with a piece of cardboard. I rip it down.

It's painted the same light blue as the wall. Nearly impossible to find just by looking, even with flashlights. Taped to the back is a manila envelope.

I take the whole thing back out into the room, where my movements have made the sailboat mobile over the toddler bed dance. Glassy-eyed bears watch as I fold up the brass tab and slide out a bunch of papers. The first thing I see is what looks like a legal contract granting Philip Sharpe immunity for past crimes. It's detailed—there are a lot of pages—but I recognize the signatures in the back. Jones and Hunt.

Behind that, though, I see three pages in Philip's looping handwriting. It's an account of whose ribs he cracked to make sure that Mom's appeal went through. I don't know what it means to find this here—whether it's with these other papers because he never gave it to the Feds or if it's here because he did.

All I know is that this could get Mom sent back to prison.

All I know is that Mom would have never forgiven him.

I push that thought out of my head as I walk back toward the living room, tucking the envelope into the waistband of my jeans and pulling my T-shirt over it. On the coffee table is a big brass ashtray, empty of all cigarette butts but one. As I walk closer, I notice it's white with a gold band. I recognize it.

It's a Gitanes. The brand Lila smoked when she came back from France all those years ago. I pick it up and look at it, see the imprint of lipstick. The first thought that occurs to me is that I didn't know she still smoked.

The second thought is that I have already seen that the Feds took stuff from Philip's apartment. I assume the ashtray is empty because the forensics team already took all the butts, along with the chunk of rug, Philip's computer, and the gun. Which means Lila came later.

The door opens and I spin around, but it's only Sam.

"I got bored," he says. "Besides, you know what's creepier than walking around your dead brother's apartment? Sitting alone in a hearse in front of his apartment."

I grin. "Make yourself at home."

He nods toward my hand. "What's that?"

"I think Lila was here," I say, holding up the remains of her cigarette. "She used to smoke these. The lipstick looks right."

He looks a bit stunned. "You think Lila killed your brother?"

I shake my head, but what I mean is that I don't think

that the cigarette proves anything. It doesn't prove that she did and it doesn't prove that she didn't.

"She must have been here *after* the place got swept for evidence," I say. "She came in here, sat on this couch, and smoked a cigarette. Why?"

"Returning to the scene of the crime," Sam says, like he's a television detective.

"I thought you liked Lila," I say.

"I *do*," he says, and suddenly looks serious. "I do like Lila, Cassel. But it's weird that she was in your brother's house after he was murdered."

"*We're* in my brother's house after he was murdered."

Sam shrugs his massive shoulders. "You should just ask her about it."

Lila loves me. She has to; she's been worked to. I don't think she would do something that would hurt me, but I can't explain that to Sam without explaining the rest. And I won't tell him about the envelope.

I don't want to even think about those three pages and what they might mean. I don't want to imagine my mother being the woman in the red gloves. I want the murderer to be someone I have never met, a hired gun. So long as it's no one I know, I am free to hate them, at least as much as I hated my brother.

Back in the car I get Sam to drive me into the parking lot of a large supermarket I spot on the way to the highway. Behind the store is a sad stretch of trees and several large Dumpsters. He watches while I fumble through my backpack for matches and make a small fire as discreetly as I can, adding scraps of nearby debris, the immunity agreement, and Philip's scrawled confession. When it's hot enough, I drop the cigarette butt into it.

"You're destroying evidence," he says.

I look up at him. "Yeah?"

He smacks his hand into his forehead. "You can't do that! What do those papers even say?"

Sam, despite everything he's seen, is a good citizen.

I watch the edges of the paper curl and the filter smoke. I knew Philip had bargained away his own secrets—and mine—but I never thought he'd bargain away Mom's, too. "The papers say that my brother was a hypocrite. He was so pissed off that I'd dare betray our family. Turns out he was just mad I did it first."

"Cassel, do you know who killed him?" There's something odd in Sam's voice.

I look at him and realize what he's thinking. I laugh. "They found video footage of a woman entering his apartment the night of his death. So *not me*."

"I didn't think it was you," he says too quickly.

"Whatever." I stand. I honestly don't blame him for being suspicious. "It'd be okay if you did. And thanks for being my wheelman."

He snorts as I disperse the blackened remains of my findings with one shoe. "Do you care if we go to Daneca's?" he asks. "I told her I was going to stop over."

"She's going to be disappointed if I tag along," I say with a smile.

He shakes his head. "She's going to want to know what you found. Remember how obsessed she was with those files?"

"You're going to tell her about this little bonfire, aren't you? Man, no wonder you want me to come along. You just want her yelling at the right person." I'm not really mad, though. I like that Sam doesn't lie to his girlfriend. I like that they are in love. I even like the way that Daneca gets on my case.

"If you tell me not to, I won't tell her," Sam says, "but I'm not sure you're really objective about this, uh, investigation."

I feel a rush of gratitude that makes me want to tell him everything, but the ashes behind us remind me not to trust anyone completely.

Sam flips on the car radio. It's set to some news program where the hosts are talking about the protest in Newark. The cops are claiming a riot broke out, but several YouTube videos show peaceful demonstrators being arrested. Some are still in custody—the numbers remain uncertain. The whole conversation deteriorates into jokes about girls with naked hands.

Sam changes the channel abruptly. I look out the window to avoid meeting his eyes. We stop at an auto parts store for a package of fuses and a new battery. Over the piped-in elevator music, he explains how to install them. I act even more incompetent with cars than I am, mostly to annoy Sam into laughing.

Minutes later, we pull into Daneca's family's fancy

Princeton driveway. A guy in a green uniform is dusting the lawn with a leaf blower. In the back I can see Mrs. Wasserman in her garden, cutting a dark orange sunflower. She's got a basket of them on her arm and waves when she sees us.

"Cassel, Sam," Mrs. Wasserman says, walking over to the gate. "What a pleasant surprise."

I thought people didn't say things like that in real life, although I guess there are exceptions for people who live in houses like hers. Mrs. Wasserman doesn't look as elegant as she sounds, though. Her cheek is smeared with dirt, her green Crocs are ragged, and her hair is pulled back into a messy ponytail. Somehow, though, her lack of effort is even more intimidating.

She doesn't look like a tireless campaigner for worker rights. You wouldn't figure her for the person who admitted on national television to being a worker. But she is.

"Oh, hi," says Sam. "Is Daneca home?"

"Inside," she says, and holds out the basket of flowers. "Can you two take these to the kitchen? I have to get the last of the zucchini. No matter how few you plant, somehow they always come in at once and then you have too many."

"Can I help?" I ask impulsively.

She gives me an odd look. "That would be great, Cassel."

Sam takes the basket of flowers and shakes his head at me, clearly guessing that I'm trying to delay answering Daneca's inevitable questions.

I follow Mrs. Wasserman into the backyard while Sam goes inside. She picks up another basket from a pile of them inside a shed. "So how are things? I heard about Ms. Ramirez's resignation. It's ridiculous what that school thinks it can get away with."

The garden is idyllic and huge, with lavender plants and blooming vines crawling up pyramids of woven sticks. Tiny red cherry tomatoes cover one raised bed, while another is bright with summer squash.

"Yeah," I say. "Ridiculous. I was wondering, though. There was something I was hoping to ask you."

"Of course." She gets down on her knees and starts to snap off striped green vegetables with a twist of her garden-gloved hands. The zucchini grow from the center of a large leafy plant with yellow flowers and seem to just sprawl heavily on the ground. After a moment I realize that offering to help her means I should be mimicking what she's doing.

"Um," I start, bending down. "I heard about this thing— this organization the federal government has. For worker kids. And I wondered if you'd heard about it too?"

Mrs. Wasserman nods, not bringing up the fact that the last time I saw her, I was insisting up, down and sideways that I wasn't a worker and wasn't interested in them either. "No one will confirm much about it, but anyone trying to legislate in favor of protections for worker kids runs into government push-back concerning their own program. I've heard it called the Licensed Minority Division."

I frown over the name for a moment. "So is it legit?"

"All I know," she says, "is that I used to correspond with a kid about your age before he got recruited by them. I never heard from him again. Worker teenagers are a valuable resource, until the blowback cripples them—and the LMD tries to recruit before the mob does. The LMD goes after other workers—sometimes for legitimately terrible crimes, sometimes for minor infractions. It can sour the soul. If someone told you about the Minority Division, then you need a lawyer, Cassel. You need someone to remind them you're still a citizen with choices."

I laugh, thinking of the holding cell, thinking of all the people who might still be in it. I guess Daneca didn't share that story with her mother. But even if I believed citizens had choices, the only person with any legal expertise I know is Barron, and all he managed was a couple years of pre-law at Princeton. Mom has a lawyer, but I can't pay him the way she does. Of course, there's Mrs. Wasserman. *She's* a lawyer, but she's not exactly volunteering. "Okay. I'll try to keep my nose clean."

She pushes back a lock of woolly brown hair and manages to paint her forehead with dirt. "I don't mean to say that they aren't a worthwhile organization. And I'm sure that some kids wind up with fine, upstanding government jobs. I just want us to live in a world where worker kids don't have to play cops or robbers."

"Yeah," I say. I can't imagine that world. I don't think I'd fit in there.

"You should go on into the house," she says, and then smiles. "I can manage the rest of the vegetable picking."

I stand up, understanding a dismissal when I hear one.

"I didn't know what I was," I say, swallowing hard. "Before. I didn't mean to lie to you."

Mrs. Wasserman looks up at me, shading her eyes with one gloved hand. For the first time in this conversation, she looks rattled.

Daneca and Sam are sitting on stools at the massive island in her kitchen. Resting on the marble counter in front of him is a glass of iced tea with a sprig of actual mint stuffed into it.

"Hey, Cassel," Daneca says. She's wearing a white T-shirt and jeans with knee-high brown suede boots. One purple-tipped braid hangs in front of her face. "You want something to drink? Mom just went to the store."

"I'm good," I say, shaking my head. I always feel awkward in Daneca's house. I can't help casing the joint.

"Why did you go investigating without me?" Daneca demands, clearly done with being a hostess. "I thought we were in this together."

"It was on the way," I say. "Sam mostly waited in the car. Anyway, the police and the Feds were already through there. I just wanted to see if I noticed anything they wouldn't."

"Like the cigarette?"

"I see Sam told you about that. Yeah, like the cigarette. But that came later, I'm pretty sure."

"Cassel, I know this is hard to hear, but she has every reason to want to kill your brother. You said he kidnapped her."

I'm probably thinking about this the wrong way, but right now I regret telling them anything. The problem with starting to talk is that the parts you leave out become really obvious. Plus there's the temptation to just reveal everything.

And I can't do that. Now that I have friends, I don't want to lose them.

"I know," I say, "but I don't think she did it. She didn't seem guilty at his funeral."

"But she *went* to the funeral," Daneca says, insisting. Sam isn't saying anything, but I can see him nod along with her. "Why would she even go to the funeral of someone she hated? Murderers do that. I've read about it."

"Revisiting the scene—," Sam starts.

"Philip wasn't killed at a funeral parlor! Besides, she came there with Zacharov," I say. "He wanted to offer me a job."

"What kind of job?" Daneca asks.

"The kind you don't talk about," I say. "The kind that gets you a big fat keloid necklace and a new nickname."

"You didn't take it, right?" she says. I am pretty sure that, like the Feds, Daneca and Sam have come to the conclusion that I'm a death worker along the lines of Grandad.

I pull at the collar of my shirt. "You want to see my throat?"

"Oh, come on," she says. "Just answer the question."

"I didn't take the job," I say. "Honest. And I have no plans to. *And* I want some of the iced tea that Sam has. *With* a mint sprig, please."

Daneca smiles tightly and hops down from her stool.

"Fine, but that doesn't mean we're done discussing Lila. I mean clearly you've got a crazy, epic thing for her—but that doesn't mean that she's not a suspect."

I try not to take it too hard that even though Lila has been worked to love me, I'm the one whose feelings are obvious. "Okay. What if she did kill my brother? Will knowing that help anyone?"

"It'll help you protect her," Sam says. "If you want to."

I look at him in surprise, because it's not at all what I expected him to say. It's also absolutely true.

"Okay," I say. "Okay. Is it really that obvious I'm into her?" I think of Audrey, practically saying the same thing outside the cafeteria. I must be pathetic.

"We went to the movies together," Daneca says. "Last night. Remember?"

"Oh, yeah," I say. "That."

Sam frowns as Daneca pours my tea.

"Maybe you should just call and *ask* if she killed Philip," Sam says.

"No!" says Daneca. "If you do that, then she's going to put on an act. Hide evidence. We have to make a plan."

"Okay." I hold up my hand. "I don't think Lila did this. I really don't. It's not that I think she's not capable of killing someone. I'm sure she is. And I'm sure she hated Philip, although if she was going to kill one of my brothers, I'm pretty sure she would have started with Barron. But she—I know this isn't going to sound convincing—she really likes me. Like, likes me so much that I don't think she'd do something that would hurt me or make me hate her."

They both exchange a glance.

"You're a charming dude," Sam says carefully. "But no one is that charming."

I groan. "No, I'm not *bragging*. She's been cursed to love me. Now do you get it? Her feelings are reliable because they're not real." My voice breaks on the last two words, and I look at the floor.

There is a long pause.

"How could you do that to her?" Daneca says finally. "That's like brain rape. That's like actual rape if you— How could you, Cassel?"

"I *didn't*," I say, biting off each word. She could have given me the benefit of the doubt for just one minute. She's supposed to be my friend. "I'm not the one who worked Lila. And I never wanted her to—I never wanted this."

"I'm going to tell her," Daneca says. "She has to be told."

"Daneca," I say, "just shut up for a minute. I already told her. What kind of person do you think I am?" Looking at Daneca's face, I can see exactly what kind of person she thinks I am, but I keep going anyway. "I told her and I've tried to stay away from her, but it's not easy, okay? Everything I do seems to be the wrong thing."

"So that's why—" Sam cuts himself off.

"Why I've been acting so weird about her?" I say. "Yeah."

"But you're not an emotion worker?" Daneca says cautiously, no longer quite so disgusted. I appreciate that she's at least trying to sort through what I've already said, but I can't help resenting that the one thing I actually didn't do is what she's accusing me of.

"No," I say. "I'm not. Of course not."

Sam looks over at the doorway, and I follow his gaze to see the blond worker kid that Mrs. Wasserman took in.

"So if you're not the one who cursed her . . . ?" Daneca asks me, whispering.

"That part's not important," I say.

The kid turns to us, his face pinched. "I already heard you. You don't have to whisper."

"Leave us alone, Chris," Daneca says.

"I'm just getting a soda." He opens the refrigerator.

"We have to do something," Daneca says. Her voice is still low. "There's some emotion worker going around hurting people. We can't just let—"

"Daneca," Sam says. "Maybe Cassel's not ready to—"

"Emotion workers are *dangerous*," Daneca says.

"Oh, shut up," says Chris suddenly. The refrigerator gapes open behind him. He has the soda in his gloved hand, and he seems ready to hurl it at one of us at any moment. "You always act like you're better than everybody else."

"This is none of your business," says Daneca. "If you don't get your soda and get out of here, I'm calling Mom."

Sam and I share the awkward look of outsiders in the middle of a family squabble.

"Oh, yeah?" Chris says. "Maybe you should tell your friends that *you're* an emotion worker instead of hiding it. Do you think they'll still listen to you then?"

For a moment everything stops.

I look at Daneca. She has the blank look of shock, eyes

wide. Her hand is raised protectively as if words could be warded off. The kid isn't lying.

Which means that Daneca has been.

Sam falls off his stool. I think he was trying to stand up and wasn't really thinking about it, but he winds up stumbling back as the stool crashes to the floor. His back hits the cabinet. The expression on his face is awful. He doesn't know her anymore. It cuts me to the bone because that's exactly how I'm afraid he'll look at me.

I lean down and right the fallen stool, glad to have something to do.

"We've got to go," Sam says. "Cassel, come on. We're out of here."

"No, *wait*," Daneca says, walking toward him. She falters as if not sure what to say, then turns back to the kid. "How could you do this to me?" Her voice is a thin wail.

"It's not my fault you're a liar," Chris says haltingly. He looks terrified. I think if he could, he'd take the words back.

Sam stumbles toward the door.

"I'll talk to him," I say to Daneca.

"*You* lie," she says, grabbing my arm, desperate. I can feel her nails through the thin leather of her gloves. "You lie to him all the time. Why is it okay when you do it?"

I shrug off her hand, not letting her see how much the words hurt. Right now all my impulses are bad ones. I hadn't realized how little Daneca trusted me until this afternoon. And if she's anything like my mother—the only other emotion worker I know—maybe I shouldn't trust her, either. "I said I would talk to him. That's all I can do."

Outside, Sam's hearse is still in the driveway but I don't see him anywhere. Not in Daneca's mother's elegant garden, not over the hedge in the neighbor's backyard with an in-ground pool. Not walking down the side of the road. Then one of the doors of the hearse swings open. Sam is lying on his back inside.

"Get in," he says. "Also, girls suck."

"What are you doing?" I climb inside. It's creepy. The roof is lined in gathered gray satin and the windows are tinted very dark.

"I'm thinking," he says.

"About Daneca?" I ask, although I can't imagine the answer is anything other than yes.

"I guess now we know why she wouldn't get tested." He sounds bitter.

"She was scared," I say.

"Did you know she was a worker?" he asks. "Be honest."

"No," I say. "*No.* I mean, I guess I thought she might be—before I really knew her—because of her being so gung ho about HEX, but I figured she *wished* she was a worker. Like I used to. But you have to understand how frightening—"

"I don't," Sam says. "I don't have to understand."

It finally occurs to me what's bothering me about the hearse. Being in the back reminds me of being in the trunk of Anton's car, next to garbage bags of bodies. I remember vividly the smell of spilled guts. "She cares about you," I say, trying to force my mind back to the present. "When you care about someone it's harder to—"

"I never asked you what kind of worker you are," Sam says, flinging the words at me like a challenge.

"Yeah," I say carefully. "And I really appreciate that."

"If I did . . ." Sam pauses. "If I did, would you tell me?"

"I hope so," I say.

He's quiet then. We lie next to each other, twin corpses waiting for burial.

CHAPTER ELEVEN

WE CAN'T STAY IN DANECA'S driveway. Instead, we go to Sam's house, steal a six-pack of his dad's beer, and drink it between us in his garage. There's an old maroon couch out there near a drum set from his older sister's band. I flop down on one side of the sofa, and he flops on the other.

"Where is your sister now?" I ask, reaching for a handful of sesame-coated peanuts—we found a bag of them near the beer. They crunch in my mouth like salted candy.

"Bryn Mawr," he says, belching loudly, "driving my parents crazy because she has a girlfriend covered in tattoos."

"Really?"

He grins. "Yeah, why? You didn't think anyone related to me could be a rebel?"

"How much of a rebel can she be in that fancy college?" I say.

He throws a musty pillow at me, but I manage to block it with my arm. It tumbles to the concrete floor.

"Didn't your brother go to Princeton?" he asks.

"Touché," I say, and gulp from the beer. It's warm. "Shall we duel for the dishonor of our siblings?"

Sam frowns at me, suddenly serious. "You know, I thought—for most of the first year we lived together—that you were going to kill me."

That makes me nearly spit out beer, I laugh so hard.

"No, look—living with you, it's like knowing there's a loaded gun on the other side of the room. You're like this leopard who's pretending to be a house cat."

That only makes me laugh harder.

"Shut up," he says. "You might do normal stuff, but a leopard can drink milk or fall off things like a house cat. It's obvious you're not—not like the rest of us. I'll look over at you, and you'll be flexing your claws or, I don't know, eating a freshly killed antelope."

"Oh," I say. It's a ridiculous metaphor, but the hilarity has gone out of me. I thought I did a good job of fitting in—maybe not perfect, but not as bad as Sam makes it sound.

"It's like Audrey," he says, stabbing the air with a finger, clearly well on his way to inebriated and full of determination to make me understand his theory. "You acted like she went out with you because you did this good job of being a nice guy."

"I am a nice guy."

I try to be.

Sam snorts. "She liked you because you scared her. And then you scared her too much."

I groan. "Are you serious? Come on, I never did anything—"

"I'm as serious as a heart attack," he says. "You're a dangerous dude. Everyone knows this."

I take the remaining throw pillow and press it over my face, smothering myself. "*Stop,*" I say.

"Cassel?" Sam says.

I peek out from under the cushion. "Don't traumatize me any more than you already—"

"What kind of worker are you?" Sam's looking over at me with the benevolent curiosity of the drunk.

I bite off what I was going to say, hesitate. The moment drags on, suspended in amber.

"You don't have to tell me," he says. "It doesn't matter."

I know what he thinks my answer is going to be. He figures I'm a death worker. Maybe he even thinks I killed somebody. If he's really clever—and at this point I have to assume he's more clever than I am, since he's saying that he figured out I was dangerous long before I did—he's got a theory that I killed one of the men the Feds are looking for. If I say I'm a death worker, he'll swallow it. He'll think I'm a good friend. He'll think I'm honest.

My palms sweat.

I want to be that friend. "Transformation," I say. It comes out like a croak.

He sits up fast, staring at me. All traces of humor are gone. "What?"

"See? I'm getting better at being truthful," I say, trying to lighten the mood. My stomach hurts. Honesty freaks me right the hell out.

"Are you crazy?" he asks me. "You shouldn't have told me that! You shouldn't tell anyone! Wait, you're really—?"

I just nod.

It takes him a long moment before he can come up with anything else.

"Wow," he says finally, awe in his voice. "You could create the best special effects *in the world*. Monster masks. Horns. Fangs. Totally permanent."

I never thought of that, never considered using working for anything fun. The corner of my lip lifts in an unexpected smile.

He pauses. "The curses *are* permanent, right?"

"Yeah," I say, thinking of Lila, and Janssen. "I mean, I can change things back to the way they were. Mostly."

Sam gives me a considering look. "So you could stay young forever?"

"That *sounds* possible," I say with a shrug. "But it's not like the world is full of transformation workers, so it must not work." The sheer enormity of what I don't know about my limitations—the stuff I don't even want to deal with—is suddenly a lot more obvious.

"How about giving yourself a huge you-know-what?"

He leans back on the couch and points to his pants with both hands. "Like, unnaturally big."

I groan. "You've got to be kidding me. That's what you want to know?"

"I've got my priorities straight," he says. "You're the one who's not asking the right questions."

"Story of my life," I say.

Sam finds a dusty bottle of Bacardi in the back of his parents' pantry. We split it.

Late Sunday afternoon I wake up to someone ringing the doorbell. I don't remember how I got home; maybe I walked. My mouth still tastes like booze, and I am pretty sure my hair is sticking straight up. I try to smooth it out as I walk down the stairs.

I don't know what I expect, really. A package that I have to sign for, maybe. Missionaries, kids selling cookies, something like that. Even the Feds. Not Mr. Zacharov, looking as crisp as a fake hundred-dollar bill, at the door of my dingy kitchen.

I flip the locks. "Hey," I say, and then realize my breath must be awful.

"Are you busy this evening?" he asks, giving every appearance of not noticing that I just rolled out of bed. "I'd like you to come with me." Behind him is a goon in a long, dark coat. He's got a tattoo of a skull on his neck, above the keloid scars.

"Sure," I say. "Okay. Can you give me a minute?"

He nods. "Get dressed. You can have breakfast on the way."

I walk back upstairs, leaving the kitchen door open so that Zacharov can come in if he wants.

In the shower, as hot water pounds down like needles onto my back, I realize that it's really, really odd that Zacharov is waiting for me downstairs. The more awake I get, the more surreal it seems.

I come back into the kitchen fifteen minutes later, chewing aspirin, in black jeans and a sweater, with my leather jacket on. Zacharov is sitting at my kitchen table, looking relaxed, fingers tapping on the worn wood.

"So," I say. "Where are we going?"

He stands and raises both steel gray eyebrows. "To the car."

I follow him out to a sleek black Cadillac. It's already running, with Stanley—a bodyguard I met before—in the driver's seat. The guy with the skull tattoo is sitting beside him. Zacharov waves me in, and I scoot across the backseat.

"Hey, kid," Stanley says. There's a steaming cup of coffee in the cup holder and a fast-food bag over on my seat. I open it up and take out the bagel and egg sandwich inside.

"Stanley," I say, nodding to him. "How's the family?"

"Never better," he says.

Zacharov sits beside me as the tinted privacy divider grinds up.

"I understand that you and my daughter spent Friday together," he says as Stanley backs the Cadillac out of my driveway.

"I hope she had fun," I say between chews. I wonder suddenly if Zacharov found out about the curse. If so, it was nice for him to let me get cleaned up and fed before he killed me.

But Zacharov has an amused curl to his lip. "And I understand that you spent some time with some federal agents the day before that."

"Yeah," I say, trying not to look too relieved. Questions about the Feds from a mob boss should not *relax* anyone. "They came to see me at school. About Philip."

He narrows his eyes. "What about Philip?"

"He was making a deal with them," I say. There's no point in lying to Zacharov about this. Philip's dead. There's no real harm in his knowing. I feel a pang of guilt nonetheless. "They say he was an informant. And then someone murdered him."

"I see," Zacharov says.

"They want me to help them find the killer." I hesitate. "At least that's what they say they want."

"But you don't think so," he says.

"I don't know," I say, and take a long swig of the coffee. "All I know is that they're assholes."

He laughs at that. "What are their names?"

"Jones and Hunt." The combination of coffee and grease is soothing my stomach. I feel pretty good, leaning back against the leather seat. I'd feel better if I knew where we were going, but for the moment I am willing to wait.

"Huh," he says. "Luck workers, both of them."

I look over at him, surprised. "I thought they hated workers."

He smiles. "Maybe they do. I just know they *are* workers. Most of the agents in the division that deals with us folks are workers themselves." By "us folks," I'm guessing he means organized crime families on the East Coast. Families like his.

"Oh," I say.

"Didn't know that, eh?" He seems pleased.

I shake my head.

"They have been worrying you about your mother, too, yes? I know how these men operate." He nods his head, clearly indicating that I can answer if I want to, but it's not required. "I could get them off your back."

I shrug my shoulders.

"Yes, you're not sure. Maybe I pushed you too hard at Philip's funeral. Lila thinks so, anyway."

"Lila?" I say.

His smile smoothes out with something like pride. "Someday she will lead the Zacharov family. Men will die for her. Men will kill for her."

I nod my head, because, of course, that's what it means to be Zacharov's daughter. It's just that his saying it makes it uncomfortably real. Makes the future seem to come too soon.

"But some men might not like to follow a woman," Zacharov says as the car takes a sharp turn. We pull into the covered garage of a building, and park. "Especially a woman he knows too well."

"I really hope you're not talking about me," I say.

The locks pop up on the doors.

"Yes," he says. "As do I."

The garage is unfinished. Just rough concrete without signs or even lines painted to delineate one space from another. Someone must have run out of money partway through the build.

I'm guessing that means screaming for help is off the table.

We get out of the car. I follow Zacharov and Stanley into the building. The tattooed goon follows me, his gloved hand giving me a little push at the base of my spine when I look around too much.

If the parking lot is new and unfinished, the building it connects to is ancient, with a plaque that reads TALLINGTON STRING-MAKERS GUILD AND NEEDLE FACTORY. It has clearly been abandoned a long time, the windows covered with nailed-up boards, and the wooden planks covered in a thick layer of sticky black dirt. I'm guessing someone wanted to convert where I'm standing into lofts before the last recession hit.

The thought rises unbidden that I've been brought here to die. Grandad told me that's how they do it. Take a guy for a ride, real friendly. Then, *pow*. Back of the head.

I stick my right hand into the pocket of my jacket and start worming off that glove. My heart's racing.

We come to stairs, and Stanley hangs back. Zacharov holds out his hand, indicating I should go first.

"You lead, I follow," I say. "Since you know where we're going."

Zacharov laughs. "Someone is cautious."

He starts toward the stairs, and Stanley follows him,

then skull tattoo guy, leaving me last. I've managed to work off my glove. I cradle it in my palm.

The hallway we come to is lit by flickering overhead fluorescents. They look yellowed and, in a few cases, burned. I follow the skull tattoo guy's suit-jacketed back until we all come to a large steel door.

"Put this on," Zacharov says, reaching into his coat and taking out a black ski mask.

I pull it over my head somewhat haphazardly with my one gloved hand. Zacharov and his guys must notice I keep the other hand in my pocket, but no one says anything about it.

Stanley knocks three times.

I don't recognize the man who swings the door open. He's tall, maybe forty, wearing stained jeans and no shirt. He's so skinny that his chest looks concave. He's covered in tattoos. Naked women being beheaded by skeletons, demons with curling tongues, blocky words in Cyrillic. No color, just black ink and an unsteady hand. It's amateur work. Jailhouse, I'm guessing. The guy's hair hangs over his cheekbones in greasy strings. One of his ears is as black-ened as Grandad's fingers. He's obviously been living for a while in the room that he ushers us into. There's a cot cov-ered in a filthy blanket. A table made from sawhorses and a single sheet of plywood rests in the center of the room, piled with cardboard pizza boxes, a mostly empty bottle of vodka, and a take-out foil container of half-eaten pelmeni.

His gaze darts hungrily from me to Zacharov, then back again.

"Him?" the guy says, and spits on the floor.

"Hey," Stanley says, stepping between us. The other body-guard was leaning against the wall near the door. He stands up a little straighter, like he's expecting trouble.

I look over at Zacharov, waiting for his reaction.

"You are going to change his face," he tells me calmly, as if he was discussing the weather. "For old times' sake. For the debt you still owe me."

"Make me pretty," the man says, coming as close to me as he can with Stanley between us. He smells like stale sweat and vomit. "I want to look like a movie star."

"Yeah, okay," I say, taking my hand out of my pocket. Bare. The air feels cool on my skin. I rub my thumb against my fingers in an unfamiliar gesture.

The man dances away. Stanley turns to see what freaked the guy out, and backs off too. Ungloved hands get attention.

"You sure he's what you say he is?" the guy asks Zacharov. "This isn't your way of getting rid of a problem, right? Or making me forget my own name?"

"No need to bring a boy to do either of those things," Zacharov says.

That doesn't seem to reassure the guy. He looks at me and gestures to his neck. "Show me your marks."

"I don't have any," I say, pulling at the front of my sweater.

"We don't have time for these pointless questions," Zacharov says. "Emil, sit down now. I am a busy man and I do not oversee murders. I also do not take pointless risks."

That seems to settle him. He pulls up a folding metal

chair and sits in it. Rust has eaten away at the joints, but he doesn't seem to notice. He's too busy watching my hand.

"What's this for?" I ask.

"I will answer all of your questions later," Zacharov says. "But for now, do as I ask."

Stanley eyes me coldly. Zacharov's not *asking*. There never were any good choices.

Emil's eyes go wide when I touch the pads of my fingers to his filthy cheek. I bet my heart is beating just as fast as his.

I've never done anything like this transformation, something requiring fine detail and finesse. I close my eyes and let myself see with that odd second sense, let every part of Emil become infinitely malleable. But then I panic. I can't think of a single movie star whose features I recall in detail. Not a guy, anyway. They're all blurs of eyes and noses and some vague sense of familiarity. The only actor that comes to mind at all is Steve Brodie as Dr. Vance in *The Giant Spider Invasion*.

I change Emil. I'm getting the hang of this. When I open my eyes, he looks like a passably hot dude from the 1970s. No more tattoos. No more scars. I fixed his ear, too.

Stanley sucks in his breath. Emil reaches up to touch his face, his eyes wide.

Zacharov is staring at me, one corner of his thin mouth lifted in a hungry smile.

Then my knees cramp and I go down hard. I can feel my body start to spread, my fingers branching out into dozens of iron nails. My back spasms and my skin feels like it's sloughing off me. I can hear a sound coming out of me, more a moan than a scream.

"What's wrong with him?" Emil yells.

"It's the blowback," Zacharov says. "Give him some space."

I hear the table being dragged back as I flop around on the floor.

"Is he going to bite his tongue?" That's Stanley's voice. "I don't think that looks right. He's going to give himself a concussion. We should at least put something under his head."

"Which one?" asks someone else. Emil? The guy by the door? I no longer know.

It hurts. It really, really hurts. Blackness rises up, looming and terrible, before breaking over me like a wave, dragging me down to the bottom of the dreamless sea.

When I wake, I'm on the cot, swaddled in Emil's stinking blanket, and only Zacharov and Stanley remain. They're sitting on the folding chairs, playing cards. The boarded-up windows have a halo of light around their edges. It's still daytime. I can't have been out for that long.

"Hey," says Stanley, spotting me shifting. "Kid's awake."

"You did good, Cassel," Zacharov says, turning his chair to face me. "You want to sleep some more?"

"No," I say, pushing myself up. It's a little awkward, like I've been sick or something. The mask is gone. They must have taken it off me while I was sleeping.

"You hungry?" he asks.

I shake my head again. I feel a little queasy after the

change, like I'm not sure where my stomach is. The last thing I want is food.

"You will be hungry later," he says, with such certainty that it seems impossible to contradict him. I'm too tired to bother, anyway.

I let Stanley help me up, and he half-carries me out to the car.

We ride for a while, with my head resting against the window. I think I fall asleep again. I drool on the glass.

"Time to wake up." Someone is shaking my shoulder. I groan. Everything is stiff, but otherwise I feel okay.

Zacharov is grinning at me from the other side of the car. His silver hair is bright against the blackness of his wool coat and the leather seats. "Give me your hands," he says.

I do. One is gloved; the other one isn't.

He takes off my remaining glove and holds my bare hands in his gloved ones, palms up. I feel uncomfortably vulnerable, even though he's the one who's in danger of being worked. "With these hands," he says, "you will make the future. Be sure it is a future in which you want to live."

I swallow. I have no idea what he means. He lets go, and I fish in my pocket for the other glove, avoiding his gaze.

A moment later the car door opens on my side. Stanley's there, holding it wide. We're in Manhattan, skyscrapers looming over us and traffic streaming past.

I shuffle out, breathing the car exhaust and roasting-peanut-scented air. I'm still blinking the sleep out of my eyes, but I realize that not being in New Jersey means that whatever I've been brought to do isn't over.

"Oh, *come on*," I say to Zacharov. "I can't. Not again. Not today."

But he just laughs. "I only want to give you some dinner. Lila would never forgive me if I sent you back on an empty stomach."

I'm surprised. I must have really looked in bad shape back at the warehouse, because I am sure he's got better things to do than feed me.

"This way," Zacharov says, and walks toward a large bronze door with a raised relief of a bear. There's no sign on the building; I have no idea what to expect when we go in. It doesn't look like a restaurant. I glance back at Stanley, but he's getting back into the driver's seat of the Cadillac.

Zacharov and I walk into a small mirrored entranceway with a polished brass elevator. There's no furniture other than a gilt and black bench and, from what I can see, no intercom or bell. Zacharov fishes around in his pocket and removes a set of keys. He puts one into a hole on an otherwise blank panel and twists. The doors open.

The inside of the elevator is richly burled wood. A video screen above the doors is showing a black-and-white movie without any sound. I don't recognize the film.

"What's this place?" I ask finally as the doors slide shut.

"A social club," Zacharov says, clasping his gloved hands in front of him. Neither of us has pushed any button. "Here, things are private."

I nod, as though I actually understand what he's talking about.

When the elevator opens, we're in a huge room—*huge* like, seriously, you can't figure this place is really in New York. The marble floor is mostly covered in an enormous carpet. Along it are islands of two or four club chairs with high backs. The ceiling far above our heads is decorated with intricate plaster moldings. Along the nearest wall is a massive bar, its marble top shining against dark wood paneling. Behind the bar, on a high shelf, are several hulking jars of clear liquor with fruits and spices floating in them: lemons, rose petals, whole cloves, ginger. Uniformed staff move through the room silently, carrying drinks and small trays to the occupants of the chairs.

"Wow," I say.

He gives me a half grin, one that I have seen on Lila's face before. It's unnerving.

An old man with sunken cheeks in a black suit walks up to us. "Welcome, Mr. Zacharov. May I take your coat?"

Zacharov shucks it off.

"Would you like to borrow a sport jacket for your friend?" the man asks him, barely glancing in my direction. I guess I'm breaking some kind of dress code.

"No," Zacharov says. "We will have drinks and then dinner. Please send someone to us in the blue room."

"Very good, sir," the man says, just like a butler in a movie.

"Come," says Zacharov.

We walk through the room, through double doors into a far smaller library. Three bearded men are sitting together, laughing. One smokes a pipe. Another has a girl in a very short red dress sitting on his knee doing a bump of cocaine off a sugar spoon.

Zacharov sees me staring. "Private club," he reminds me. Right.

In the third room a fire is blazing. The room is smaller than the other two, but there's only one set of doors—the ones we came through—and no one else inside. Zacharov motions that I should sit. I sink into the soft leather. There's a small, low table between us. A crystal chandelier swings gently above us, scattering bands of colored light across the room.

A uniformed attendant appears. He looks me over, obviously skeptical, then turns to Mr. Zacharov. "Would you care for a drink?"

"I will take Laphroaig with a single cube of ice to begin, and Mr. Sharpe will have—"

"A club soda," I say lamely.

"Very good," says the attendant.

"After that you will bring us three ounces of the Iranian osetra with blinis, chopped egg, and plenty of onion. We will both take a little Imperia vodka with that, very cold. Then a turbot with some of the chef's excellent mustard sauce. And finally two of your *pains d'amandes*. Any objections, Cassel? Anything you don't care for?"

I have never eaten most of the things he named, but I am unwilling to admit it. I shake my head. "Sounds great."

The attendant nods, not even looking at me now, and walks off.

"You are uncomfortable," Zacharov says, which is true but seems like an uncharitable observation. "I thought Wallingford prepared you to take your place in society."

"I don't think they expect my place to be anywhere near *this* place," I say, which makes him smile.

"But it could be, Cassel. Your gift is like this club—it makes you uncomfortable. It's a bit too much, isn't it?"

"What do you mean?"

"A man may daydream of how he would spend a million dollars, but playing the same game with a billion dollars sours the fantasy. There are too many possibilities. The house he once wished for with all his heart is suddenly too small. The travel, too cheap. He wanted to visit an island. Now he contemplates buying one. I remember you, Cassel. With all your heart you wanted to be one of us. Now you're the best of us."

I look into the fire, turning back only when I hear the clink of our drinks being set down on the table.

Zacharov picks up his Scotch and swirls the glass, making the amber liquor dance. He pauses another moment. "Do you recall being thrown out of Lila's birthday party because you had a fight with some kid from her school?" He laughs suddenly, a short bark of sound. "You really cracked his head on that sink. Blood everywhere."

I touch my ear self-consciously and force a grin. I stopped wearing an earring when I enrolled at Wallingford, and the hole has almost closed up, but I still have the memory of her with the ice and the needle that same night, her hot breath against my neck. I shift in the chair.

"Back then I should have seen you were worth watching," he says, which is flattering but pretty obviously not true. "You know I'd like you to come work for me. I know you have some reservations. Let me answer them."

The attendant returns with our first course. The tiny gray pearls of caviar pop on my tongue, leaving behind the briny taste of the sea.

Zacharov seems like a benevolent gentleman, loading his blini with chopped egg and crème fraiche. Just a distinguished guy in a perfectly tailored suit with a bulge under one arm where his gun rests. I'm thinking he's not the best person in whom to confide my moral quandaries. Still, I've got to say something. "What was it like for my grandfather? Did you know him when he was younger?"

Zacharov smiles. "Your grandad's from a different time. His parents' generation still thought of themselves as good people, thought of their powers as gifts. He was part of that first generation to be *born* criminals. Desi Singer came into the world—what?—not ten years after the ban was passed. He never had a chance."

"Dab hands," I say, thinking of Mrs. Wasserman's version of this story.

He nods. "Yes, that's what we used to be called, before the ban. Did you know that your grandfather was conceived in a worker camp? He grew up tough, like my father did. They had to. Their whole country had turned on them. My grandfather, Viktor, was in charge of the kitchens; it was his job to make sure everybody got fed. He did whatever he had to do to make the meager rations go around—made deals with the guards, made his own still and distilled his own booze to trade for supplies. That's how the families started. My grandfather used to say that it was our calling to protect one another. No matter how much money we had or how much power, we should never forget where we came from."

He stops speaking as the attendant returns, setting the fish down before us. Zacharov calls for a glass of 2005 Pierre Morey Meursault, and it comes a moment later, lemon pale, the base of the glass cloudy with condensation.

"When I was a young man of twenty, I was in my second year at Columbia. It was the late seventies, and I thought the world had changed. The first Superman movie was on the big screen, Donna Summer was on the radio, and I was tired of my father being so old-fashioned. I met a girl in class. Her name was Jenny Talbot. She wasn't a worker, and I didn't care."

The fish is cooling in front of us as Zacharov strips off one of his gloves. His bare hand is striped with scars. They're a ruddy brown and pulled like taffy.

"Three boys cornered me at a party in the Village and pressed my hand against one of the burners on an electric coil stove. Seared through my glove, fused the cloth into my flesh. It felt like someone was flaying me to the bone. They said I should stay away from Jenny, that the thought of someone like me touching her made them sick."

He takes a long swallow of wine and pokes his fork into the turbot, one hand still bare.

"Desi came to the hospital after my father and mother left. He wanted my sister Eva to wait in the hall. When he asked me what happened, I was ashamed, but I told him. I knew he was loyal to my father. After I'd finished the story, he asked me what I wanted done to those boys."

"He killed them, didn't he?" I ask.

"I wanted him to," says Zacharov, taking a bite of the fish and pausing to swallow. "Every time the nurse changed the dressing on my hand, every time they dug tweezers into blistered skin to pull out cloth, I imagined those boys dead. I told him so. Then your grandfather asked me about the girl."

"The girl?" I echo.

"That's exactly what I said, in that exact incredulous tone. He laughed and said that someone put those boys up to what they did. Someone told them something to rile them up. Maybe she liked to have boys fighting over her. But he was willing to bet that that girl of mine wanted to end our relationship and had decided to throw me out like garbage. It was easier, after all, if she seemed like a victim rather than the kind of girl who liked messing around with workers.

"Your grandfather was right. She never came to the hospital to see me. When Desi finally paid a visit to the boys, he found Jenny in one of their beds."

Zacharov pauses to eat a few bites. I eat too. The fish is amazing, flaky and redolent of lemon and dill. But I don't know what to make of the story he's telling.

"What happened to her?" I ask.

He pauses, fork in hand. "What do you think?"

"Ah," I say. "Right."

He smiles. "When *my* grandfather said we had to protect one another, I thought he was a sentimental old man. It wasn't until *your* grandfather said it that I understood what it meant. They hate us. They might give us a smile. They might even let us into their beds, but they still hate us."

The door opens. Two attendants have arrived with coffee and pastries.

"They'd hate you most of all," says Zacharov.

The room's warm, but I feel very cold.

It's late when Stanley drops me back at the house. I've only got maybe twenty minutes to get my stuff and get back to Wallingford before room check.

"Stay out of trouble," Stanley says as I hop out of the back of the Cadillac.

I unlock the door and head for the back room, gather up my books and backpack. Then I look for my keys, which I thought were right with my bag but aren't. I stick my hands beneath the cushions of the couch. Then I kneel down to see if they fell underneath. I finally find them on the dining room table, hidden by some envelopes.

I start to head out when I remember that my car is still busted. I'm not even sure I brought the battery and fuses home from Sam's house. In a panic, I run upstairs to my bedroom. No battery. No fuses. I retrace what my drunken steps must have been, all the way back to the kitchen. I discover that the coat closet is slightly ajar and, amazingly, the auto parts bag is inside of it, resting alongside an empty beer can. A coat is wadded up in the back, like maybe I knocked it off its hanger. I lift it, intending on putting it back where it goes, when I hear a metallic thunk.

A gun rests on the linoleum. It's silver and black with the Smith & Wesson stamp on the side. I stare at it, and stare, like I'm seeing it wrong. Like it's going to turn out to be a toy. After a moment I hold up the wide-collared coat. Black. Big. Like the one on the video.

Which makes that gun the one that killed my brother.

I put both the coat and the gun back, carefully, thrusting the evidence as far into the closet as it will go.

I wonder when she decided to shoot Philip. It must have been after she came back from Atlantic City. I can't believe that she knew about his deal with the Feds before then. Maybe she went to Philip's house and saw some of the papers—but, no, he wouldn't be that stupid. Maybe she spotted Agent Jones or Hunt talking to Philip. It would take only a single look at either one of them to know they were law enforcement.

But even that doesn't seem like enough. I don't know why she did it.

I only know that this is my mother's house, and my mother's closet, making that my mother's coat.

Making that my mother's gun.

CHAPTER TWELVE

AT SCHOOL MONDAY morning I catch up with Lila on my way to French class. I touch her shoulder, and she spins around, her smile tinged with longing. I hate having so much power over her, but there is a sinister creeping pleasure in knowing I am so much in her thoughts. A pleasure I have to guard against.

"Did you go to Philip's house?" I ask.

She opens her mouth uncertainly.

"I found one of your cigarettes," I say before she can lie.

"Where?" she asks. Her arms wrap around her chest protectively. She grips her shoulder tightly with one gloved hand.

"Where do you think? In his ashtray." I see her expression darken, and I abruptly change my mind about what's going to make her talk. She looks utterly closed to me, a house locked against burglars, even ones she likes. "Tell me it wasn't yours and I'll believe you."

I don't mean that for a second, though. I know the cigarette was hers. I just also know the best way to get into a locked house is to be let in the front door.

"I have to go to class," she says. "I'll meet you outside at lunch."

I lope on to French. We translate a passage from Balzac: *La puissance ne consiste pas à frapper fort ou souvent, mais à frapper juste.*

Power does not consist in striking hard or often, but in striking true.

She's waiting for me by the side of the cafeteria. Her short blond hair looks white in the sunlight, like a halo around her face. She's got on white stockings that stop at her thighs, so that when she swishes her rolled-up skirt, I can almost see skin.

"Hey," I say, determined not to look.

"Hey yourself." She smiles that crazy, hungry smile she has. She's had time to pull her act together, and it shows. She's decided what to tell and what to hide.

"So . . . ," I say, gloved hands in my pockets. "I didn't know you still smoked."

"So, let's take a walk." She pushes off the wall, and we start down the path toward the library. "I started again this summer. Smoking. I didn't really mean to, but everyone around my father smokes. And besides, it was something to do with my hands."

"Okay," I say.

"It's hard to quit. Even here at Wallingford, I take a paper towel tube, stuff it with fabric softener sheets, and exhale into that. Then I brush my teeth a million times."

"Rots your lungs," I say.

"I only do it when I'm really nervous," she says.

"Like when you're in a dead man's apartment?"

She nods quickly, gloves rubbing against her skirt. "Like that. Philip had something that I wanted to make sure no one found." Her gaze darts to my face. "One of the bodies."

"Bodies?" I echo.

"One of the people that you . . . changed. I've heard there's ways to tell if an amulet is real and, well, maybe someone—the cops or the Feds—could use that to tell if an object has been worked. I was worried for you."

"So why didn't you tell me?" I ask.

She turns to me, eyes blazing. "I want you to *love* me, you idiot. I thought that if I did something for you, something huge, then you would. I wanted to save you, Cassel, so that you'd have to love me. Get it now? It's horrible."

For a moment I don't know why she's so angry. Then I realize that it's because she's embarrassed. "Gratitude isn't love," I say finally.

"I should know that," she says. "I'm grateful to you and I hate it."

"You didn't do me any other favors you haven't mentioned,

right?" I ask, not relenting. "Like murdering my brother?"

"No," she says sharply.

"You had every reason to want him dead," I say, thinking of Sam and Daneca's accusations in the kitchen of Daneca's fancy house.

"Just because I'm glad he's dead doesn't mean I killed him," she says. "I didn't order him killed either, if that's what you're going to ask next. Is that what those agents wanted? To tell you I murdered your brother?"

I must look blank, because she laughs. "I go to this school too. Everyone knows you got cuffed and thrown into the back of a black car by guys in suits."

"So, what do most people think?"

"There's a rumor going around that you're a narc," she says, and I groan. "But I think the jury's still out."

"I don't know what the suits want with me any more than the school does," I say. "I'm sorry I asked you about the cigarette. I just had to know."

"You're getting very popular," she says. "Not enough Cassel to go around."

I look up. We've walked past the library. We're almost to the woods. I swing around, and she does the same. We walk back together quietly, lost in separate thoughts.

I want to reach out for her hand, but I don't. It's not fair. She'd have to take it.

I'm heading toward Physics when Sam stops me in the hall.

"Did you hear?" he asks. "Greg Harmsford went crazy and trashed his own laptop."

"When?" I ask, frowning. "At lunch?"

"Last night. Apparently everyone on his hall woke up to him drowning it in a sink. The screen was already cracked like he'd been punching it." At that, Sam can no longer contain his laughter. "Serious anger management problem."

I grin.

"He says that he did it in his sleep. Way to steal your excuse," says Sam. "Besides, everyone could see that his eyes were open."

"Oh," I say, the grin sliding off my face. "He was sleep-walking?"

"He was *faking*," Sam says.

I wonder where Lila was while I drove around with her father. I wonder if she visited Greg's room, if he asked her to come in, if she slowly removed her gloves before she ran her hands through his hair.

Sam turns to me to say something else.

Then, thankfully, the bell rings and I have to run to class. I sit down and listen to Dr. Jonahdab. Today she's talking about the principal of momentum and how hard it is to stop something once it has been set in motion.

Daneca rushes past me out of the room at the end of Physics. She heads for Sam's class and stands near the door, waiting for him. The expression she's wearing makes it clear that Sam hasn't started talking to her yet.

"Please," she says to him, hugging her books to her chest, but he walks past her without even hesitating. The skin around her eyes is red and swollen with recent tears.

"Everything's going to be okay," I say, although I'm not sure I believe it. It's just something people say.

"I guess I should have expected it," she says, pushing back a lock of purple-tipped hair and sighing. "My mom said lots of people want to know workers but would never date one. I thought Sam was different."

My stomach growls, and I remember that I skipped lunch. "No, you didn't," I say. "That's why you lied to him."

"Well, I was right, wasn't I?" she asks plaintively. She wants to be contradicted.

"I don't know," I say.

My next class—ceramics—is held across the quad at the Rawlings Fine Arts Center. I'm surprised when Daneca follows me onto the green; I really doubt her next class is there too.

"What do you mean?" she asks. "Why do you think he's like this?"

"Maybe he's mad you didn't trust him. Maybe he's mad you didn't tell him the real reason you didn't want to be tested. Maybe he's just happy to be in the right for once—you know, enjoying having the upper hand."

"He's not like that," she says.

"You mean he's not like me?" I ask. In the nearby parking lot a tow truck is starting to pull out with a car attached.

She blinks, as if startled. I have no idea why; it's not like she doesn't keep assuming terrible things about me. "I didn't say that."

"Well, you're right. I *would* like it, even if I didn't want to admit it. Everyone likes a little power, especially people who feel powerless." I think of Sam at the start of the semester, feeling like he could never measure up to Daneca, but I doubt she has any idea about that.

"Is that how you are with Lila?" If she wasn't judging me before, she's judging me now.

I shake my head, trying to keep the annoyance out of my voice. "You know it's not the same—not real. Haven't you ever worked—"

I stop speaking as I realize the car being towed is mine. "What the hell?" I say, and take off running.

"Hey!" I shout as I see the bumper of my car smack against the last speed bump before the road. All I can see of the guy driving is that he's got a cap on, pulled low enough to shade his eyes. I can't even see the license on the tow truck, since my own car is obscuring it. I can see the name airbrushed on the side of the truck, though. Tallington Towing.

"What just happened?" Daneca asks. She's standing in the empty parking spot where my Benz used to be.

"He stole my car!" I say, utterly baffled. I turn and sweep my hand to indicate all the other vehicles in the parking lot. "Why not one of these? These are nice cars! Why my crappy broken down piece of—"

"Cassel," Daneca says sternly, interrupting me. She points to the ground in front of her. "You better take a look at this."

I walk over and spot a small black jewelry box with a black bow sitting in the middle of the empty space. I squat down and touch the small tag, flip it over. There on the black paper, in even blacker ink, is a crude drawing of the crenellations of a castle. Frowning at it, I feel the familiar pull of the shadow world of crime and cons. This is a gift from that world.

Castle.

Cassel.

I pull the ribbon, and it comes free easily. Before I lift the lid, I briefly consider that there's going to be something unpleasant inside—a bomb or a finger—but if there's really a body part inside, waiting's only going to make everything worse. I open the box. Inside, nestled in cut black foam, is a square Benz key. Shiny. Silver edged and so newfangled that it looks more like a flash drive than anything to do with a car.

I lift it up and click the unlock button. Headlights flicker in a car across from where I'm standing. A black Roadster with chrome trim.

"Are you kidding me?" I say.

Daneca walks over and presses her face against the window. Her breath fogs the glass. "There's a letter inside."

I hear the bell ring faintly from inside the academic center. We're officially late for class.

Daneca seems not to hear it. She opens the door and takes out an envelope. Her gloved fingers make quick work of it, ripping open the flap before I can stop her.

"Hey," I say. "That's mine."

"Do you know who it's from?" she asks, unfolding the paper.

Sure. There's only one person it could be from. Zacharov. But I'd rather she didn't know that.

I make a grab for the letter, but she laughs and holds it out of reach.

"Come on," I say, but she's already reading.

"Iiiiinteresting," Daneca says, her gaze rising to meet mine. She holds out the note:

A taste of your future.
—Z

I snatch it out of her hand and crumple it. "Let's take a drive," I say, holding the key up in front of her. "We're already cutting class—at least we can have some fun."

Daneca slides into the passenger seat without protest, shocking me. She waits until I've buckled myself in before she asks, "So, what's that note about?"

"Nothing," I say. "Just that Zacharov wants me to join his merry band of thieves."

"Are you going to keep this?" she asks, brushing gloved fingers over the dashboard. "It's a pretty expensive bribe."

The car is beautiful. Its engine hums and the gas pedal responds to even the lightest touch.

"If you keep it," Daneca says, "he'll have his claws in you."

Everyone has their claws in me. Everyone.

I pull out onto the street and head for the highway. We ride in silence for a few moments.

"Before—when we were heading to class—you asked me if I ever worked anyone." Daneca looks out the window.

"Please know that I am seriously the last person in the world to judge you."

She laughs. "Where are we going anyway?"

"I thought we'd get coffee and a doughnut. Brain food."

"I'm more of an herbal tea girl," Daneca says.

"I'm shocked," I say, taking one hand off the wheel and placing it over my heart. "But you were about to tell me all your secrets. Please, continue."

She rolls her eyes, leans forward, and fiddles with the radio. The speakers are just as fantastic as the rest of the car. No hiss. No distortion. Just full, clear sound. "There's not much to tell," she says, adjusting the volume down. "There was this guy I liked when I was twelve, right before I came to Wallingford. His name was Justin. We were both at this arts-focused middle school and he was a kid actor. He'd done some commercials and everything. I was just on the edge of his friends circle, you know."

I nod. I survive at the edge of friends circles.

"And I followed him around like a puppy dog. Every time he talked to me, I felt like my heart was in my throat. I wrote a haiku about him."

I look over at her, eyebrows raised. "Seriously? A haiku?"

"Oh, yeah—want to hear it? 'Golden blond hair and eyes like blue laser beams. Why won't you notice me?'"

I laugh, snorting. She laughs too.

"I can't believe you remember that," I say.

"Well, I remember it because he *read it*. The teacher hung up all of our haikus without telling us she was going to, and a girl in class told him about mine. It was horrible. Humiliating. All his friends would tease me about it and he would just look at me with this smug smirk. Ugh."

"He sounds like a jerk."

"He was a jerk," Daneca says. "But I still liked him. I think in some weird way I liked him more."

"So, did you work him?"

"No," Daneca said. "I worked *me*. To stop feeling the way I did. To feel nothing."

I didn't expect that. "You're a good person," I say, humbled. "I give you a hard time about it, but I really do admire you. You care so much about doing the right thing."

She shakes her head as I pull into a coffee shop. "It was weird. Every time I looked at him afterward, I had that tip-of-the-tongue feeling, like I couldn't quite remember a word I ought to have known. It felt wrong, Cassel."

We get out of the car. "I'm not saying that working yourself is a great idea . . ."

The coffee place has tin ceilings and a counter full of fresh-baked cookies. Its tables are filled with students and the self-employed, tapping away on laptops and clutching cups with a reverence that suggests they just crawled out of bed.

Daneca orders a maté chai latte, and I get a regular cup of coffee. Her drink comes out a vivid grass green.

I make a face. We head to the only free table, one next to the door and the racks of newspapers. As I sit down, one of the headlines catches my eye.

"Don't look like that," Daneca says. "It's good. Want a sip?"

I shake my head. There is a photograph of a man I know beside the words "Bronx Hitman Jumps Bail." The type under the picture says "Death worker Emil Lombardo, also known as the Hunter, missing after being indicted for double homicide." They didn't even bother to lie to me about his name.

"Do you have a quarter?" I ask, fishing around in my pockets.

Daneca reaches into her messenger bag and feels around until she finds one. She slaps it down on the table. "You know what the weirdest thing about me working myself over that boy was?"

I find fifty cents and feed our combined change into the machine. "No, what?"

I lift out the paper. The double homicide was of a thirty-four-year-old woman and her mother. Two witnesses to another crime—something about the Zacharovs and real estate. There are smaller pictures of the dead women beneath the fold. They both look like nice people.

Nice people. Good people. Like Daneca.

"The weirdest thing," Daneca says, "is that after I stopped liking him, he asked me out. When I turned him down, he was really hurt. He didn't know what he'd done wrong."

I touch my gloved finger to the murdered women's faces, letting the leather smear the ink. Last night I helped their killer get away. "That is weird," I say hollowly.

When we get back to school, it's just in time for my computer class. I walk in as the bell stops ringing.

"Mr. Sharpe," says Ms. Takano without looking up.

"They're looking for you in the office." She hands me her official hall pass, a large plastic dinosaur.

I take my time walking across the green. I think about my new car, gleaming in the sun. I think of the sophomore-year production of *Macbeth*, and Amanda Kerwick as Lady Macbeth, holding up her bare hands, looking for blood.

But there is no mere spot on me. As her husband says, "I am in blood/Stepp'd in so far that, should I wade no more,/ Returning were as tedious as go o'er."

I shake my head. I'm just looking for excuses to keep the car.

When I walk into the office, Ms. Logan frowns. "I didn't think you'd be back so soon. Cassel—you know you're supposed to sign out when you leave campus."

"I know," I say contritely. I'm hoping that Northcutt gives me only a single demerit for cutting class. Not a week ago I was bragging to Lila about my strategies to get off campus without trouble. Then I drove off without implementing a single one.

But Ms. Logan just shoves the sign-in folder at me. "Put the time you left here," she says, brushing her gloved finger over the line. "And when you came back, here."

I write them down faithfully.

"Good," she says. "The lawyer said you were a bit dazed when he called to remind you about the meeting. Northcutt wants you to know that you don't have to go back to class if you're not ready."

"I'm okay," I say slowly. Something's going on. I better figure out what before I screw it up.

"We just want you to know that we're very sorry for your loss, Cassel. And I hope everything went as well as it could today."

"Thank you," I say, trying to look somber.

I head for the door, thinking over what just happened. One of Zacharov's people must have called and pretended to be the family lawyer—maybe it was even the fellow driving the tow truck—to give me not only the car, but time to tool around in it. Being courted by a mobster sure is sweet. Hard for the offers of the federal agents to compare.

I am crossing back toward my computer class when I see Daneca come out of the office.

"Hey," I say. "I didn't see you in there."

"I was in Northcutt's office," she says dejectedly. Then she kicks a clod of dirt off the quad. "I can't believe I let you talk me into that."

Looks like Daneca just got her first demerit for cutting class.

"Sorry," I say.

She makes a face like she knows I'm not that sorry. "So, what's Lila up to?"

"Lila?" I am feeling very stupid lately.

"You know, your *girlfriend*? Blonde? Cursed to love you? Ringing any bells yet?" Daneca holds out her phone to show me a text from Lila: *Come to Spanish classroom. Third floor. Urgent.*

"No idea," I say, looking at the words. I pull out my phone, but there are no messages.

Daneca laughs. Her voice is teasing. "So, wait, you *don't* know who Lila is?"

I realize my mistake and laugh. But it makes me think. The Lila I remember was fourteen. She hadn't spent three years as an animal in a cage and hadn't been forced to feel anything, and even then she was a mystery to me. I wonder if I have any idea who Lila is after all.

We find Lila sitting on one of the desks in the empty classroom, swinging her legs, when we walk in. Propped in another is Greg Harmsford. He's wearing sunglasses, but his head is tilted all the way back and it's clear he's unconscious. At least I hope he's unconscious. In front of him are two cans of Coke, both open.

"What did you do?" I ask.

"Oh, hi, Cassel." A faint blush has started at the tips of her ears. She holds out a piece of paper. It's a printout of an e-mail. I take it from her but don't really look.

Daneca clears her throat and points to Greg's prone body, widening her eyes to emphasize that she wants me to *do something*.

"Is he dead?" I ask. Someone's got to.

"I roofied him," Lila says matter-of-factly. The late afternoon light has turned her blond hair to gold. She's wearing a crisp white shirt and tiny blue stones in her ears that match one of her eyes. She looks like the last girl in the world who would drug a boy in the middle of the day. *Like butter wouldn't melt in her mouth*, the old folks in Carney would say.

"Look what I found on his computer," Lila says.

I finally look at the page in my hand. It's from Greg and is addressed to a bunch of e-mail addresses I don't know. The text informs parents that "Wallingford supports a club encouraging criminal activities" and that "worker kids are allowed to openly brag about their illegal exploits." I look at the e-mail addresses again. I guess they're the addresses of our parents. There are photos attached, and although Lila has printed out only the first page, the two there make it pretty obvious that he attached stills of everyone at the HEX meeting. "Wow," I say, and pass the paper to Daneca.

I don't mention that to get that off his computer before he tried to drown it in his dorm sink, she must have been working him. I don't mention that Greg's passed out now, asleep, vulnerable to any invasion of his dreams.

"I'm going to *kill* him," Daneca says. She looks angrier than I have ever seen her.

Lila takes a deep breath, then lets it out slowly. "This is all my fault."

"What do you mean?"

She shakes her head, avoiding my gaze. "It's not important. What matters is that I'm going to make it right. We're going to get him back. For Ramirez and the video. For that e-mail. I have a plan."

"Which is . . . ?" I ask.

Lila hops off the desk.

"Greg Harmsford is about to join HEX," she says. "He's going to attend his first meeting today. Right now, hopefully. Before he wakes up." Her eyes are brimming with manic glee, and I realize how much I've missed her like this, ferocious. Missed the fearless girl who used to beat me at races and order me around.

I laugh. "You are *evil*," I tell Lila.

"Flatterer," she says, but she seems pleased.

"I don't know if I can get anyone to come out for a meeting," Daneca says. She walks to the door and checks the hallway, then looks back at us. "Do you think people would believe it? Could we pull it off?"

Lila reaches into her bag and pulls out a tiny silver camera. "Well, we'll have pictures. Besides, stuff like this is in the news all the time. Government officials who are all anti-worker turn out to be workers themselves. It's totally believable. The fact that he got the footage the first time will make him seem guiltier."

I grin. "I guess we better make some calls if we want to convene an entire HEX meeting."

It takes Daneca a lot of begging to get even a small group together. No one wants to be associated with HEX right now. They've all got stories about being hassled. Some even have stories about classmates' parents trying to hire them to do shady things. They're freaked, and I don't blame them.

Daneca gives each one the same song and dance about how important it is that we stick together. Lila gets on the line and swears up and down that it'll be funny. I try to prop up Greg Harmsford.

Posing an unconscious body isn't easy. Greg's not comatose, just sleeping. He still moves when I put him in an uncomfortable position, still makes a face and pushes away my hands when I try to make him sit up. I search around in the desk until I find some tape and pencils. I use those to build a kind of splint on the back of Greg's head. From the front he might look like he's slouching, but at least he'll seem awake since his head will be upright. He makes a protesting sound as I attach the tape, but after a minute, he seems to get used to it.

"Nice work," Lila says absently. She's busy writing "HEX MEETING" in chalk on the board.

"How long will he be like that?" Daneca asks, poking Greg's shoulder. He twitches a little, almost shifting enough to ruin the effect of my pose, but not quite. Daneca smothers a shriek with both her hands.

"I'm not really sure, but when he wakes up, he'll probably be sick. Side effect." Lila says distractedly. "Cassel, can you put Greg's arm up on the chair or something? I don't think he looks very natural."

"We should get Sam," I say with a sigh. "Special effects are his area of expertise. I have no idea what I'm doing."

"No," says Daneca, taking my phone out of my hand and setting it down on a desk. "We're not calling him."

"But he's—," I start.

"No," she says.

Lila looks at us in confusion.

"They're having a fight," I explain.

"Oh," she says, then tilts her head and squints at Greg. "There's something still off. Maybe if we had some junk food? We've always got stuff at real meetings. Daneca, can you go to the vending machine before people start showing up? Cassel, maybe you can look and see if there are empty chip bags in the trash? They'd just be props. I could run to the store—"

"I'll go if Cassel promises not to call Sam," Daneca says.

I groan. "I'll pinky swear if you want."

Daneca gives me a dark look and heads into the hall-way. Instead of following, I turn toward Lila, who's rifling through her bag.

"Why do you think this is your fault?" I ask.

Her gaze darts from me to Greg. "There's not a lot of time. We should . . ."

I wait, but she doesn't say anything else. Her cheeks pink and she turns her gaze to the floor.

"Whatever happened," I say, "you can tell me."

"It's nothing you don't already know. I was jealous and stupid. After I saw you and Audrey together, I went and talked to Greg. Flirted with him, I guess. I knew he had a girlfriend and it was a mean, bad thing to do, but I didn't think things would get—I didn't think it would be as bad as it was. Then he asked about you, wanted to know if we were together. I told him 'sorta.'"

"Sorta," I echo.

She rubs her hand over her eyes. "Everything was so complicated between us. I didn't know *what* to say. Once he heard that we were—whatever—he started really hitting on me. And I just wanted to feel something—something other than the way I felt."

"I'm not—," I start to say. *I'm not worth that.* I reach out and tuck a loose strand of hair behind her ear.

She shakes her head, almost angrily. "The next day, I

can tell he was bragging about me. One of his friends even asks me about it. So I go over to Greg and think of the worst possible thing I can say. I tell him that if he doesn't shut up about me, I will swear up and down that he's awful in bed. That he's hung like a worm."

I give a snort of incredulous laughter.

She's still not looking at me, though. And her cheeks are, if anything, redder. "He's all, 'You know you liked it.' And I say—"

She stops. I can hear people in the hallway. In a few moments, they'll be inside.

"What?" I ask.

"You have to understand," she says, quickly. "He got really mad. Really, really mad. And I think that's why he went after HEX."

"Lila, what did you *say*?"

She closes her eyes tightly. Her voice is almost a whisper. "I said I was thinking about you the whole time."

I'm glad her eyes are closed. I'm glad she can't see my face.

People start filing in. Nadja, Rachel, and Chad are the first to arrive and Lila, still blushing, doesn't waste any time directing them. Soon, everyone is arranging chairs.

I fake my way through seeming calm and collected. Daneca comes in a few moments later with snacks.

It's not your fault, I want to tell Lila. But I don't say that. I don't say anything.

We take picture after picture with the backdrop of the blackboard and the scrawled "HEX MEETING" on it. Ones with someone standing in the center of a circle of chairs, talking earnestly. Ones with everyone laughing and a girl on Greg's lap. Halfway through our photo shoot, he wakes up enough to pull the pencils off the back of his neck and push up his sunglasses. He looks at all of us in confusion, but not with any real alarm.

"What's going on?" Greg slurs.

I want to snap his neck. I want to make him sorry he was ever born.

"Smile," says Daneca. He gives a lopsided grin. A girl throws her arm over his shoulder.

Lila keeps clicking away.

Eventually Greg goes back to sleep, head cradled in his arms on a desk. Lila, Daneca, and I go to the corner store and use the booth there to print out all the photos from the SIM card.

They look great. So good that it would be a crime not to share them with everyone at Wallingford.

Most people never report being conned, for three reasons. The first reason is that con artists don't usually leave a lot of evidence. If you don't really know who did this to you, there's no point in reporting them. The second reason is that usually you, the mark, agreed to do something shady. If you report the con artist, you have to report yourself along with him. But the third reason is the simplest and most compelling. Shame. You're the dummy who got conned.

No one wants to look stupid. No one wants to be thought of as gullible. So they hide how dumb and gullible they were. Con artists barely have to cover up at all, with marks so eager to cover up for them.

Greg Harmsford insists he was Photoshopped into the pictures, loudly and to anyone who will listen. He's furious when his story gets questioned. Eventually the teasing gets to him and he punches Gavin Perry in the face.

He's suspended for two days. All that because he doesn't want to admit that he got had.

I'm sitting in my room for study hall, working on my world ethics homework, when my phone rings. I don't know the number, but I pick it up.

"We have to meet," says the voice on the other end. It takes me a moment to realize I'm talking to Barron. His voice sounds colder than usual.

"I'm at school," I say. I'm not in the mood for more sneaking around. "I can't get out of here before the weekend."

"What a coincidence," Barron says. "I'm at Wallingford too."

The fire alarm sounds. Sam jumps up and starts shoving his feet into sneakers.

"Grab the PlayStation," he says to me.

I shake my head, covering the phone. "It's a prank. Someone pulled it." Then I nearly spit into the phone, "You idiot. Even if you wanted me to leave, there's no way I can now. They will take a head count. They will make absolutely sure we're all back in our rooms."

Sam ignores me and starts unhooking his game system.

"I already made your hall master forget you," Barron says. The words send a chill up my spine.

I file out with Sam and all the other kids to stand on the grass. Everyone's looking up at the building, waiting for wisps of smoke to unfurl or flames to light the windows. It's easy to back away until I'm near trees and shadows.

No one's looking for me. No one but Barron.

His gloved hand comes down on my shoulder heavily. We walk away from the school, along the sidewalk, toward houses bathed in the flickering blue light of televisions. It's only around nine, but it feels much later.

It feels too late.

"I've been thinking about the Zacharovs," says Barron too casually. "They're not the only game in town."

I should never have let my guard down.

"What do you mean?" It's hard to look at Barron now, but I do. He's smirking. His black hair and black suit make him into a shadow, as if I conjured some dark mirror of myself.

"I know what you did to me," he says, and although he's trying to keep his tone even, I can hear rage bleeding through. "How you took advantage of the holes in my memory. How for all your bellyaching about doing the right thing, you're no different from me or Philip. I met two nice men from the FBI—Agent Jones and Agent Hunt. They had a lot to tell me about my big brother—and about my little one. Philip told them how you turned me against him. How somehow you'd messed up my head so that I didn't remember that I'd been in on his plan to make Anton head of the

Zacharov family. At first I didn't believe them, but I went back and looked at my notebooks again."

Oh, crap.

There are master forgers in the world, folks who know exactly what chemicals ink had in it in the sixteenth century versus the eighteenth. They have sources for paper and canvases that will carbon date correctly; they can create perfect craquelure. They practice the loops and flourishes of another hand until it is more familiar than their own.

It probably goes without saying that I am not a master forger. Most forgeries get by because they are good enough that no one checks them. When I sign my mother's name to a permission slip, so long as it looks like her handwriting, no one brings in a specialist.

But if Barron compared the notebook I hastily forged to his older ones, the fake would be obvious. We are all specialists in our own handwriting

"If you know what I did to you," I say, trying not to seem rattled, "then you know what you did to me, too."

That brings out his lopsided grin. "The difference is that I'm willing to forgive you."

That's so unexpected that I have no reply. Barron doesn't seem to need one. "I want to start over, Cassel," he says, "and I want to start at the top. I'm going to the Brennan family. And for that I need you. We'll be an unstoppable team of assassins."

"No," I say.

"*Ouch.*" He doesn't sound all that put out by my refusal. "Think you're too good for such a dirty job?"

"Yeah," I say. "That's me. Too good."

I wonder if he really could rationalize what I did to him, really treat betrayal like the slight transgression of a recalcitrant business partner. I wonder if I hurt him.

If he can rationalize what I did to him, it's easy to imagine how he rationalized what he did to me.

"Do you know why you agreed to change all those people into inanimate objects? Why you agreed to kill them?"

I take a deep breath. It sucks to hear the words out loud. "Of course I don't. I don't remember anything. You *stole all my memories*."

"You would follow Philip and me around like a little puppy," Barron says. I can hear the violence in his voice. "Begging to do a job with us. Hoping we'd see your black heart and give you a chance." He pokes me in the chest.

I take a step back. Rage flashes through me, sudden and nearly overwhelming.

I was their baby brother. Sure, I idolized them. And they kicked me in the teeth.

Barron grins. "It's pretty clever, really. I made you believe you'd killed before. That's all! I made you believe that you were what I wanted you to become. You loved it, Cassel. You loved being a goddamn assassin."

"That's not true," I say, shaking my head, willing myself to shut out his words. "You're a liar. You're the prince of liars. And since I don't remember, you know you can say anything. I would be stupid to believe you."

"Oh, come on," Barron says. "You know your own nature. You know if something *feels* true."

"I'm not going to do it," I say. "You and the Brennans can go to hell together."

He laughs. "You will do it. You already have. People don't change."

"No," I say.

"Like I said, those federal agents came to see me," Barron says. I start to interrupt him, but Barron just raises his voice. "I didn't give them anything important. Nothing like I could have. If I told them what you are, it would just be a matter of time before they connected the dots and figured out you're the murderer they're looking for."

"They'd never believe you," I say, but I feel unsteady. The world has already tilted. I can feel myself falling.

"Of course they would," Barron says. "I can show them a body. The one you left in the freezer in Mom's house."

"Oh," I say faintly. "That."

"Sloppy," Barron says. "I was the one who told you about him, after all. Didn't you think I would look?"

"I don't know what I thought." Truly, I don't.

"Then they can make you that same crap offer they made Philip, get what they want, and lock you away for a thousand years."

"Philip had immunity," I say. "I saw the contract."

Barron laughs. "I saw it too. Too bad Philip didn't show it to me before he sold them his soul. I was pre-law, remember? That contract's worthless. Agents can't offer immunity; it wasn't worth the paper it was printed on. It was for show. They could have taken Philip in whenever they wanted."

"Did you tell him that?" I ask.

"Why bother?" Barron says. "Philip didn't want to hear it. He just wanted to say good-bye before they shipped him off to witness protection land."

I can't tell if Barron's lying or not. I have a sinking feeling that this time he's telling the truth.

Which means I can't trust the Feds.

But Barron's going to go to the Feds if I don't throw in my lot with the Brennans.

And Zacharov will have me killed in a heartbeat if I do work for the Brennans.

There's no way out.

I think about what Zacharov said at Philip's funeral. *There are people close to you that you will have to deal with eventually.*

You will do it, Barron said. *You already have. People don't change.*

I look over at him. He smirks. "Not a tough choice when I lay it all out for you, is it, Cassel?"

It's not.

CHAPTER THIRTEEN

BARRON WALKS ME BACK to my dorm. I get there before lights-out at eleven. The hall master looks surprised to find someone occupying the other half of Sam's room when he comes in for the final hall check, but he doesn't say anything. He must figure that he's getting old, to be forgetting things like which students he's supposed to be responsible for. He must worry about dementia, Alzheimer's, getting enough sleep. It's a trick that wouldn't have worked at any other time but the beginning of the year.

It did work, though. Barron's clever.

"What happened to you during the fire drill?" Sam asks, pulling on a ratty Dracula T-shirt. His sweatpants have a hole on the knee.

"Went for a walk," I say, peeling off my gloves. "Fresh air."

"With Daneca?" Sam asks.

I frown. "What?"

"I know you took her out in that new, fancy car of yours. You got her in trouble, man."

"Yeah, I'm sorry about that." Then I grin. "But it was kind of funny. I mean, she never does anything bad, and now she's cutting class, getting thrown in jail . . ."

Sam isn't smiling. "You're going to treat her the same way you treated Audrey, aren't you? Barely noticing if you hurt her. I always knew Daneca liked you. Girls *like* you, Cassel. And you ignore them. And then they like you more."

"Hey," I say. "Wait a minute. She skipped class because she was miserable over *you*. We talked about *you*."

"What did she say?" I can't tell if he believes me, but at least I've distracted his focus.

I sigh. "That you're a bigot who doesn't want to date a worker girl."

"I'm not!" Sam says. "That's not even why I'm mad at her."

"I told her that." I chuck a pillow at him. "Just before we leaped into each other's arms and made out passionately, like weasels on Valentine's Day, like those really magnetic magnets, like greased-up eels—"

"Why am I your friend?" Sam moans, flopping back onto the bed. "Why?"

A knock on the door startles us just before our hall master jerks it open. "Is there a problem? Lights-out was fifteen minutes ago. Keep it down in here and go to sleep or I'm giving you both a Saturday detention."

"Sorry," we both mumble.

The door closes.

Sam snickers and pitches his voice low. "Okay, fine. I get it. I'm insecure. But look, I'm a fat dork. Girls aren't exactly getting in line, you know? And then there's this girl, and I figure she's too good for me so there has to be some kind of catch, and then there *is*. She's hiding that she's a worker. She doesn't trust me. She's not taking me seriously."

"You ignoring Daneca is making you both insane," I say. "She made a mistake. I've made plenty of mistakes. It doesn't mean she doesn't like you. It means she wants you to like her and she thought she had to lie to make that happen. Which makes her less perfect, sure. But isn't that a relief?"

"Yeah," he says quietly, his pillow half-covering his mouth. "I guess. Maybe I should talk to her."

"Good," I say. "I need you to be happy. I need one of us to be happy."

It's a dream. I'm pretty sure it's a dream, but I am back in my grandfather's basement in Carney, lying on top of Lila, and my hands are tightening on her arms, and it's really hard to concentrate on anything but the smell of her hair and the feel of her skin. Except then I look down at her and she's staring up at the ceiling, her face slack and pale.

And in the dream I lean down to kiss her anyway, even though I can see that her neck is slit with the worker's smile, cut too deep, running with blood. Even though she's dead.

Then I'm teetering on the roof of my old dorm, slate tiles biting into the pads of my feet. Leaves rustle overhead. I look down at the empty quad, just like I did last spring.

This time I jump.

I'm awake, sweating through the sheets, hating myself for the hot shudder that's running through my body. On the other side of the room, Sam is snoring gently.

I reach for my cell phone before I think better of it.

Stop it, I type to Lila.

What? she texts back a moment later. She's awake.

And then I'm pushing open the window and sneaking out to the quad in the middle of the night, in just a T-shirt and boxers. It's stupid, stupid like driving off campus with no plan. I'm acting like I want to get caught, like I want someone to stop me before I have to make the decisions I am careening toward.

Once, a year ago, I would never have believed how easy it was to just walk out of one building and into another. The front doors of the dorms aren't even locked. Each floor door *is* locked, but not with anything challenging. No bolt. Just a quick twist and swipe, and I'm walking across her floor and into her room, like getting caught is the last thing on my mind.

"*You*," I say, my voice low but not low enough. She's huddled in blankets and peering up at me owlishly.

"I can't keep having these dreams," I whisper. "You have to stop giving them to me."

"Are you crazy?" She rolls onto her back, kicking off

the blanket and sitting up. She's only got on a tank top and underwear. "You're going to get us both thrown out of school."

I open my mouth to bargain with her, but I feel suddenly undone by despair. I am like a clockwork automaton whose gears just locked.

She touches my arm, bare skin on bare skin. "I'm not giving you any dreams. I'm not working you. Can't you believe there's one person in your life who's not out to get you?"

"No," I say, too honest by half. I sit down on the bed and put my head in my hands.

She puts her hand on my cheek. "There's something really wrong, isn't there?"

I shake my head. "It's just dreams."

I don't want Lila to see that I hoped the dreams were from her, wanted them to be clues that added up to something, wished for them to be something that could just stop. I didn't want more evidence that the inside of my head is an ugly place.

She drops her hand and looks at me, head tilted to one side. For a moment I am flooded with nostalgia for us being kids, for my own uncomplicated and completely impossible yearning.

"Tell me," she says.

"I can't," I say, shaking my head again.

There is a sound in the hallway, a door shutting and then footsteps. Lila looks toward her closet, and I start to pad my way toward it. Then I hear the flush of a toilet.

I sigh and lean against the wall.

"Come here," she whispers recklessly, opening the covers. "Get under. You'll be hidden if someone comes in."

"I don't know if that's such a—," I begin.

"*Shhhh.*" She cuts me off, smiling in a way that suggests that she's mocking her own motivations before I get the chance. "Come on. Quick."

It's not that I don't know that it's a bad idea. It's that, lately, bad ideas have a particular hold over me. I get under the covers. They're warm from being against her skin, and they carry her smell—soap and the faint trace of ash. When she throws an arm over my torso, urging me to press against her, I do.

Her skin is soft and scorchingly hot after the cool night air. Her leg twines around mine. It feels so good, I have to choke back a gasp.

It's so easy. Wrong, but easy. There are so many things I want to say to her, and they're all unfair. I kiss her instead, smothering the unutterable *I love you. I have always loved you* against her tongue. Her mouth opens under mine with a whimper.

When she pulls her tank top over her head and throws it onto the floor, I am hollowed out, empty of everything but gnawing self-hate. When her bare fingers thread through my hair, even that fades away. There is nothing but her.

"I'm a good pretend girlfriend," she says, like she's telling a joke that's just between us.

We should really stop.

Everything slows to her skin, the swell of her lip

between my teeth, the arch of her bare back. My hands slide to her hip bones and the edge of her cotton underpants.

"The best," I say. My voice sounds unfamiliar, like I've been screaming.

Lila's mouth moves against my shoulder. I can feel her smile.

I push her hair gently back from her cheek. I can feel her heartbeat throbbing in the pulse at her throat, measuring out the moments before she's gone.

The moment she was cursed, I lost her. Once it wears off—soon—she will be embarrassed to remember things that she said, things she did, things like this. No matter how solid she feels in my arms, she is made of smoke.

I should stop, but there's no point in stopping. Because I'm not strong enough—eventually, I won't stop.

I thought the question was "Will I or won't I?"

But that's not the question at all.

It's "When?"

Because I will.

It's just a matter of time. It's now.

Lila kisses me again, and even that thought spirals away. I close my eyes.

"We can do whatever you want," I say, voice ragged. "But you have to tell me—"

The sound of shattering glass seems impossibly loud. I am up on my knees in the bed, cold air from outside sobering me before I really understand what's happening. But then I see the tableau: the jagged outline of what's left of the window, a rock lying in the glittering fragments on the floor, and a girl turning to run.

For a moment my gaze locks with Audrey's. Then she's halfway across the quad, rain boots sinking in the dirt.

Lila's bent over the stone, looking dazed, a crumpled piece of paper in her hand. "There was a note taped to it. It says 'Die, curse worker.'" She looks out the window. Too late. Audrey's gone.

I hear footsteps in the hall, the banging of doors. Voices.

"You have to hide," Lila whispers. She's still bare to the waist. It's really distracting.

I look around the room instead of looking at her. There's nowhere to go—under the bed and in the closet might work for a quick room check, but not something like this.

All I can think to do is change myself.

I have never transformed myself beyond a slight changing of my hands, and only the terror of getting both of us thrown out of school is enough to make me concentrate. I jerk my body into shifting. It happens fast; I'm getting better. I fall forward onto the pads of four feet. I want to shout, but what comes out of my mouth is a yowl.

"A black cat?" Lila snorts, leaning down. Her fingers sink into my fur as she lifts me up. I'm glad she's holding me, because the shift in perspective is dizzying. I'm not sure how to manage my feet.

Someone, probably her hall master, bangs on the door. "What's going on in there? Ms. Zacharov, you better open up."

Lila leans out the remains of the window, swinging my new body over the quad. My tail lashes back and forth without my knowing how I'm making that happen. It's a long way down.

"Too far," she says suddenly. "You're going to hurt your—"

She's forgotten that I'm not going to look like a normal cat in a moment. I squirm, twisting until I can bite her hand.

"Ow!" she yells, and lets go.

The air rushes past me, too fast for me to make any sound. I try to keep my limbs loose, not to brace myself for impact, but hitting the ground feels like a punch in the chest. My breath goes out of me.

I barely manage to crawl into the bushes before the blowback hits.

Everything aches. I lift my head to see a pink light glowing behind the stretch of trees near the track. Morning.

I'm still a cat.

Blowback as something smaller than yourself is even more bizarre than usual. Nothing feels real or right. No part of your body is your own. Even perspective is all wrong.

Waking up in an unfamiliar body is stranger still.

My senses are heightened to a surreal degree. I can hear insects moving through blades of grass. I can smell mice burrowing into the soft wood. I feel very small and very scared.

I'm not sure I can walk. I push myself up, leg by leg, and wobble until I'm sure I've got my balance. Then I shift one front paw and one back one, moving in a staggered limp across the quad in the early morning light.

It feels like it takes hours. By the time I make it to beneath my own window, I'm exhausted. The window is just as I left it, slightly lifted from the sill, but not so wide that Sam would be woken by the breeze.

I yowl hopefully. Sam, predictably, hears nothing.

Closing my eyes against the pain, I force the transformation. It *hurts*, like my skin was still raw from shifting the first time. I push open the window and hop inside, falling onto the floor with a thump.

"Hrm," Sam says muzzily, turning over.

"Help me," I say, lifting my arm to touch the metal edge of his bed. "Please. The blowback. You've got to keep me from being loud."

He's staring at me with wide eyes. They only get wider when my fingers start to curl like vines. My leg starts shaking.

"It hurts," I say, shamed by the whine in my voice.

Sam is getting up, throwing his comforter over me. Two pillows come down on either side of my head so I can't thrash it around too badly. He's totally awake now, looking at me with true adrenaline-pumping horror.

"I'm sorry," I manage to get out before my tongue turns to wood.

I feel a sharp nudge on my side. I turn stiffly and blink up at Mr. Pascoli.

"Get up, Mr. Sharpe," our hall master says. "You're going to be late for class."

"He's sick," I hear Sam say.

I am cocooned in blankets. Just moving is hard, like the air has turned semi-solid. I groan and then close my eyes again. I have never felt so worn out. I had no idea that back-to-back blowback could do this to me.

"What is he doing on the floor?" I hear Pascoli say. "Are you hungover, Mr. Sharpe?"

"I'm sick," I slur, borrowing Sam's excuse. My mind isn't working fast enough to come up with one of my own. "I think I have a fever."

"You better get down to the nurse, then. Breakfast is almost over."

"I'll take him," Sam says.

"I want to see a copy of that slip, Mr. Sharpe. And you better get one. If I find out you've been drinking or using, I don't care what's going on with your family, you're going to be off my hall. Understand?"

"Yeah." I nod. Right now I am willing to say whatever I think will make Pascoli go away faster.

"Come on," Sam says, picking me up under my arms and dumping me onto my bed.

I struggle to stay sitting up. My head swims. I'm not really sure how I pull on jeans, gloves, and boots, which I fumble over and finally decide not to lace.

"Maybe we should call someone," he whispers once Pascoli is out of the room. "Mrs. Wasserman?"

I frown, trying to concentrate on his words. "What do you mean?"

"Last night you seemed way screwed-up. And today? You look pretty bad."

"Just tired," I say.

He shakes his head. "I've never seen anything like—"

"Blowback," I say quickly, reluctant to hear his description of what it looks like. "Don't worry about it."

He narrows his eyes but waits for me to get up. He follows as I shuffle dazedly across campus.

"I need one more thing," I say, "when we get to the nurse's office."

"Sure, man," he says, but I don't think he's decided yet. I'm freaking him out.

"When we go in there, I am going to have a coughing fit, and you are going to volunteer to get me a glass of water. But you're going to get me *hot* water—as hot as you can get it out of the tap. Okay?"

"Why?" asks Sam.

I force a grin. "Easiest way to fake a fever."

Even semiconscious I can still manage a minor con.

Hours later I wake up in the nurse's office, drooling on a pillow. I'm ravenously hungry. I get up and realize I'm still wearing my boots. I lace them and pad out to the front room.

The school nurse is gray-haired, short, and round. She moves around her white room, with its anatomical posters, with purpose born of the fact that she believes that all student problems can be cured with (a) rest on one of her cots,

(b) two aspirin, or (c) Neosporin and a bandage. Luckily, there's nothing else I need.

"Hey," I say. "I'm feeling better. I'm going to go back to my room now if that's okay?"

Nurse Kozel's in the middle of giving pills to Willow Davis. "Cassel, why don't you sit down and let me check your temperature. It was pretty high before."

"Okay," I say, slouching in a chair.

Willow swallows her medicine with a sip from a paper cup as Nurse Kozel crosses to the other side for the thermometer.

"You might as well lie down in the back until the pills start working," Kozel calls. "I'll come in a little while to check on you."

"I'm so hungover," Willow says to me under her breath.

I smile the conspiratorial smile of people who have used the nurse's office to sleep off the night before.

She heads for the back, and I get a thermometer stuck under my tongue. While I wait, I consider for the first time what happened—and didn't happen—with Lila.

It's just a matter of time.

Even in the light of day, the thought feels no less true.

Temptation is tempting. I like my shiny new Mercedes-Benz; I like getting fancy dinners with the head of a crime family; I like the Feds off my back and my mom safe. I like having Lila kiss me as if we could have some kind of future. I like it when she says my name as though I'm the only other person in the world.

I like it so much that I'll probably do anything to get it.

Ignore that Lila doesn't really love me. Kill my own brother. Become a hired assassin. Anything.

I thought that I could never betray my family, never work someone I loved, never kill anyone, never be like Philip, but I get more like him every day. Life's full of opportunities to make crappy decisions that feel good. And after the first one, the rest get a whole lot easier.

CHAPTER FOURTEEN

THE GREAT THING ABOUT a sick day is that it's not hard to walk out of school. I do. I could drive, but I worry they'd notice my car missing. I can't afford to take any more chances.

Besides, right now I'm not sure I should be trusted with nice things.

I have woken with a new resolution. No more stupid risks. No more trying to get caught. No more leaving things up to fate. No more waiting for the other shoe to drop. I walk until I get far enough off campus to be safe. Then I call a cab with my cell phone.

Barron doesn't want to go to the Feds. If he tells them everything, then he gets nothing from the Brennans. But if he really believes I'm not going to cave to his demands, he might turn me in, and I need to tidy things up before he gets the chance. Especially because I know something that he can't—there isn't evidence just of what I've done at the old house. There's evidence of Mom's crime too.

First things first, I have to get rid of that.

I'm her son. It's my job to keep her safe.

I wait on the tree-lined sidewalk in front of a bunch of nice-looking houses. Ones with backyards and swings. A white-haired lady smiles at me when she ducks out to get her mail from a polished brass box.

I smile back automatically. I bet those fat pearls she's got in her ears are real. If I asked politely, she'd probably let me wait on her porch. Maybe even make me a sandwich.

My stomach grumbles. I ignore it. After another moment she goes back inside, the screen door slamming on my chances for lunch.

The trees shake with a sudden gust of wind, and a few still-green maple leaves fall around me. I toe one with my booted foot. It doesn't look it, but it's already dead.

The cab pulls up, the driver frowning when he sees me. I slide into the back and give him directions to the garbage house. Happily, he doesn't ask any questions about picking up a kid three blocks away from a high school. Probably he's seen a lot worse.

He drops me off, and I hand him the cash from a few recent wagers. I'm low on funds and I'm spending money that I don't really have. An unexpected dark horse bet coming in could clean me out.

I head up the hill toward the old place. It looks ominous, even in the day. Its shingles are gray with neglect, and one of the windows in the upper story—the one to Mom's old room—is broken with a bag taped over it.

Barron had to know I might come here. He had to think I might hide the body, now that he warned me that he knows where it is. But whatever surprises he left for me must be in the basement, because the kitchen looks identical to the way I left it on Sunday. My half cup of coffee is still sitting in the sink, the liquid inside looking ominously close to mold.

The coat is right where I left it too, in the back of the closet, gun still rolled inside. I kneel down and pull the bundle out just to be sure.

I picture my mother, pressing the barrel against Philip's chest. He couldn't have believed she'd shoot—he was her firstborn. Maybe he laughed. Or maybe he knew her better than I did. Maybe he saw in her expression that no amount of love was worth her freedom.

But the more I try to imagine it, the more I see myself in his place, feel the cold barrel of the gun, see my mother's smeary lipsticked mouth pull into a grimace. A shudder runs down my back.

I force myself up, grab a knife from the block and a plastic bag from under the sink. I need to stop *thinking*. I start chopping the buttons off the coat instead. I'm going to burn the cloth, so I want to make sure any hooks or solid parts go into the plastic bag with the gun. After that I plan on weighting it with bricks and sinking it in the Round Valley Reservoir up near Clinton. Grandad once told me that half of New Jersey's criminals have dropped something down there—it's the deepest lake in the state.

I turn the pockets inside out, checking for coins.

Red leather gloves tumble onto the linoleum floor. And something else, something solid.

A familiar amulet, cracked in half. At the sight of it I know who killed Philip. Everything snaps into place. The plan changes.

Oh, man, I am an *idiot*.

I call her from a pay phone, just like Mom taught me.

"You should have told me," I say, but I understand why she didn't.

On the cab ride back to school, I get a text from Audrey.

I remember how there was a time when that would have thrilled me. Now I open my phone with a sigh.

mutually assured destruction

meet me @ the library tomorrow @ lunch

I have been too busy worrying about my immediate problems to really consider who to tell—or even *whether* to tell anyone—that Audrey threw a rock through Lila's window, but Audrey raises an interesting point. If I report Audrey, then Audrey reports seeing me in Lila's room. I'm not sure which crime they'll think is worse, but I don't want to get tossed out of Wallingford in our senior year, even if I get tossed out with someone else.

And I do know which one of us Northcutt thinks is more trustworthy.

I text her back: *i'll be there*

I'm exhausted. Too tired to do anything more than drag myself back to the dorm and eat the rest of Sam's Pop-Tarts. I fall asleep on top of my blankets, still in my clothes. For the second time that day, I don't even remember to take my boots off.

Wednesday afternoon, Audrey is waiting for me on the library steps, red hair tossed by the wind. She's sitting with her hands in bright kelly green gloves, clasped in the lap of her Wallingford pleated skirt.

Seeing her makes me think ugly thoughts. Zacharov's story about Jenny. The words scrawled on the paper. Shards of glass shining at Lila's feet.

"How could you?" Audrey spits when I get close, like she's the one with a reason to be angry.

I'm taken aback. "What? You *threw a rock—*"

"So what? Lila took everything from me. Everything." Her neck has gone red and blotchy, like it always does when she's upset. "And then you're there, in her room, in the middle of the night like you don't care if you get caught. How could you do that after what she—what she—"

Tears stream down her cheeks.

"What?" I ask. "What did she do?"

She just shakes her head, incoherent with weeping.

I sigh and sit beside her on the steps. After a moment

I put my arm around her shoulders, drawing her shaking body against me. She tucks her head into my neck, and I inhale the familiar floral scent of her shampoo. I know that she'd probably hate me if she knew what I was really like or what I could really do, but she was my girlfriend once. I can't help caring.

"Hey," I say softly, meaninglessly. "It's okay. Whatever it is."

"No, it's not," Audrey says. "I hate her. I hate her! I wish the rock smashed her face in."

"You don't mean that," I say.

"She got Greg suspended, and then his parents wouldn't let him come home." She gives a wet gasp. "They saw those stupid pictures your friends took. He had to beg for his mother to—to even listen through the door." She's crying so hard that her breaths are more like big hiccupping gulps of air. She fights to get words out between sobs. "So they finally took him to get tested. And when they found out he wasn't a worker, they decided to enroll him at Southwick Academy."

Audrey stops trying to talk at that point. It's as though she's possessed by grief, as if something other than herself has hold of her body.

Southwick Academy is famously anti-worker. It's in Florida, close to the Georgia border, and requires all student applications to come with a copy of their hyperbathygammic test. A test with clear negative results. If the student is accepted, then he or she is retested by the on-staff physician.

Sending Greg to Southwick means that his reputation, and presumably the reputation of his parents, is saved. I'd feel bad, if I didn't think he'd enjoy being at a school where everyone feels the way he does about workers.

"We'll all be out of high school in less than a year," I say. "You'll see him again."

After a few moments Audrey pulls away and looks up at me with red-rimmed eyes. Then she shakes her head. "He told me about Lila before he left. How he cheated on me. That she worked him to make him want—"

"That's not true," I say.

She takes a long, shuddering breath. Then she wipes her cheeks with her kelly green gloves. "That just makes it worse. That you want her and he wants her and no one was forced and she's not even nice."

"Greg's not nice," I say.

"He was," she says. "To me. When we were alone. But I guess it didn't mean anything. Lila made it not mean anything."

I get up. "No, she didn't. Look, I get why you're pissed. I even get why you smashed her window, but this has to stop. No more rocks. No more slurs."

"She cheated on you, too," Audrey says.

I just shake my head.

"Fine," she says, standing and dusting off her skirt. "If you don't tell anyone what I did, I won't say that you were in her room."

"And you'll leave Lila alone?"

"I'll keep your secret. This time. I'm not promising anything else." Audrey stalks down the steps and across the quad without looking back once.

My shirt is still wet with her tears.

Classes go about as well as usual. Lately, I can't seem to get it together. Emma Bovary and her basket of apricots blur together with information asymmetries and incomplete markets. I close my eyes in one class and when I open them, I'm in another.

I walk into the cafeteria for dinner and pile food onto my plate. Tonight's main course is chicken enchiladas with salsa verde. My stomach is so empty that even the smell of the food makes it churn. I'm early, so I have a few minutes at the table alone. I use them to shovel food into my face.

Eventually, Sam sits down across from me. He grins. "You look slightly less close to death."

I snort, but most of my attention is on watching Lila walk in and pick up a tray of food. Looking at her brings a hot flush of memory to my skin. I'm ashamed of myself and I want to touch her again, all at once.

She and Daneca come to the table and take seats. Daneca looks over toward Sam, but he's staring at his plate.

"Hey," I say as neutrally as I can.

Lila points her fork at me. "I heard a rumor about you."

"Oh?" I can't tell if she's teasing or not, but she's not smiling.

"I heard that you were taking bets about me." Lila rubs her gloved hand across her forehead, pushing back her bangs. She seems tired. I'm guessing she didn't get any sleep last night. "Me and Greg. Me being crazy. Me being in a prison in Moscow."

I glance quickly at Sam, who is wearing an expression of almost comical surprise. He's been helping me keep the books for bets, since his stint running the business, so he knows what's come in and what's gone out. He knows we're busted.

"Not because I wanted to," I say. "If I didn't, I was afraid people would make too much of it. I mean, I take bets on *everything*."

"Like who's a worker?" she asks. "You're making money off those bets too, aren't you?"

Daneca narrows her eyes at me. "Cassel, is that true?"

"You don't understand," I say, turning to her. "If I suddenly pick and choose what bets to take, then it would seem like I knew something—like I was protecting someone. I sit with you three; everyone would assume I was protecting one of you. Plus people would stop telling me what's going on—what rumors are being spread. And I couldn't spread any rumors of my own. I wouldn't be any help."

"Yeah, and you'd have to take a stand, too," Lila says. "People might even think *you're* a worker. I know how much you would hate that."

"Lila—," I say. "I swear to you, there's a stupid rumor about every new kid that comes to Wallingford. No one believes them. If I didn't take those bets, I would basically confirm that you and Greg—" I stumble over the words and start over, not wanting to piss her off any worse than

I already have. "It would make everyone think the rumor was true."

"I don't care," Lila says. "You're the one that's making me into a joke."

"I'm sorry—", I start, but she cuts me off.

"Don't con me." She reaches into her pocket and slaps five twenty-dollar bills down on the table. The glasses rattle, liquid sloshing. "A hundred bucks says that Lila Zacharov and Greg Harmsford did it. What are my odds?"

She doesn't know that Greg's never coming back to Wallingford. She doesn't know that Audrey hates her guts. I look automatically toward his old table, hoping that Audrey can't overhear any of this.

"Good," I force out. "Your odds are good."

"At least I'll make a profit," she says. Then she gets up and stalks out of the dining hall.

I rest my forehead against the table and fold my arms on top of my head. I really can't win today.

"You gave back that money," Sam says. "Why didn't you tell her?"

"Not all of it," I say. "I didn't want her to know that they were betting on her, so I just took whatever envelopes people handed me when Lila was around. And I *did* take bets on who was a worker. I thought I was doing the right thing. Maybe she's right. Maybe I was just covering my ass."

"I took those bets about who was a worker too," says Sam. "You were right. It was the only thing we could do to have any leverage." He sounds more sure than I feel.

"Cassel?" Daneca says. "Wait a second."

"What?" Her voice sounds so odd—tentative—that I look up.

"She shouldn't have been able to do that," Daneca says. "Lila just *told you off.*"

"You can love someone and still argue with—," I start to say, and stop myself. Because that's the difference between real love and cursed love. When you really love someone, you can still see them for who they are. But the curse makes love sickly and simple.

I look in amazement toward the doors Lila walked through. "Do you think she could be—better? Not cursed?"

The hope that blooms inside of me is terrifying.

Maybe. Maybe she could come out of this and not hate me. Maybe she could even forgive me. Maybe.

I cross the quad, heading back to my dorm room, Sam next to me. I'm smiling, despite knowing better. Despite knowing my own luck. I'm dreaming dreams where I'm clever enough to weasel my way out of all my problems. Sucker dreams. The kind of dreams con artists love to exploit.

"So," Sam says slowly, his voice low. "It's always like that? When you transform?"

Yesterday morning seems so long ago. I remember Sam's look of terror as he stared down at me, sprawled on the floor. I can still feel the blowback creeping up my spine. I want to deny any of it happened; in those moments I felt more naked than I ever have in my life. So naked I was turned inside out.

"Yeah," I say, watching moths circling the dim lights

along the path. The moon overhead is just a sliver. "Pretty much. That was worse than usual because I worked myself twice in one night."

"Where were you?" Sam asks. "What *happened*?"

I hesitate.

"Cassel," Sam says. "Just tell me if it's bad."

"I was in Lila's room."

"Did you break her window?" he asks. I should have realized the story was all over campus. Everyone knows about the rock, about the threat.

"No," I say. "The person who did that couldn't have known I was there."

He looks over sharply, a line appearing over the bridge of his nose, between his eyebrows, as he frowns. "So you know who it was? Who broke the window?"

I nod my head, but I don't volunteer Audrey's name. Telling Sam isn't like telling Northcutt, but I still feel bound to keep the secret.

"When it rains, it pours," Sam says.

As we head into the building, my phone buzzes in my pocket. I open it against my chin and put it to my ear. "Yeah?"

"Cassel?" Lila says softly.

"Hey," I say. Sam turns and gives me a knowing look, then keeps walking, leaving me to sit on the steps to the second floor.

"I'm sorry I yelled at you," she says.

My heart sinks. "You are?"

"I am. I get why you took those bets. I'm not sure I like it, but I get it. I'm not mad."

"Oh," I say.

"I guess I just freaked out," she says. "After last night. I don't want this to be just pretend." She's speaking so quietly now that I can barely make out the words.

"It's not," I say. The words feel ripped out of my chest. "It never was."

"Oh." She's quiet for a long moment. Then, when she does speak, I can hear the smile in her voice. "I still expect my winnings, Cassel. You can't sweet-talk me out of those."

"Ruthless as usual," I say, grinning, looking down at the stair. Someone dropped their gum, someone else stepped on it. Now it's a streak of grimy pink.

I'm such a fool.

"I love you," I say, because I might as well now, when it no longer matters what I do. I've made up my mind. Before she can reply, I close my phone, hanging up on her.

Then I rest my head on the cold iron railing. Maybe the curse would fade eventually, but I will never be sure it's completely gone. So long as she's fond of me, I will never know whether it's forced. Curses are subtle. Sure, emotion work is supposed to wear off, but how can anyone *know*? I have to be certain, and I never will be.

There never were any good choices.

I call Agent Jones. I've lost his card, so I just call the main number for the agency in Trenton. After a couple of transfers, I get an answering machine. I tell him that I need more time, just a couple more days, just until Monday, and then I'll give him his murderer.

* * *

Once you decide you have to do something, it's almost a relief. Waiting is harder than doing, even when you hate what you're about to do.

The longer I look for alternatives, the darker those alternatives get.

I have to accept what is.

I am a bad person.

I've done bad things.

And I'm going to keep on doing them until somebody stops me. And who's going to do that? Lila can't. Zacharov won't. There's only one person who can, and he's shown himself to be pretty unreliable.

Sam's up in our room, paging through *Othello* when I come in. His iPod is plugged into our speakers, and the sound of Deathwërk rattles the windows.

"You okay?" he shouts over the guttural vocals.

"Sam," I say, "remember how at the beginning of the semester you said you went to that special effects warehouse and cleaned it out? How you were ready for anything."

"Yeah ...," he says, suspicious.

"I want to frame someone for my brother's murder."

"Who?" he asks, turning down the sound. He must be used to me saying crazy things, because he's totally serious. "Also, why?"

I take a deep breath.

Framing someone requires several things.

First you have to find a person who makes a believable villain. It helps if she's already done something bad; it helps even more if some part of what you're setting her up for is true.

And since she's done something bad, you don't have to feel so terrible about picking her to take the fall.

But the final thing you need is for your story to make sense. Lies work when they're simple. They usually work a lot better than the truth does. The truth is messy. It's raw and uncomfortable. You can't blame people for preferring lies.

You especially can't blame people when that preference benefits you.

"Bethenny Thomas," I say.

Sam frowns at me. "Wait, what? Who's that?"

"Dead mobster's girlfriend. Two big poodles. Runner." I think of Janssen in the freezer. I hope he'd approve of my choice. "She put out a hit on her boyfriend, so it's not like she hasn't murdered *someone*."

"And you know that how?" Sam asks.

I'm trying really hard to be honest, but telling the whole thing to Sam seems beyond me. Still, the fragments sound ridiculous on their own. "She said so. In the park."

He rolls his eyes. "Because the two of you were so friendly."

"I guess she mistook me for someone else." I sound so much like Philip that it scares me. I can hear the menace in my tone.

"Who?" Sam asks, not flinching.

I force my voice back to normal. "Uh, the person who killed him."

"*Cassel*." He groans, shaking his head. "No, don't worry, I'm not going to ask why she would think that. I don't want to know. Just tell me your plan."

I sit down on my bed, relieved. I'm not sure I can endure another of my confessions, despite the fact that I have so much yet to confess.

I used to stake out joints for robberies with my dad sometimes, back when I was a kid. See what people's patterns were. When they left for work. When they returned. If they ate at the same place each night. If they went to bed at the same time. The more tight a schedule, the more tidy a robbery.

What I remember most, though, are the long stretches of sitting in the car with the radio on. The air would get stuffy, but I wasn't allowed to roll down the windows far enough to get a good breeze. The soda would get stale, and eventually I'd have to piss into a bottle because I wasn't supposed to get out of the car. There were only two good things about stakeouts. The first thing was that Dad let me pick out anything at the gas station mart that I wanted snack-wise. The second was that Dad taught me how to play cards. Poker. Three-card monte. Slap. Crazy eights.

Sam's pretty good at games. We spend Friday night watching Bethenny's apartment building and gambling for cheese curls. We learn that the doorman takes a couple of smoking breaks when no one's around. He's a beefy dude who tells off a homeless guy harassing residents for change out front. Bethenny takes her dogs for a run in the evening and walks them twice more before she goes out for the night. At dawn the doormen change shifts. The guy who comes in is skinny. He eats two doughnuts and reads the newspaper before residents start coming downstairs. It's late Saturday morning by then, and Bethenny's still not back, so we bag it and go home.

I drop Sam off at his place around eleven and crash for a few hours at the garbage house. I wake up when the cordless phone rings next to my head. I'd forgotten that I brought it into the room days ago. It's tangled in the sheets.

"Yeah?" I grunt.

"May I speak with Cassel Sharpe?" my mother asks in her chirpiest voice.

"Mom, it's me."

"Oh, sweetheart, your voice sounded so funny." She seems happier than I've heard her in a long time. I shove myself into a sitting position.

"I was sleeping. Is everything okay?" My automatic fear is that she's in trouble. That the Feds have gotten tired of waiting and have picked her up. "Where are you?"

"Everything's perfect. I missed you, baby." She laughs. "I've just been swept up in so many new things. I met so many nice people."

"Oh." I cradle the phone against my shoulder. I should probably feel bad that I suspected her of murder. Instead I feel guilty for not feeling guilty. "Have you seen Barron recently?" I ask. I hope not. I hope she has no idea he's blackmailing me.

I hear the familiar hiss of a cigarette being lit. She inhales. "Not in a week or two. He said he had a big job coming up. But I want to talk about *you*. Come see me and meet the governor. There's a brunch on Sunday that I think you'd just love. You should see the rocks some of the women wear, plus the silverware's *reeeal*." She draws the last part out long, like she's tempting a dog to a bone.

"Governor Patton? No, thanks. I'd rather eat glass than eat with him." I carry the phone downstairs and pour out the old coffee in the pot. I dump in new water and fresh grounds. The clock says its three in the afternoon. I have to get moving.

"Oh, don't be like that," says Mom.

"How can you sit there while he goes on and on about proposition two? Okay, fine. He's a really tempting mark. I'd love to see him get conned, but it's not worth it. Mom, things could get really bad. One mistake and—"

"Your mother doesn't make mistakes." I hear her blow out the smoke. "Baby, I know what I'm doing."

The coffee is dripping, steam rising from the pot. I sit down at the kitchen table. I try not to think about her the way she was when I was a kid, sitting right where I am now, laughing at something Philip said or ruffling my hair. I can almost see my dad, sitting at the table, showing Barron how to flip a quarter over his knuckles while she makes breakfast. I can smell my dad's cigarillos and the blackening bacon. The back of my eyes hurt.

"I don't know what *I'm* doing anymore," I say. You might think I'm crazy, telling her that. But she's still my mother.

"What's wrong, sweetheart?" The concern in her voice is real enough to break my heart.

I can't tell her. I really can't. Not about Barron or the Feds or how I thought she was a murderer. Certainly not about Lila. "School," I say, resting my head in my hands. "I guess I'm getting a little overwhelmed."

"Baby," she says in a harsh whisper, "in this world, lots of people will try to grind you down. They need you to be small so they can be big. You let them think whatever they want, but you make sure you get yours. *You get yours.*"

I hear a man's voice in the background. I wonder if she's talking about me at all. "Is someone there?"

"Yes," she says sweetly. "I hope you'll think about coming on Sunday. How about I give you the address and you can think about it?"

I pretend to copy down the location of Patton's stupid brunch. Really I'm just pouring myself a cup of coffee.

CHAPTER FIFTEEN

WAKING UP IN THE MIDDLE of the day always leaves you with a slightly dazed feeling, as though you've stepped out of time. The light outside the windows is wrong. My body feels heavy as I force it up and into clothing.

I stop at the store for more coffee and a prop, then head over to Daneca's house. I walk across the green lawn, up to the freshly painted door between two manicured bushes. Everything is as pretty as a picture.

When I ring the bell, Chris answers. "What?" he says. He's got on a pair of shorts and flip flops with an oversize shirt. It makes him look even younger than he is. There's a smudge of something blue in his hair.

"Can I come in?"

He pushes the door wide. "I don't care."

I sigh and walk past him. The scent of lemon polish fills the hallway, and there's a girl in the living room running a vacuum. For some reason it never occurred to me that Daneca grew up with maids, but of course she did.

"Is Mrs. Wasserman here?" I ask the girl.

She takes headphones out of her ears and smiles at me. "What was that?"

"Sorry," I say. "I was just wondering if you know where Mrs. Wasserman is."

The girl points. "In her office, I think."

I walk through the house, past the artwork and the antique silver. I knock on the frame of a glass-paneled door. Mrs. Wasserman opens it, hair pulled up into a makeshift bun with a pencil shoved through her mass of curls. "Cassel?" she says. She's got on paint-stained sweatpants and is holding a mug of tea.

I hold out the violets I bought at the garden supply store. I don't know much about flowers, but I liked how velvety they looked. "I wanted to say thanks for the other day. For the advice."

Gifts are very useful to con men. Gifts create a feeling of debt, an itchy anxiety that the recipient is eager to be rid of by repaying. So eager, in fact, that people will often overpay just to be relieved of it. A single spontaneously given cup of coffee can make a person feel obligated to sit through a lecture on a religion they don't care about. The gift of a tiny, wilted flower can make the recipient give to a charity they dislike. Gifts place such a heavy burden that even throwing away the gift doesn't remove the debt. Even if you hate coffee, even if you didn't want that flower, once you take it, you want to give something back. Most of all, you want to dismiss that obligation.

"Oh, thank you," Daneca's mother says. She looks surprised, but pleased. "It was no trouble at all, Cassel. I'm always here if you want to talk."

"You mean that?" I ask, which is maybe laying it on really thick, but I need to push her a little. This is her chance to repay me. It doesn't hurt that I know she's a sucker for hard-luck cases.

"Of course," she says. "Anything you need, Cassel."

Bingo.

I like to think it's the gratitude that makes her overgenerous, but I guess I'll never know. That's the problem with not trusting people—you never find out if they'd have helped you on their own.

Daneca is on her computer when I come into her room. She looks up at me in surprise.

"Hey," I say. "Your little brother let me in." I'm already not being entirely honest by failing to mention I talked with her mother, but I'm determined to do nothing more dishonest than that. I hate myself enough already without conning one of my only friends.

"Chris is not my brother," Daneca says automatically. "I don't even think it's legal for him to live here." Her room looks exactly like I would have expected. Her bedspread is batik, studded with silver discs. Fringed scarves drape over the tops of the linen curtains. The walls are covered in posters of folk singers, in poems, and with a big worker rights flag. On her bookshelf, next to copies of Ginsberg and Kerouac and *The Activist's Handbook,* is a line of horses. White and brown, speckled and black, they're arranged like a chorus line.

I lean against the doorjamb. "Okay. Some kid who's always hanging around at this address let me in. He was pretty rude about it too."

She half-smiles. I can see past her to the paper she's writing, the letters like black ants on the screen. "Why are you here, Cassel?"

I sit down on her bed and take a deep breath. If I can do this, then I can do everything else.

"I need you to work Lila," I say. The words come easily to my lips, but my chest hurts as I speak them aloud. "I need you to make her not love me anymore."

"Get out," Daneca says.

I shake my head. "I need you to do it. Please. Please just listen." I'm afraid my voice is going to break. I am afraid she is going to hear how much this hurts.

"Cassel, I don't *care* what reason you have. There is *no* reason good enough to take away someone's free will."

"It's already been taken! Remember when I said that I tried to stay away from Lila?" I say. "I've stopped trying. How's that for a good reason?"

She doesn't trust me. Surely she can understand if I don't trust myself either.

The look Daneca gives me is full of disgust. "There's

nothing I can do anyway. You know that. I *can't* take the curse off her."

"Work her so that she feels nothing for me," I say. My vision blurs. I wipe the dampness away from my eyes angrily. "Let her just feel nothing. Please."

She looks at me in an odd, stunned way. When she speaks, her voice is soft. "I thought the curse was fading. It might already be gone."

I shake my head. "She still likes me."

"Maybe she likes you, Cassel," Daneca says carefully. "Without the curse."

"No."

She waits for a long moment. "What about you? How are you going to feel when she—"

"It doesn't matter about me," I say. "The only way that Lila could be sure—that anyone could be sure—the curse was over is if she didn't love me."

"But—," Daneca begins.

If I can just get through this, then nothing else can hurt me. I will be capable of anything. "It has to be this way. Otherwise I'll create reasons to believe that she wants me, because I'd like that to be true. I can't be trusted."

"I know that you're really upset—," Daneca says.

"*I can't be trusted.* Do you understand me?"

She nods, once. "Okay. Okay, I'll do it."

I exhale all at once, a dizzy rush of breath.

"But this is a onetime thing. I will never do this again. I will never do anything like this again. Do you understand me?"

"Yes," I say.

"And I'm not even sure how to do it, so there are no guarantees. Plus the blowback is going to make me act all weird and emotional, so you are responsible for baby-sitting me until I am stable. Okay?"

"Yes," I say again.

"She won't care about you." Daneca tilts her head to one side, like she's seeing me for the first time. "You'll just be some guy she once knew. Everything she feels about you—everything she felt about you—it will all be gone."

I close my eyes and nod my head.

The first thing I do when I get back home is go down into the cellar. I open the cooler. Janssen is right where I left him—milk pale, with sunken eyelids and frosty hair. He looks like a demented marble sculpture—portrait of a killer, killed. All the blood must have made its sluggish way to his back before it froze. I bet if I turned him over, he'd be purple.

I strip off my right-hand glove and place my hand on his chest, pushing aside the stiffened fabric of his undershirt, letting my fingers rest against his icy skin.

I turn his heart to glass.

The change takes only a moment, but recovering from it takes longer. Once the blowback wears off, I rub my head where I smacked it against the floor. Everything aches, but I'm getting used to that.

Then I go upstairs, take the gun out of the plastic bag, close my eyes, and shoot two bullets into the ceiling of the parlor. Dust rains down on me, covering the room in a powdery cloud. A single chunk of plaster nearly brains me.

Cons aren't glamorous. They're hauling out the ancient vacuum from the closet, changing the bag, and making sure you get up most of the dust. They're sweeping in the basement to hide that you were recently rolling around after a transformation. They're fieldstripping the gun according to instructions on the Internet and carefully buffing off any fingerprints with a lightly oiled cloth, then wrapping the whole thing in paper towels. They're driving a mile to an abandoned stretch of road and soaking the murderess's coat and gloves with enough lighter fluid that they burn to ash. They're waiting to make *sure* they burn to ash and then scattering that ash. They're smashing any remaining buttons from the coat with a hammer, then tossing them along with the vacuum bag and any hooks or metal parts in different Dumpsters far from where you burned the clothes. Cons are all in the details.

By the time I'm done, it's late enough to call Sam and get the next part of the plan under way.

My mother's a purist when it comes to scamming people. She's got her thing, and it's pretty effective. Glamorous clothes, a touch of her hand, and most people are willing to do what she wants. But I'd never really thought about costumes or props until I met Sam. I have my computer open to Cyprus View's website. They have examples of the layout of their apartments for prospective renters. Very helpful.

Sam's expectantly holding up a fake wound on a thin rubbery piece of silicone. "Look, you said yourself that guard wanted to be a hero," Sam is telling me.

It might be true that I said that. I don't remember. I said a lot of things on the stakeout, mostly boring observations about the place or completely exaggerated claims about how I was going to beat Sam at cards. "But then we need another person," I say. "That's a three-person job."

"Ask Lila," he says.

"She's all the way in the city," I say, but it's a halfhearted objection. The thought of seeing her one last time before I lose her is poisonously compelling.

"Daneca and I are still . . . I don't know. Besides, she's not the best actress."

"She did fine at Zacharov's fund-raiser," I say, thinking of the way she smiled in my brother's face moments after she slipped me a fake blood packet.

"I had to give her a pep talk on the way," he says. "How about if I'm the one who calls Lila?"

Mutely I hand him my phone. I want her to come. If I resist this, I don't think I will have any resistance left.

We pick Lila up at the train station in Sam's hearse. He works on her in the back while I fiddle with the radio nervously in the front seat and eat a slice of pizza.

"Almost done?" I call, looking at the clock on the dashboard.

"Don't rush the artist," Lila says. Her voice goes through me like a knife, leaving a wound so clean I know it won't even hurt until the knife's pulled out.

"Yeah," I say. "Sorry, Sam."

Finally she climbs into the front seat. She's got a bruise painted on her cheek. It looks real, partially hidden by curls of a long blond wig.

I reach out automatically to touch her face, and then jerk my hand back.

"Don't mess me up," she says with a lopsided grin.

"We ready to go?" I call into the back.

"One second," Sam says. "I just have to get this scrape on my mouth, and it's not sticking."

Lila leans toward me, nervous and determined. "That thing you said before you hung up the phone," she half-whispers. "Did you mean it?"

I nod.

"But I thought it was all fake—" She stops and bites her lip, like she can't quite bring herself to ask the rest of the question, for fear of my answer.

"I faked faking," I say softly. "I lied about lying. I couldn't think of another way to make you believe we couldn't be together."

She frowns. "Wait. Then why tell me now?"

Crap. "Because I am about to be devoured by poodles," I quip. "Remember me always, my love."

Mercifully Sam picks that moment to lean into the front. "Okay, all done," he says.

"Here's what you asked me for," Lila says, pulling a green glass bottle out of her backpack. It's wrapped in a T-shirt. "Is this what you're going to plant in her house?"

I take it, careful not to touch the neck of the bottle. It's bizarre to think that this small thing is what Lila took from

Philip's house. It's even more bizarre to know it used to be a living person. "Nope," I say. "My plan is even more secret than that."

She rolls her eyes.

I pull my pizza delivery boy cap low and start the engine.

The plan is pretty simple. First we wait until Bethenny Thomas leaves the building without her dogs. This is the twitchiest part, because she might decide to spend her Saturday night at home, curled up in front of the television.

At ten, she gets into a cab, and we're on.

I go into the building with three boxes of pizza. I'm wearing the cap—which was pretty easy to lift from the busy shop where we ordered the pizzas—and regular clothes. Keep my head down in front of the security cameras. I say I have a delivery for the Goldblatts. We picked them because, of all the people we were able to identify as living in the building—thanks to the white pages online—they were the first not to answer when we called.

The big guy behind the desk looks up at me and grunts. He lifts the phone, pressing a button. I try very hard to act like I am bored, instead of nearly jumping out of my skin with adrenaline.

Sam comes roaring out of the darkness, hitting the glass wall of the lobby like he barely notices it. He starts screaming, pointing at the bushes. "Stay away from me. Stay the hell away!"

The guard stands up, still holding the phone but no longer paying any attention to it.

"What the hell?" I say.

Lila runs up the path toward Sam. She slaps him so hard that all the way inside the lobby, I can hear the crack of leather glove against skin. I sincerely hope that he taught her some kind of stage trick, because otherwise that had to hurt.

"I saw you looking at her," Lila shrieks. "I'm going to scratch out your eyes!"

If he was a different person, the front desk guy might just call the cops. But when I saw him toss that homeless guy off the property Friday night, I realized that he's not the type to call anyone if he thinks he can handle it.

Now I just have to hope I read him right.

When he puts down the receiver, I let out a breath I shouldn't have been holding. That's no way to look casual.

"Wait a sec," he says to me. "I got to get these kids out of here."

"Man," I groan, trying to sound as exasperated as possible. "I need to deliver these pizzas. There's a fifteen-minute guarantee."

He barely even looks at me as he heads for the door. "Whatever. Go on up."

As I step into the elevator, I hear Lila yell about how the front desk guy better mind his own business. I grin as I hit the button.

The door to Bethenny's apartment is identical to all the others. White doors in a white hallway. But when I slip my pick into the keyhole, I hear the dogs start barking.

The lock is easy, but there's a dead bolt on top that takes longer. I can smell someone frying fish across the hallway and hear someone else playing classical music with the sound turned way up. No one comes out into the hallway. If they had, I would have asked them for a number that's on a different floor and headed for the elevators. Lucky for me, I make it inside Bethenny's apartment without a lot of detours.

The minute I'm inside, the dogs run toward me. I close the front door and sprint for the bedroom, slamming the door in their snouts. They scratch against the wood, whining, and all I can hope is that they aren't scarring the door too deeply. I silently thank the building again for putting the layout of their apartments online.

Inside I dump the boxes onto the wood floor and open them up. The first has the remains of an actual pizza in it. The few slices we didn't eat are covered in pepperoni and sausage—in a pinch that might effectively distract the dogs.

The second contains the gun, wrapped in paper towels; baggies to put over my feet; bleach-soaked wipes; and disposable gloves.

The third pizza box has my getting-out-of-the-building outfit. A suit jacket and pants, glasses, and a soft leather briefcase. I change clothes quickly and then gear up.

As I tie the plastic over my feet, I glance around the room. The walls are a sea blue, hung with framed photographs of Bethenny in various tropical settings. She smiles at me, cocktail in hand, from a hundred pictures, reflected a thousandfold in the mirrors on her closet doors. I can't help seeing myself too, dirty hair hanging in my face. I look like I haven't slept in weeks.

The dogs stop whining and start barking. Over and over, a chorus of sound.

Dresses are strewn around the opening of her closet in frothy, glittering profusion, and shoes are scattered all over the room. On top of a white dresser, a tangle of gold chains droops into a drawer overstuffed with satiny bras.

I touch nothing except for the mattress. Lifting up one end, I get ready to shove my gun on top of the box spring.

Another gun's already there.

I stare at the large silver revolver. It makes the pistol in my hand look dainty.

I am so thrown that I momentarily have no idea what to do. *She already has a gun under her mattress.*

I start to laugh, the hysteria bubbling up out of my throat. All of a sudden it overwhelms me. I can't help it. I am crouched down in front of the bed, sucking in deep breaths, tears starting to run out of my eyes, I am laughing so hard. I'm laughing so hard that I am making no sound at all.

It feels as helpless as blowback, as helpless as grief.

Finally I get it together enough to put the Smith & Wesson between the mattress and box spring near the foot of the bed. I figure no one grabs for a gun there, and no one lifts up their mattress really high when they're grabbing for a different gun.

Then I break down the pizza boxes, shoving them into the briefcase along with the jeans and jacket I was wearing when I came in. I dump the extra pizza, paper towels, and wipes in too. I change my gloves. Then I run a bleach-soaked wipe over the floor to get rid of any crumbs, grease, or hairs. I toe it along to the door just to be safe.

Outside the room the poodles' barking has reached a fever pitch. I tuck the wipe into my pocket.

I hear one of the dogs thump against the knob, and suddenly, horribly, it turns. One of them must have caught it with a paw. A moment later they rush in, barking furiously. I barely jump up onto the bed in time to avoid getting bitten.

Okay, I know what you're thinking. They're poodles, right? But these things aren't little fuzzy toy poodles. They're *standard* poodles, huge and snapping at me, white teeth bared and a growl rumbling up their throats when I make a move toward the edge of the mattress. I look at the chandelier hanging above me and contemplate trying to swing from it.

"Hey," I hear a voice call. "Beth? How many times do I got to tell you to keep those dogs of yours quiet?"

Oh, *come on*. This cannot be happening.

Of course, it wouldn't be happening if I'd thought to lock the apartment door after I picked the lock. Cons are all in the details. They're about the little things that you either remember or you don't.

"If you don't shut them up, I'm gonna call the police," the guy yells. "This time I mean it—Hey, what the—"

He stands in the doorway, looking at me, astonishment silencing him. In a moment he's going to yell. In a moment he's going to rush into his apartment and dial 911.

"Oh, thank God," I say, trying to give him my most grateful look. I clear my throat. "We got a report—one of the neighbors complained. I had an appointment with—"

"Who the hell are you? What are you doing in Bethenny's apartment?" The neighbor is a guy, balding and probably in his early forties. He's sporting a pretty heavy beard and mustache. His worn T-shirt has the faded logo of a construction company.

"The apartment manager sent me to evaluate the situation with these dogs," I shout over the din of barking. "The door was open, and I thought that perhaps Ms. Thomas was in. She's been avoiding my calls, but I finally got her to agree to a meeting. I didn't expect them to attack."

"Yeah," the guy shouts. "They're high strung. And spoiled all to hell. If you want to get down from there, you better give them a treat or something."

"I don't have a treat." I decide I better move, if I want to be convincing. I jump down from the bed, grab my briefcase, and run for the neighbor. I feel teeth close on my leg.

"Augh," I yell, nearly falling.

"You *stay*," the neighbor shouts at the poodles, which miraculously seems to make them pause long enough for us to slam the bedroom door.

I lean down and pull up the hem of my pants. My left ankle is bleeding sluggishly, soaking my sock. I have only a couple of minutes before my blood spills over the plastic covering my feet and hits the floor.

"This is ridiculous!" I say. "She told me this was the only time that she could meet, even though it was extremely inconvenient for me. And she's not even here—"

The guy looks back toward the door of the apartment. "Do you want a bandage or something?"

I shake my head. "I'm going immediately to a hospital so that the wound can be photographed and entered into evidence. It's extremely important right now that Ms. Thomas not know the building is trying to put together a case against her. Can I rely on your discretion?"

"Are you trying to get Bethenny kicked out?" he asks. I adjust my answer when I see his expression.

"Our first step is going to be suggesting that Ms. Thomas enroll her dogs in intensive obedience classes. If that doesn't work, we may have to ask her to place them elsewhere."

"I'm tired of all their noise," he says. "I'm not going to say anything to her, so long as you're not trying to mess with her lease."

"Thank you." I glance down at the floor, but I don't see any blood. Good. I head for the hallway.

"Aren't you kind of young to work for the management?" the neighbor says, but he seems more amused than suspicious.

I push the glasses up the bridge of my nose the way Sam does. "Everyone says that. Lucky me, I've got a baby face."

I limp through the lobby. The change in the way I walk probably helps my disguise—the desk guy barely looks up.

I walk out the door, going over all the things I could have done wrong. I make my way stiffly down to the street and then over to the supermarket parking lot, where the hearse is idling.

Lila hops out of one side and comes running toward me. The wig's gone, bruise makeup is smeared across her nose, and she's laughing.

"Did you see our performance? I think you missed the part where we convinced Larry that he'd accidentally punched me. He wound up begging us not to press charges." She throws her arms around my neck, and all of a sudden her legs are around my waist and I'm holding her up.

I spin around to hear her giggling shriek, ignoring the pain in my ankle. Sam is getting out of the car, grinning too.

"She's such a con artist," he says. "Better than you, I think."

"Don't sass me," I say. I stop spinning, walking over to Sam's car and setting her down so she's sitting on the hood. "I know she's better."

Lila grins and doesn't unlock her legs from my waist. Instead she pulls me toward her for a kiss that tastes of greasepaint and regret.

Sam rolls his eyes. "How about we hit a diner? Larry paid us fifty bucks to go away."

"Sure," I say. "Absolutely."

I know I will never be this happy again.

CHAPTER SIXTEEN

MONDAY MORNING I pull into the parking lot of the FBI office in my shiny mob-bought Benz. I feel pretty good with the built-in GPS reassuring me that I've arrived at my destination, the leather seats heating my ass, and the surround-sound speakers blasting music from my iPod loudly enough that I can feel it in my bones.

I get out, throw my backpack over my shoulder, hit the button so that the alarm sets, and walk into the building.

Agent Jones and Agent Hunt are waiting for me inside the lobby. I follow them into the elevator.

"Nice car," Agent Hunt says.

"Yeah," I say. "I like it."

Agent Jones snorts. "Let's go upstairs, kid, and see what you've got to say. You better have something this time."

We get to the fourth floor, and they march me into a different room. No mirror this time. I'm sure it's bugged, though. Simple furniture. Table, metal chairs. The kind of room someone could lock you in for a long time.

"I want immunity," I tell them, sitting down at the table. "For any and all past crimes."

"Sure," Agent Jones says. "Look, here's my verbal agreement. You're just a kid, Cassel. We're not interested in busting you for whatever little—"

"No," I say. "I want it in writing."

Agent Hunt clears his throat. "We can do that. Not a problem. Whatever makes you feel the most comfortable. Give us a little while and we'll get something put together for you. Whatever you say to us, we can guarantee that no prosecutor will ever file charges against you. You'll have your deal. We want you on board."

I reach into my backpack and take out three copies of a contract.

"What's this?" Agent Jones says. He doesn't sound happy.

I swallow. My fingers dampen the paper with sweat. I hope they don't notice. "These are my terms. And, unlike the deal you made with my brother, I need this to be authorized by an attorney in the Justice Department."

The two agents exchange a look. "Philip was a special case," Agent Hunt says. "He had some information we needed. If you're proposing a trade, you have to give us something."

"I'm a special case too. Philip told you—or at least he strongly implied—that he knew the identity of a transformation worker, right? So do I. But I'm not a sucker like him, okay? I don't want a bunch of empty promises. I want this contract signed by *an attorney from the Justice Department*. Not by you two jokers. Then I fax it to my lawyer. When I get her okay, I'll tell you everything."

Agent Hunt looks a little stunned. I don't know if they guessed the killer was a transformation worker or not, but I can't take chances. Besides, I have only a few cards to play.

"And if we can't do that?" Agent Jones asks. He doesn't seem so friendly right at the moment.

I shrug my shoulders. "I guess neither of us gets what we want."

"We could pick up your mother. You think we don't know what she's been up to?" Agent Hunt says.

"I don't know what she's been up to," I say, keeping my voice as mild as I can. "But if she's done something wrong, then I guess she's going to have to pay for it."

Agent Jones leans in across the table. "You're a death worker, right, kid? You strongly implied that the last time you were here. Maybe something went wrong before you knew how to control your work? It happens, but you think we aren't going to find out about a missing kid somewhere in your past? Then it's going to be too late for deals."

It's going to be too late for deals much sooner than that, I think.

I wonder what it would be like working for the Brennan family. I wonder what it's like to kill someone when you have to remember it.

"Look," I say, "I have outlined my conditions in the document in front of you. In exchange for immunity I will give you the full name and location of the transformation worker and proof of one or more crimes committed by that person."

"It's Lila Zacharov, isn't it?" Agent Hunt says. "We already know that. Not much of a secret you've got there. She disappears, and her father suddenly gets a new assassin."

I touch the top of the paper, tracing the words, willing myself not to react. Finally I look up at them both. "Every minute you spend talking to me is a minute you're not talking to the Justice Department. And in a couple of minutes I am going to get up and walk out of here and take my offer with me."

"What if we don't let that happen?" Agent Hunt says.

"Unless you plan on bringing in a memory worker to actually go through my brain like it's a deck of cards, you can't force me into a deal—and, let's face it, if you were going to do that, you would have already done it. I guess you could physically keep me here, but you can't keep me interested."

"You better really have the goods," Agent Jones says, standing up. "I can't make any promises, but I'll make the call."

They leave me alone in the room. I figure I'm going to be there a while. I brought my homework.

*   *   *

When they bring me back the first contract, I call my lawyer. Unfortunately, she doesn't know she's my lawyer quite yet.

"Hello?" Mrs. Wasserman says.

"Hi, it's Cassel," I say, letting all the fear I actually feel creep into my voice. The agents have left me alone in the room, but I have no doubt that they are recording everything I say. "Remember when you told me I should ask you if I needed anything?"

I hear the hesitation in her voice. "Did something happen?"

"I really need a lawyer. I need you to be my lawyer." I have no doubt that right now she's wishing she never took those violets from me.

"I don't know," she says, which isn't no. "Why don't you tell me what happened?"

"I can't really explain." Knowing people is important to conning them. I know Mrs. Wasserman wants to help worker kids, but she also likes to know things. It doesn't hurt to add a little incentive. "I mean, I want to tell you, but if you're not my lawyer . . . I shouldn't put you in that position."

"Okay," she says quickly. "Consider me your lawyer. Now explain what's going on. My caller ID has you calling from an unlisted number. Where are you?"

"Trenton. The federal agents here are putting together a contract to try to get me immunity if I give up the identity of a transformation worker—a *murderer*," I say, in case she starts feeling protective of the unnamed worker. "But I need you to make sure the immunity deal is airtight. Plus, they want me to work for them. I need to make sure I can finish out the year at Wallingford before I start. And there's one other thing—"

"Cassel, this is very serious. You never should have tried to work out a deal like this on your own."

"I know," I say, happy to be chastised.

It takes hours and I wind up having to call Daneca's mother four times with changes before she approves the paperwork. Finally I sign. The Justice Department signs. And since I am still a minor, Mrs. Wasserman sends over the page with my mother's forged signature—the one I prepared in advance and left on Mrs. Wasserman's desk on Saturday, flipped over so it looked like just another piece of blank paper. She doesn't, of course, know that it's forged although I imagine she must *guess*.

Then I tell the Feds who the transformation worker is.

That really doesn't go well.

Agent Jones taps his fingers irritably against the press-board top of the table. The bottle rests in front of him, light making the green glass glow softly. "Let's go through your story one more time."

"We've gone through it twice already," I say, pointing to the paper he's making notes on. "I've given you a written statement."

"One more time," says Agent Hunt.

I take a deep breath. "My brother Barron is a memory

worker. My other brother—my dead brother—Philip—was a physical worker. He was employed by a guy named Anton. Anton was the one who ordered the hits. No one else knew what he was doing. We were his private execution squad. I'd transform someone, and then Barron would make me forget about it."

"Because he didn't think you'd go along with this whole deal?" Agent Jones asks.

"I think—I think that Philip thought he was doing right by me. That I was just a kid. That if I didn't know, then it was no big deal." My voice cracks, which I hate.

"Would you have killed those people?" Agent Hunt asks. "Without magical coercion?"

I imagine my brothers coming to me and telling me that I was important, needed. That I would be in on the jokes, be a real part of the family, no longer an outsider. I could have everything I wanted, if I would just do this one thing for them. Maybe Barron was right about me. "I don't know," I say. "I don't even know if I thought they were dead."

"Okay," says Agent Jones. "When did you discover that you were a transformation worker?"

"I figured out there was something wrong with my memory, so I bought a couple of charms and kept them on me. When I changed something by accident, I figured out what I was. Barron couldn't make me forget, because of the charms. Philip told me the rest." It's weird to tell it so blandly, without all the horror or the betrayal. Just the facts.

"So you knew that we were talking about people you killed that first time you were in this office?"

I shake my head. "But I figured it out when I looked at the files. And I was able to remember enough to find that bottle."

"But you don't know where any of the other bodies are? And you don't know whose body that is?"

"True. I really don't know. I wish I did."

"Is there any special significance to the bottle? Why did you pick that?"

I shake my head again. "I have no idea. Probably it just came to mind."

"Why don't you tell us about Philip's murder again. You're saying you did not shoot your brother, correct? Are you sure? Maybe you don't remember it."

"I don't know how to use a gun," I say. "Anyway, I know who shot my brother. It was Henry Janssen. He broke into my mom's house and tried to kill me, too. I wasn't wearing gloves, so I just . . . I reacted."

"And what day was this?" asks Hunt.

"Monday the thirteenth."

"What did you do exactly?" Jones asks.

It's like remembering lines for a play, Sam said.

"Mom had signed me out of Wallingford to go to a doctor's appointment and get lunch. After, I figured I had some time to kill, so I went home."

"Alone?" asks Agent Hunt.

"*Yes.* Like I said twice before, *alone.*" I yawn. "The front door was kicked in."

I think of Sam, with an oversize shoe on his foot, slamming the sole against the door. The wood splintered around the lock. He looked satisfied and also startled, like he'd never been allowed to do anything so violent.

"But you weren't worried?"

I shrug. "I guess I was, a little. But the house is pretty busted up. I assumed that Barron and Mom had a fight. There's not much worth stealing. It made me a little more alert, maybe, but I honestly didn't think there was anyone inside."

"Then what?" Agent Jones crosses his arms over his chest.

"I took off my jacket and my gloves."

"You always take off your gloves at home?" asks Agent Hunt.

"Yeah," I say, looking Hunt in the eye. "Don't you?"

"Okay, go on," says Agent Jones.

"I turned on the television. I was going to watch some TV, eat a sandwich, and then go back to school. I figured I had about an hour to hang."

Agent Hunt scowls. "Why go home at all? None of that sounds very exciting."

"Because if I went back to school, I'd have to do after-school stuff. I'm lazy."

They share another look, not a very friendly one.

"This guy comes out, pointing a gun at me. I hold up my hands, but he comes right up to me. He starts telling me this story about how Philip was supposed to kill him and he had to take off in the middle of the night, leave everything behind. I was with Philip, although I don't remember it, and he blamed me, too. Which, I guess, is fair. He goes on, saying that he and his girlfriend capped Philip and that I'm next."

"And he told you all this?"

I nod my head. "I guess he wanted to be sure I was afraid."

"Were you afraid?" asks Agent Jones.

"Yeah," I say, nodding. "Of course I was scared."

Agent Hunt scowls. "Was he alone?"

"The girlfriend was there. Beth, I think. Her picture was in those files you gave me. I don't think she's a professional. She didn't act like one. I guess that's how she wound up walking in front of a camera."

"How come he came back now, after all this time?"

"He said that Philip no longer had Zacharov's protection."

"Is that true?"

"I don't know," I say. "I'm no laborer. At the time I didn't really care. I had to do something, so I rushed him."

"Did the gun go off?"

"Yeah," I say. "Two in the ceiling. Plaster everywhere. My hand hit his skin and I changed his heart to glass."

"Then what?" Agent Jones asks.

"The woman screamed and grabbed for the gun," I say. My hands feel clammy. I concentrate on minimizing my tells. Thinking of the last time I told this story, I make sure not to use the same language, so it doesn't seem like a memorized speech. "She ran."

"Did she shoot at you?"

I shake my head. "Like I said, she ran."

"Now, why do you think that is? Why not take a shot at you? You were right there. Blowback was going to knock you out in a minute. She probably could have carved you up slow." It doesn't comfort me that Agent Hunt knows so much about the way transformation blowback works, but the delight in his voice when he talks about what she could have done to me worries me even more.

"I have no idea," I say. "I guess she freaked out. Maybe she didn't know. I'm not telling you anything new here. I don't know, and no matter how many times you ask me, all I can do is guess."

"So you put him in the freezer? Sounds like you've disposed of a body before." Agent Jones says it like he's joking, but he's not.

"I watch a lot of television," I say with a meaningless wave of my hand. "Turns out bodies are heavier in real life."

"Then what? You went back to school like nothing happened?"

"Yeah, kind of," I say. "I mean, I went back to school like I'd just killed a guy and put him in my freezer. But I'm not sure you can tell the difference from the outside."

"You're a pretty cool customer, huh?" says Agent Hunt.

"I hide my inner pain under my stoic visage."

Agent Hunt looks like he would like to put his fist through my stoic visage. Then Agent Jones's phone rings and he gets up, walking out of the room. Agent Hunt follows him. His last look in my direction is some combination of suspicion and alarm, like he suddenly thinks I might be telling the truth.

I go back to my homework. My stomach growls. According to my watch it's nearly seven.

It takes them twenty minutes to come back.

"Okay, kid," Agent Hunt says when they do. "We found the body in the freezer, just like you said. Just one last question. Where are his clothes?"

"Oh," I say. For a moment my mind goes blank. I knew I forgot something. "Oh, yeah." I force a shrug. "I dropped them into the river. I thought maybe it would suggest he'd drowned, if someone found them. No one did, though."

Hunt gives me a long look, then nods once. "We also visited Bethenny Thomas and recovered two guns, although ballistics will still need to match the bullets. Now let's see you transform something."

"Oh, right. The show," I say, standing up.

I strip off my gloves slowly and press my hands down onto the cool, dry surface of the table.

At eleven that night I call Barron from my car.

"Okay," I say. "I made my decision."

"You really had no choice," he says, smug. He sounds very big-brotherly, like he already warned me not to cross the street by myself and there I am on the other side, cars whizzing by and no way back. Just as casual as that. I wonder if Barron really doesn't feel violated, if he's so steeped in magic and violence that he believes cursing and blackmailing one another is just what brothers do.

"No," I say. "No choice at all."

"Okay," he says, laughter in his voice. He sounds relaxed now, no longer wary. "I'll let them know."

"I'm not doing it," I say. "*That's* my decision. I'm not working for the Brennans. I'm not going to be an assassin."

"I could go to the Feds, you know," he says stiffly. "Don't be an idiot, Cassel."

"Go, then," I say. "Go ahead. But if you do, then they'll know what I am. You'll lose the ability to control me. I'll be common property." It's easy to bluff now, when the Feds already know what I am.

There is a long pause on the other end of the line. Finally he says, "Can we talk about this in person?"

"Sure," I say. "I can sneak out of Wallingford. Pick me up."

"I don't know," he says sourly. "I don't want to encourage your delinquency."

"There's a store near the school," I say. "Be there or be square."

"It'll take me fifteen minutes."

When we hang up, I look out the window of the car. My chest feels tight, cramped, the way my legs would sometimes get after running—a pain so sudden that it would wake me from a sound sleep.

There's only one thing to do when that happens. You wait for it to pass.

I figure that the Benz will make Barron nervous about my loyalties, so I wait for him on foot, leaning against the concrete wall. Mr. Gazonas, who owns the corner store, looked at me sadly from behind the counter when I came in and bought a coffee.

"You should be in school," he said, then looked at the clock. "You should be asleep."

"I know," I said, putting my money on the counter. "I've got family troubles."

"No trouble ever got fixed late at night," he said. "Midnight is for regrets."

I don't like to think about that as I sip coffee and twiddle my thumbs, but everything else I've got to think about, I like even less.

Barron's only a half hour late. He pulls up and rolls down his window. "Okay," he says. "Where do you want to go?"

"Somewhere private," I say, getting into the car.

We drive a couple of blocks until we come to an old cemetery. He pulls onto the pebbled road, past a NO TRESPASSING sign.

"Look," I say. "I get that you have something on me. You could run your mouth. Tell people what I am and what I've done. Hell, you could scream it from every rooftop. I would be screwed. My life would be over."

He frowns. I can't tell if he's considering what I said or just scheming.

"The thing is," I say, "I could change my face and start a totally different life. All I'd need is a name and a Social Security number. I'm pretty confident that Mom raised me well enough to commit a little identity theft."

He looks startled, like he'd never even considered that.

"I don't want to be a murderer," I say.

"Don't think of it like that," he says, leaning over and picking up my coffee from the cup holder. He takes a long swallow. "The people we'd be taking out aren't good guys. Let me explain how this would work. The Brennans don't even have to meet you. They'll just get to see your work. I'm your agent and accomplice and fall guy. I help you set up the crimes, and I hide your identity."

"What about school?"

"What about it?" he asks.

"I'm not leaving Wallingford."

He nods, lip curling up. "Now that Lila's at Wallingford, I just bet you don't want to leave. It always comes back to her, doesn't it?"

I frown. "So why couldn't I do this on my own? Cut you out?"

"Because you need me to do the research," he says, clearly relieved to be asked a question he can easily answer. "I'll make sure we find the right person on the right night. And, of course, I'll make sure the witnesses don't remember anything."

"Of course," I echo.

"So?" he says. "Come on. We could make a lot of money. And I could even make you forget—"

"No," I say, cutting him off. "I don't think so. I don't want to do it."

"Cassel," he says desperately. "Please. Look, you've *got* to. *Please*, Cassel."

For a moment I am uncertain about everything.

"I don't," I say finally. The inside of the car feels stuffy, cramped. I want to get out. "Just take me back to Wallingford."

"I already took a job," he says. "I was so sure that you'd say yes."

I freeze. "Barron, come on. You can't manipulate me like this. I'm not going to—"

"Just this once," he says. "One time. If you hate it, if it goes to hell, we never have to do it again."

I hesitate. After I changed Barron's notebooks, he became the brother I always wanted. There's always a price. "So instead of pizza night, we're supposed to bond over murder?"

"So you'll do it?" he asks.

I feel sick. For a moment I really think I am going to throw up. He looks so genuinely pleased by the idea that I might agree. "Who?" I ask, leaning my head against the cool glass of the window. "Who's this victim?"

He waves his hand in the air dismissively. "His name's Emil Lombardo. No one you know. Total psycho."

I am glad my face is turned, so he can't see my expression. "Okay," I say. "Just this once."

He claps me on the shoulder just as a car pulls between the pillars behind us. Red and blue lights whirl, sending the gravestones into bizarre strobing relief.

Barron punches the dashboard. "*Cops.*"

"It does say no trespassing," I remind him, pointing toward the sign.

He leans down and peels off one of his gloves.

"What are you doing?" I ask.

He raises his eyebrows, his lip quirking on one side. "Getting out of a ticket."

The floodlight on the cop car turns on suddenly, making spots dance behind my eyes.

I look nervously through the rear window. One of the officers has gotten out and is walking toward us. I take a deep breath.

Barron rolls down the window, a grin splitting his face. "Good evening, sir."

I grab Barron's wrist in my gloved hand before he can strike. He looks at me, too shocked to register that he ought to be angry, as Agent Hunt lowers the barrel of a gun to his face.

"Barron Sharpe, step out of the car," Hunt says.

"What?" he demands.

"I'm Agent Hunt, remember?" Agent Hunt looks pleased for the first time since I've met him. "We had a nice conversation about your brother. You told us a bunch of things that didn't quite check out."

Barron nods his head, glances at me. "I remember you."

"We just heard your very interesting proposition," Agent Hunt says. In the side mirror, I see Agent Jones get out of the car.

He walks around to my side and opens the door. Barron turns toward me.

I do the only thing I can think of. I lift up my shirt to show him the wire.

"Sorry," I say. "But I figured that if you could force me to work for someone, then you couldn't be too mad if I did the same to you. I enrolled us in a program."

He looks like he doesn't quite agree with my logic.

I think of Grandad sitting in his backyard, looking up at the sky, wishing things could have been different for us kids. I'm sure this wasn't what he was picturing.

So what if I led the horse directly to water, I tell myself. *It's not like I made him drink.*

They slap the cuffs on Barron. Good thing I've already negotiated his deal, because Hunt and Jones look like they'd much rather lock him in a deep dark hole than work with him. I recognize the look. It's the same one they give me.

CHAPTER SEVENTEEN

THE HARDEST THING IS making sure that I don't have a tail. Agent Hunt gave me a lift back to my car at Wallingford, which made me nervous. I drive around aimlessly for about an hour, until I'm sure there's no one behind me.

The streets are nearly empty. This late at night, there are few good reasons to be on the road.

Finally I head to the hotel. I park in the far back, near the Dumpsters. The night air is like a slap in the face. It seems too early in the season for the temperature to have dropped so abruptly. Maybe it's just colder at three in the morning.

The hotel she picked is brick, with a central building and then a couple of other buildings that form a C-shape around a greenish pool. All the rooms open onto the outdoors, so there's no need to walk through a lobby.

She's in room 411. Upstairs. I knock three times. I hear the chain slide, and then the door opens.

My brother's widow looks less gaunt than she did the last time I saw her, but her eyes are as bruised as ever. Her hair is a silky brown tangle, and she's wearing a tight black dress that I in no way deserve.

"You're late." She motions me inside and locks the door. Then she leans against it. Her hands and feet are bare, and I have to remind myself that she's not a worker.

Her suitcase is open in one corner, and her clothes are spread across the floor. I move a slip off the one chair in the room and sit down. "Sorry," I say. "Everything takes longer than you think it will."

"You want a drink?" Maura asks me, indicating a bottle of Cuervo and a couple of plastic cups.

I shake my head.

"I knew you'd figure it out." She drops a couple of cubes into the cup and gives herself a generous pour. "You want to hear the story?"

"Let me tell it," I say. "I want to see how much I actually figured out."

She takes her glass and goes over to the bed, where she lies down on her stomach. I'm pretty sure this isn't her first drink.

"Philip and you had one of those relationships that was all ups and downs, right? Highs and lows. Lots of screaming. Passionate."

"Yeah," she says, looking at me oddly.

"Oh, come on," I say. "He was my brother. I know what *all* his relationships were like. Anyway, maybe the fighting got to be too much for you, or maybe it was different after you had the baby, but at some point Barron got involved. Started making you forget fights you'd had with Philip. Made you forget you'd decided to leave him."

"That's when you gave me the amulet," she says. I think of handing it to her in the kitchen of the apartment, my nephew howling in the background, Grandad snoring on a chair in the living room.

I nod. "He made me forget a lot too."

She throws back a good portion of the liquid in her glass.

"And you'd already started to get some pretty bad side effects." I think of her sitting at the top of the stairs, legs dangling off the edge, her whole body moving in time with a song I couldn't hear.

"You mean the music," she says. "I miss it, you know?"

"You said it was beautiful."

"I used to play the clarinet in middle school—did you know that? I wasn't very good, but I can still read music." She laughs. "I tried to write down snatches of it—a few notes, even—but it's all gone. I may never hear it again."

"It was an auditory hallucination. I get headaches. Be glad it's gone."

Maura makes a face. "That is a very unromantic explanation."

"Yeah." I sigh. "So anyway. You realized what Barron and Philip were doing to you and you split. Took your son."

"Your nephew has a name," she says. "It's Aaron. You never say it. Aaron."

I flinch. For some reason I never connected the kid with me. He was always Philip's son, Maura's son, not my *nephew*. Not someone with a name who'll grow up to be another screwed-up member of my screwed-up family.

"You took Aaron," I say. "Philip guessed that I had something to do with you two leaving, by the way."

She nods. There's a story there, one about the slow realization of how betrayed she really was, one where she jumped a little as she felt the amulet pinned under her shirt splitting. One where she had to think fast and not gasp, and keep pretending even when she must have felt drowned by horror. But she doesn't move to tell it, and it's her story to tell or not tell. My brothers did this to her. She doesn't owe me anything.

"So you've got a big family, right? Or a best friend who moved to the South. Someone you thought you'd be safe staying with in Arkansas. You get in your car and just go. Maybe trade it in for another vehicle. You're using your maiden name, and even though you figure Philip is going to freak out about you taking his son, you know that you've got lots on him. You're sure that he's going to be afraid of you going to the police, so you never even consider that *he* will.

"You're careful, but not careful enough. Maybe it's hard to find you, but far from impossible. So when the Feds call, looking for you, with stories about your husband going into witness protection and wanting you with him, you freak out. The Feds need you—Philip wouldn't give them what they wanted until he saw you—so I'm sure they didn't care about your feelings. Your country needed you."

Maura nods.

"You realize you'll never get away from him. Legally, with the Feds helping him out, he might be able to get joint custody of your son. You might even be forced to live nearby—and then maybe a couple of his friends would come over. Either they'd work you or they'd work you over, but you knew he could get you back. You knew that you were in danger."

She's watching me like I'm a snake, coiling back and ready to strike.

"You know where Philip keeps his guns. You drive up from Arkansas, you take one, and you shoot him."

At the word "shoot" she flinches. Then she swallows the rest of her tequila.

"You wear a big coat and those very lovely red gloves. Security had put in cameras outside the condos recently. Luckily for you, all they could tell was that the person who entered Philip's apartment that night was a woman."

"What?" She sits up and stares at me like I've finally surprised her. She presses both her hands to her mouth. "No. There was a camera?"

"Don't worry," I say. "After, you toss the clothes and the gun someplace where you figure they'll be safe. My house. Mom's out of jail, after all. You figure she'll be hoarding again in no time. A garbage house really would be a great place to hide evidence—under so much crap that even cops aren't going to have the patience to sort through it all."

"I guess I'm no criminal genius, though," she says. "You found them. And I had no idea about being taped."

"There's just one thing I didn't figure out," I say. "When I talked to the Feds, they said they spoke to you in Arkansas the morning after Philip's murder. That's at least a twenty-hour drive. There's no way you shot him and got back in time to take that call. How did you do it?"

She smiles. "You and your mother taught me. The agents called my house. Then my brother called me on a prepaid cell phone with an Arkansas area code. He conference-called me and then called back the federal agents. Simple. It looked like I was returning their call from home. Just like how I had to help your mother make all those calls from jail."

"I am all admiration," I say. "I actually thought the coat and gloves and gun belonged to Mom, until I saw the amulet I gave you. The one you left in the pocket."

"I made a lot of mistakes. I see that now," she says, pulling a gun from underneath the covers and leveling it at me. "You understand I can't afford to make any more."

"Oh, absolutely," I say. "So you sure don't want to kill the guy who just framed someone for his own brother's murder."

The gun wavers in her hand.

"You didn't," she says. "Why would you?"

"I tried to protect Philip when he was alive." I'm sincere, although I'm sure she's used to sincere liars. "I don't think he believed that, but I did. Now that he's dead, I'm trying to protect you."

"So you're really not going to tell anyone," she says.

I stand, and the gun comes up.

"I'll take it to my grave," I say, and grin. She's not smiling.

Then I turn and walk out of the hotel room.

For a moment I think I hear a click, and my muscles stiffen, anticipating the bullet. Then the moment's past and I keep moving—out of the room, down the stairs, and into my car. There's this old Greek myth about this guy named Orpheus. He goes down to Hades to get his wife back, but he loses her again because on the way out of hell, he looks behind him to see if she's really there.

That's how I feel. Like if I look back, the spell will be broken. I'll be dead.

It's only when I pull out of the parking lot that I can breathe again.

I don't want to go back to Wallingford. I just can't face it. Instead I drive down to Carney and bang on Grandad's door. It's well past the middle of the night, but eventually he answers, wrapped in a bathrobe.

"Cassel?" he says. "Did something happen?"

I shake my head.

He waves to me with his good hand. "Well, get in here. You're letting in all the cold air, standing in the doorway."

I walk into his dining room. There's some mail on the table, along with a bunch of wilted flowers from the funeral. It seems like it happened so long ago, but really it's just been a few weeks since Philip died.

On the sideboard are a bunch of photos, most of them of the three of us kids when we were little, doing a lot of running through sprinklers and posing awkwardly, our arms around one another, on lawns. There are other photos too, older ones of Grandad with Mom in her wedding dress, Grandma, and one of Grandad and Zacharov at what looks like Lila's parents' wedding. The expensive-looking wedding band on Zacharov's finger is pretty distinctive.

"I'm going to put on the kettle," he says.

"That's okay," I say. "I'm not thirsty."

"Did I ask you?" Grandad looks at me sternly. "You take a cup, you drink it, and then I'll make up a bed for you in the spare room. Don't you have school tomorrow?"

"Yeah," I say, chastened.

"I'll call them in the morning. Tell them you're going to be a little late."

"I've been late a lot," I say. "Missed a lot of classes. I think I'm failing physics."

"Death messes you up. Even a fancy school like yours knows that." He goes into the kitchen.

I sit down at the table in the dark. Now that I'm here, I feel a calm settle over me that I can't explain. I just want to be here, sitting at this table, forever. I don't want to move.

Eventually there is a metallic whistle from the kitchen. Grandad comes back, setting down two mugs. He flicks a switch on the wall, and the electric lights of the chandelier glow so brightly that I shade my eyes.

The tea is black and sweet, and I'm surprised that I've finished half of it in a single gulp.

"You want to tell me what's going on?" he asks finally. "Why you're here in the middle of the night?"

"Not really," I say as forthrightly as I can manage. I don't want to lose this. I wonder if he'd even let me into his house if he knew I was working for the government, no less that I blackmailed my brother into joining me. I'm not even sure they allow federal agents into the worker town of Carney.

He takes a slug from his cup and then winces, like maybe his doesn't have tea in it. "Are you in some kind of trouble?"

"I don't think so," I say. "Not anymore."

"I see." He stands and shuffles over to put his ruined hand on my shoulder. "Come on, kid. I think it's time for you to get to bed."

"Thanks," I say, getting up.

We go into the back room, the same room where I slept when I spent the summers in Carney. Grandad brings in some blankets and a pair of pajamas for me to sleep in. I think they might be an old pair of Barron's.

"Whatever's eating you," he says, "it's never worse in the morning."

I sit down on the corner of the mattress and smile wearily. "G'night, Grandad."

He pauses in the doorway. "You know Elsie Cooper's oldest son? Born crazy. He can't help it. No one knows how come he turned out like that—he just did."

"Yeah," I say vaguely. I remember people in Carney talking about how he never left the house, but I can't recall much else. I look over at the folded pajamas. My limbs feel so heavy that even thinking about putting them on is an effort. I have no idea where Grandad's story is supposed to be going.

"You were always good, Cassel," he says as he closes the door. "No idea how you turned out that way—you just did. Like the crazy Cooper kid. You can't help it."

"I'm not good," I say. "I play everybody. *Everybody.* All the time."

He snorts. "Goodness don't come for free."

I'm too tired to argue. He switches off the light, and I'm asleep before I even crawl underneath the covers.

Grandad calls school to tell them I won't be there for classes today, and I basically just sit around his house all morning. We watch *Band of the Banned* reruns and he makes some kind of turmeric beef stew in the Crock-Pot. It comes out pretty good.

He lets me stretch out on the couch with an afghan, like I'm sick. We even eat in front of the television.

When it's time to go, he packs up some of the stew into a clean Cool Whip container and hands it to me along with a bottle of orange soda. "You better go study that physics," he says.

"Yeah," I say.

He pauses when he sees the shiny new Benz. We look at each other silently over the hood for a moment, but all he says is, "Tell that mother of yours to give me a call."

"I will, Grandad. Thanks for letting me spend the night."

His brows furrow. "You better not say anything stupid like that to me again."

"All right." I grin, holding up my hands in a gesture of surrender. Then I get into the car.

He slaps the hood. "Bye, kid."

I drive off. I get twenty minutes out of Carney before I drink the orange soda. By the time I arrive at Wallingford, I've missed most of the day. I roll into the break period after study hall and before lights-out.

Sam is sitting on the striped couch of the common lounge, next to Jeremy Fletcher-Fiske. A newscaster is on the television, talking about football. Some guys are playing cards on a folding table. Another senior, Jace, is watching a carrot on a plate rotate in the microwave.

"Hey," I say, waving.

"Dude," says Sam. "Long time, no see. Where have you been?"

"Just family stuff," I say, sitting down on the arm of the couch.

Tomorrow I am going to have to get my homework from teachers. I'm going to have to start buckling down if I want to pass everything this semester, but I figure that tonight I might as well just relax.

On the screen another announcer starts in on the local news. He says that on Sunday, Governor Patton held a brunch where his unexpected and controversial announcement had his constituents up in arms.

They show a clip of a big ballroom covered in tables and Patton up on a podium with a blue curtain behind him and my mother standing nearby, along with another guy in a suit. Her hair is pulled back and she's wearing a yellow dress with short white gloves. She looks like a costumer's idea of a politician's wife. I am so busy trying to make out her expression that for a moment I don't realize what Patton's saying on the clip.

"—and furthermore, after consideration, I have come to realize that my stance was an unrealistic one. While having access to information regarding who is or is not hyperbathygammic would be convenient for law enforcement, I now see that the price for that convenience is too high. Worker rights groups have made the point that it's unlikely the information would remain confidential. As governor, I cannot countenance any risk to the privacy of New Jersey citizens, especially when that privacy may protect their lives and livelihoods. Even though I have been in the past a strong supporter of proposition two, I am withdrawing that support as of this moment. I no longer believe that mandatory testing for workers is something this government should tolerate, no less dictate."

I must be staring at the screen in horror.

"Crazy, right?" asks Jeremy. "Everyone's saying that the guy got paid off. Or worked."

Sam flinches. "Oh, come on. Maybe he just grew a conscience."

That's the brunch my mother invited me to, the one she said I'd love. *Baby, I know what I'm doing.*

A shiver runs down my back. The news has moved on to coverage of an earthquake, but I am still stuck with the memory of my mother's face on that clip. If you didn't know her, you wouldn't notice it, but she was fighting back a smile.

She worked him. There is no doubt in my mind.

I want to scream. There's no way to get her out of this. There's no way it won't be discovered.

Sam is speaking, but the buzzing in my head is so loud, it drowns out all other sounds.

I call my mother dozens of times that night, but she never picks up. I fall asleep with the phone still in my hand and wake up when its alarm goes off the next morning. I drag myself through my classes. I'm behind in everything. I stumble through answers, fail a quiz in statistics, and botch a French translation to great hilarity.

When I get up to my room, I find Daneca waiting for me. She's sitting on Sam's bed, her clunky brown shoes kicking the bed frame absently. Her eyes are red-rimmed.

"Hey," I say. "I don't know where Sam is. I haven't seen him since I passed him in the hall on the way to Physics."

She pushes a thick braid off her shoulder and straightens up like she's steeling herself to do something unpleasant. "He already went to play practice. He's still acting weird, and I'm not here to see him, anyway. I have to talk to you."

I nod, although I'm not in the frame of mind to say anything remotely sensible. "Sure. Fine."

"It's about Lila."

She couldn't go through with it, I realize. "That's okay,"

I say lightly. "Maybe it was a terrible idea anyway."

"No, Cassel," Daneca says. "You don't understand. I really screwed up."

"What?" My heart is a drum, beating out of time. I toss my backpack onto my bed and sit down beside it. "What do you mean—'screwed up'?"

Daneca looks relieved that I finally seem to understand her. She scoots forward, leaning in toward me. "Lila caught me. I'm an idiot. It must have been obvious what I was trying."

I picture Daneca trying to get off her glove without Lila noticing. It didn't occur to me until now how hard it must have been. Daneca doesn't know how to brush someone accidentally, the way you need to for a working or to lift a wallet. She's no expert at sleight of hand.

"So you didn't—," I say. "So you didn't work her?" All I feel is relief so intense that I almost laugh.

I'm glad. Horribly, shockingly glad.

I can learn to live with guilt. I don't care about being good. I can learn to live with anything if it means being with Lila too.

Daneca shakes her head. "She made me tell her everything. She can be really frightening, you know."

"Oh," I say. "Yeah, she can be."

"She made me promise not to say anything to you," Daneca says, voice low.

I look out the window. There are so many thoughts running through my head, it's like I'm not thinking at all. But still I force myself to give her a quick smile. "She didn't think you would break a *promise*? We've got to do something about that reputation of yours, Goody Two-shoes."

"I'm sorry," Daneca says, ignoring my attempt at humor.

"It's not your fault," I say. "I shouldn't have asked you. It wasn't fair."

She stands up and starts toward the door.

"See you at dinner," she says, looking at me with surprising fondness.

As the door closes behind Daneca, I feel a terrible wave of emotion sweep through me, reckless joy and horror so mixed up that I don't know what to feel first.

I tried to make myself do the right thing. Maybe I didn't try hard enough. All I know right now is that I love Lila, and for a little while she'll love me back.

When I find Lila, she's heading toward the library. The collar of her shirt is open and the white silk scarf around her throat flutters in the wind. She looks like she's about to go for a drive in a car with the top down.

"Hey," I say, jogging up alongside her. "Can we talk for a minute?"

"Cassel," she says, like my name tastes sour on her tongue. She doesn't slow.

"I know you're probably furious about Daneca," I say, walking backward so I can look at her while I'm talking. "And you have every right to be. But let me explain."

"Can you?" Lila says, stopping abruptly. "I'm not a toy you can just turn off."

"I know that," I say.

"How could you think that it would be okay to work me? How would it be any different from what your mother did?" She looks like she feels a little bit sorry for me and a little bit disgusted. "The curse is over. We're over."

"Oh." Of course. I grit my teeth against the reflexive flinch. All I can hear is my mother's words in Atlantic City: *She wouldn't have given you the time of day, Cassel.*

"It wasn't enough for you to have your joke, pretending to love me, pretending you weren't pretending—" She stops herself, closing her eyes for a moment. When she opens them again, they're bright with fury. "I'm not cursed anymore. I'm not going to grovel for your attention. It must have been thrilling to have me sigh over *every one* of your thoughtless smiles, but that's never going to happen again."

"That's not what it was like," I say. I'm stunned, all of my months of pain and panic reduced, in her eyes, to gloating.

"I'm not weak, Cassel. I'm not the kind of girl who cries over you." Her voice shakes. "I'm not the girl who does whatever you want whenever you want it."

"That's why I asked Daneca—," I say, but I can't finish. It's not even true. I asked Daneca to work her because I was starting to believe the illusion. Daneca was trying to save me from myself.

"You wanted to make me feel nothing for you?" Lila says. "Well, let me do you one better. I *hate* you. How about that? I hate you, and you didn't have to do a thing to make me."

"Come on, now," I say. I can hear the self-loathing in my voice. "I did plenty." I lost Lila the moment my mother cursed her. Everything else was just a pathetic game of pretend. None of it real.

Her expression wavers, then smoothes out into a mask of blandness. "Good-bye, Cassel," she says, and turns to go. Her head is bent and her scarf must have shifted, because I glimpse redness along her throat. From this angle it looks like the edge of a burn.

"What is that?" I say, walking after her, pointing to my own collar.

"*Don't*," she says warningly, holding up her gloved hand. But there is something in her face that wasn't there a moment ago—fear.

I grab one end of her scarf. It comes unknotted with a single pull.

Her pale throat is cut, one side to the other, newly scabbed and dark with ash. The criminal's second smile. A glittering choker of dried blood.

"You're—," I start. But of course, she always was. A crime boss's daughter. Mobster royalty.

Talking with someone who just signed up to be a federal agent.

"The ceremony was on Sunday," she says. "I told you I was going to be the head of the Zacharov family someday. No one starts at the top, though. I have a long way to go. First I have to prove my loyalty. Even me."

"Ah." Lila has always known who she was and what she wanted. There is something horrifyingly final about her scar, like a shut door. She's not afraid of her future. "Brave," I say, and I mean it.

For a moment she looks like she wants to tell me more. Her mouth opens, and then I see her swallow those words, whatever they were. She takes a deep breath and says, "If you don't stay away from me, I'll make you sorry you were ever born."

There's nothing to say to that, so I say nothing. I can already feel numbness creeping into my heart.

She continues her walk across the quad.

I watch her go. Watch the shadow of her steps and her straight back and the gleam of her hair.

I remind myself that this is what I wanted. When that doesn't work, I tell myself that I can survive on memories. The smell of Lila's skin, the way her eyes shine with mischief, the low rasp of her voice. It hurts to think of her, but I can't stop. It ought to hurt.

After all, hell is supposed to be hot.

ACKNOWLEDGMENTS

Several books were really helpful in creating the world of the curse workers. In particular, David W. Maurer's *The Big Con*; Sam Lovell's *How to Cheat at Everything*; Kent Walker and Mark Schone's *Son of a Grifter*; and Karl Taro Greenfeld's *Speed Tribes*.

I am deeply indebted to many people for their insight into this book. Thanks to Cassandra Clare, Robin Wasserman, Sarah Rees Brennan, and Delia Sherman, who were always kind enough to stop what they were doing and help me work through problems during our Mexican writing retreat. Thanks to Libba Bray and Jo Knowles for helping me enormously with the push to the end. I am grateful to Justine Larbalestier for talking with me about liars and to Scott Westerfeld for his detailed notes. Thanks to Joe Monti for his enthusiasm and book recommendations. Thanks to Elka Cloke for her medical expertise. Thanks to Kathleen Duey for pushing me to think about the larger world issues. Thanks to Kelly Link, Ellen Kushner, Gavin Grant, Sarah Smith, and Joshua Lewis for looking at very rough drafts. Thanks to Steve Berman for his help working out many, many details, especially in that last draft.

Most of all, I have to thank my agent, Barry Goldblatt, for his encouragement; my editor, Karen Wojtyla, who pushed me to make the book far better than I thought it could be; and my husband, Theo, who gave me lots of advice about private school and scams, and who let me read the whole thing to him out loud.

KEEP READING FOR YOUR FIRST HINT OF *BLACK HEART*, THE THIRD BOOK OF THE CURSE WORKERS SERIES

BLACK
HEART

HOLLY BLACK

NEW YORK TIMES BESTSELLING AUTHOR

MY BROTHER BARRON

sits next to me, sucking the last dregs of milk tea slush noisily through a wide yellow straw. He's got the seat of my Benz pushed all the way back and his feet up on the dash, the heels of his pointy black shoes scratching the plastic. With his hair slicked back and his mirrored sunglasses covering his eyes, he looks like a study in villainy.

He's actually a junior federal agent, still in training, sure, but with a key card and an ID badge and everything.

To be fair, he's also a villain.

I tap my gloved fingers impatiently against the curve of the wheel and bring a pair of binoculars to my eyes for about the millionth time. All I see is a boarded-up building on the wrong side of Queens. "What is she *doing* in there? It's been forty minutes."

"What do you think?" he asks me. "Bad things. That's her after-school job now. Taking care of shady business so Zacharov's gloves stay clean."

"Her dad won't put her in any real danger," I say, but the tone of my voice makes it pretty obvious I'm trying to convince myself more than I'm trying to convince my brother.

Barron snorts. "She's a new soldier. Got to prove herself. Zacharov couldn't keep her out of danger if he tried—and he's not going to be trying real hard. The other laborers are watching, waiting for her to be weak. Waiting for her to screw up. He knows that. So should you."

I think of her at twelve, a skinny girl with eyes too large for her face and a nimbus of tangled blond hair. In my memory she's sitting on the branch of a tree, eating a rope of red licorice. Her lips are sticky with it. Her flip-flops are hanging off her toes. She's cutting her initials into the bark, high up, so her cousin can't claim she's lying when she tells him she got higher than he ever will.

Boys never believe I can beat them, she told me back then. *But I always win in the end.*

"Maybe she spotted the car and went out the back," I say finally.

"No way she made us." He sucks on the straw again. It makes that rattling empty-cup sound, echoing through the car. "We're like ninjas."

"Somebody's cocky," I say. After all, tailing someone isn't easy, and Barron and I aren't that good at it yet, no matter what he says. My handler at the agency, Yulikova, has been encouraging me to shadow Barron, so I can learn second-hand and can keep myself safe until she figures out how to tell her bosses that she's got hold of a teenage transformation worker with a bad attitude and a criminal record. And since Yulikova's in charge, Barron's stuck teaching me. It's supposed to be just for a few months, until I graduate from Wallingford. Let's see if we can stand each other that long.

Of course, I'm pretty sure this isn't the kind of lesson Yulikova's been imagining.

Barron grins, white teeth flashing like dropped dice. "What do you think Lila Zacharov would do if she knew you were tailing her?"

I grin back. "Probably she'd kill me."

He nods. "Probably she would. Probably she'd kill me twice for helping you."

"Probably you deserve it," I say. He snorts.

Over the last few months I got every last thing I ever wanted—and then I threw it all away. Everything I thought I could never have was offered up on a silver platter—the girl, the power, a job at the right hand of Zacharov, the most formidable man I know. It wouldn't even have been that hard to work for him. It probably would have been fun. And if I didn't care who I hurt, it would still all be mine.

I lift the binoculars and study the door again—the worn paint striping the boards and crumbling like bread crumbs, the chewed-up bottom edge as ragged as if it had been gnawed on by rats.

Lila would still be mine.

Mine. The language of love is like that, possessive. That should be the first warning that it's not going to encourage anyone's betterment.

Barron groans and throws his cup into the backseat. "I can't believe that you blackmailed me into becoming Johnny Law and now I have to sweat it out five days a week with the other recruits while you use my experience to stalk your girlfriend. How is that fair?"

"*One*, I think you mean the extremely dubious benefit of your experience. *Two*, Lila's not my girlfriend. *Three*, I just wanted to make sure she was okay." I count off these points on my leather-covered fingers. "And *four*, the last thing you should want is *fairness.*"

"Stalk her at school," Barron says, ignoring everything I've just said. "Come on. I have to make a phone call. Let's pack in this lesson and get a couple of slices. I'll even buy."

I sigh. The car is stuffy and smells like old coffee. I'd like to stretch my legs. And Barron is probably right—we should give this up. Not for the reason he's saying but for the one that's implied. The one about it not being okay to lurk around outside buildings, spying on girls you like.

My fingers are reaching reluctantly for my keys when she walks out of the worn door, as though my giving up summoned her. She's got on tall black riding boots and a steel gray trench. I study the quicksilver gestures of her gloved hands, the sway of her earrings, the slap of her heels on the steps, and the lash of her hair. She's so beautiful, I can barely breathe. Behind her follows a boy with his hair braided into the shape of two antelope horns. His skin is darker than mine. He's got on baggy jeans and a hoodie. He's shoving a folded-up wad of something that looks like cash into an inside pocket.

Outside of school Lila doesn't bother wearing a scarf. I can see the grim necklace of marks on her throat, scars black where ash was rubbed into them. That's part of the ceremony when you join her father's crime family, slicing your skin and swearing that you're dead to your old life and reborn into wickedness. Not even Zacharov's daughter was spared it.

She's one of them now. No turning back.

"Well, now," says Barron, gleeful. "I bet you're thinking we just observed the end of a very naughty transaction. But let's consider the possibility that actually we caught her doing something totally innocent yet embarrassing."

I look at him absently. "Embarrassing?"

"Like meeting up to play one of those card games where you have to collect everything. Pokémon. Magic the Gathering. Maybe they're training for a tournament. With all that money she just handed him, I'm guessing he won."

"Funny."

"Maybe he's tutoring her in Latin. Or they were painting miniatures together. Or he's teaching her shadow puppetry." He makes a duck-like gesture with one gloved hand.

I punch Barron's shoulder, but not really hard. Just hard enough to make him shut up. He laughs and adjusts his sunglasses, pushing them higher on his nose.

The boy with the braids crosses the street, head down,

hood pulled up to shadow his face. Lila walks to the corner and raises her hand to hail a cab. The wind whips at her hair, making it a nimbus of blown gold.

I wonder if she's done her homework for Monday.

I wonder if she could ever love me again.

I wonder just how mad she'd be if she knew I was here, watching her. Probably really, really mad.

Cold October air floods into the car suddenly, tossing around the empty cup in the backseat.

"Come on," Barron says, leaning on the door, grinning down at me. I didn't even notice him getting out. "Grab some quarters for the meter, and your stuff." He jerks his head in the direction of the boy with the braids. "We're going to follow him."

"What about that phone call?" I shiver in my thin green T-shirt. My leather jacket is wadded up in the backseat of my car. I reach for it and shrug it on.

"I was bored," Barron says. "Now I'm not."

This morning when he told me we were going to practice tailing people, I picked Lila as my target half as a joke, half out of sick desire. I didn't think that Barron would agree. I didn't think that we'd actually see her leaving her apartment building and getting into a town car. I for sure didn't think that I would wind up here, close to actually finding out what she's been doing when she's not in school.

I get out of the car and slam the door behind me.

That's the problem with temptation. It's so damn tempting.

"Feels almost like real agent work, doesn't it?" Barron says as we walk down the street, heads bowed against the wind. "You know, if we caught your girlfriend committing a crime, I bet Yulikova would give us a bonus or something for being prize pupils."

"Except that we're not going to do that," I say.

"I thought you wanted us to be good guys." He grins a too-wide grin. He's enjoying needling me, and my reacting only makes it worse, but I can't stop.

"Not if it means hurting her," I say, my voice as deadly as I can make it. "Never her."

"Got it. Hurting, bad. But how do you excuse stalking her and her friends, little brother?"

"I'm not excusing it," I say. "I'm just doing it."

Following—*stalking*—someone isn't easy. You try not to stare too hard at the back of his head, keep your distance, and act like you're just another person freezing your ass off in late October on the streets of Queens. Above all you try not to seem like a badly trained federal agent wannabe.

"Stop worrying," Barron says, strolling along beside me. "Even if we get made, this guy will probably be flattered. He'd think he was moving up in the world if he had a government tail."

Barron is better at acting casual than I am. I guess he should be. He's got nothing to lose if we're spotted. Lila couldn't possibly hate him more than she does. Plus, he probably trains for this all day, while I'm at Wallingford studying to get into the kind of college there is no way I am ever going to attend.

It still annoys me. Since I was a kid, we've competed over lots of things. Mostly, all those competitions were ones I lost.

We were the two youngest, and when Philip would be off with his friends on the weekends, Barron and I would be stuck doing whatever errands Dad needed doing, or practicing whatever skill he thought we needed to learn.

He particularly wanted us to be better at pickpocketing and lock-picking than we were.

Two kids are the perfect pickpocket team, he'd say. *One to do the lift, the other one to distract or to take the handoff.*

We both practiced dips. First identifying where Dad kept his wallet by looking for a bulge in a back pocket or the way one side of his coat swung heavily because something was inside. Then the lift. I was pretty good; Barron was better.

Then we practiced distraction. Crying. Asking for directions. Giving the mark a quarter that you claim they dropped.

It's like stage magic, Dad said. *You've got to make me look over there so I won't notice what's happening right in front of my face.*

When Dad didn't feel like fending off our clumsy attempts at lifts, he'd bring us to the barn and show us his collection: He had an old metal tackle box with locks on all the sides, so you had to run the gauntlet of seven different locks to get into it. Neither Barron nor I ever managed.

Once we learned how to open a lock with a tool, we'd have to learn to pick it with a bobby pin, with a hanger, then with a stick or some other found object. I kept hoping that I'd be naturally great at locks, since I was pretty sure I wasn't a worker back then, and since I already felt like an outsider in my family. I thought that if there was one thing I was better at than all of them, that would make up for everything else.

It sucks to be the youngest.

If you get into the supersecure box, we'll sneak into the movie of your choice, Dad would say. Or, *I put candy in there.* Or, *If you really want that video game, just open the box and I'll get it for you.* But it didn't matter what he promised. What did matter was that I only ever managed to pick three locks; Barron managed five.

And here we are again, learning a bunch of new skills. I can't help feeling a little bit competitive and a little bit disappointed in myself that I'm already so far behind. After all, Yulikova thinks Barron has a real future with the Bureau. She told me so. I told her that sociopaths are relentlessly charming.

I think she figured I was joking.

"What other stuff do they teach you at federal agent school?" I ask. It shouldn't bother me that he's fitting in so well. So what if he's faking it? Good for him.

I guess what bothers me is him faking it better than I am.

He rolls his eyes. "Nothing much. Obvious stuff—getting people to trust you with mirroring behavior. You know, doing whatever the other person's doing." He laughs. "Honestly, undercover's just like being a con man. Same techniques. Identify the target. Befriend. Then betray."

Mirroring behavior. When a mark takes a drink from his water glass, so should you. When he smiles, so should you. Keep it subtle, rather than creepy, and it's a good technique.

Mom taught it to me when I was ten. *Cassel,* she said, *you want to know how to be the most charming guy anyone's ever met? Remind them of their favorite person. Everyone's favorite person is their own damn self.*

"Except now you're the good guy," I say, and laugh.

He laughs too, like I just told the best joke in the world.

But now that I'm thinking about Mom, I can't help worrying about her. She's been missing since she got caught using her worker talent—emotion—to manipulate Governor Patton, a guy who hated curse workers to begin with and now is on national news every night with a vein popping out of his forehead, calling for her blood. I hope she stays hidden. I just wish I knew where she was.

"Barron," I say, about to start up a conversation we've already had about a million times, the one where we tell each other that she's fine and she'll contact us soon. "Do you think—"

Up ahead the boy with the braids steps into a pool hall.

"In here," Barron says, with a jerk of his head. We duck into a deli across the street. I'm grateful for the warmth. Barron orders us two coffees, and we stand near the window, waiting.

"You ever going to get over this thing with Lila?" he asks me, breaking the silence, making me wish I'd been the one to do it, so that I could have picked another subject. Any other subject. "It's like some kind of illness with you. How long have you been into her? Since you were what, eleven?"

I don't say anything.

"That's why you really wanted to follow her and her new hire, right? Because you don't think that you're worthy of her, but you're hoping that if she does something awful enough, maybe you'll deserve each other after all."

"That's not how it works," I say, under my breath. "That's not how love works."

He snorts. "You sure?"

I bite my tongue, swallowing every obnoxious taunt that comes into my mind. If he doesn't get a rise out of me, maybe he'll stop, and then maybe I can distract him. We stand like that for several minutes, until he sighs.

"Bored again. I'm going to make that phone call."

"What if he comes out?" I ask, annoyed. "How am I going to—"

He widens his eyes in mock distress. "Improvise."

The bell rings as he steps out the door, and the guy at the counter shouts his customary "Thanksforcomingcome-again."

On the sidewalk in front of the deli, Barron is flirting like crazy as he paces back and forth, dropping the names of French restaurants like he eats off a tablecloth every night. He's got his phone cradled against his cheek, smiling like he's buying the line of romantic nonsense he's selling. I feel sorry for the girl, whoever she is, but I am gleeful.

When he gets off the phone I will never stop making fun of him. Biting my tongue won't be enough to keep me from it. I would have to bite off my whole face.

He notices me grinning out the window at him, turns his back and stalks to the entranceway of a closed pawnshop half a block away. I made sure to waggle my eyebrows while he was looking in my direction.

With nothing else to do, I stay put. I drink more coffee. I play a game on my phone that involves shooting pixelated zombies.

Even though I've been waiting, I'm not really prepared when the boy with the braids walks out of the pool hall. He's got a man with him, a tall guy with hollow cheekbones and greasy hair. The boy lights a cigarette inside his cupped palm, leaning against the wall. This is one of those moments when a little more training would help. Obviously running out of the deli and waving my arms at Barron is the wrong move, but I don't know the right one if the boy starts moving again. I have no idea how to signal my brother.

Improvise, he said.

I walk out of the deli as nonchalantly as I can manage. Maybe the kid's just hit the street for a smoke. Maybe Barron will notice me and come back over on his own.

I spot a bus stop bench and lean against it, trying to get a better look at the boy.

This isn't a real assignment, I remind myself. It doesn't matter if he gets away. There's probably nothing to see. Whatever he's doing for Lila, there's no reason to think that he's doing it now.

That's when I notice the way that the boy is gesturing grandly, his cigarette trailing smoke. Misdirection, a classic of magic tricks and cons. *Look over here,* one hand says. He must be telling a joke too, because the man is laughing. But I can see his other hand, worming out of his glove.

I jump up, but I'm too late. I see a flash of bare wrist and thumb.

I start toward him, not thinking—crossing the street, barely noticing the screech of a car's brakes until I'm past it. People turn toward me, but no one is watching the boy. Even the idiot guy from the pool hall is looking in my direction.

"Run," I yell.

The hollow-cheeked man is still staring at me when the boy's hand clamps around the front of his throat.

I grab for the boy's shoulder, too late. The man, whoever he was, collapses like a sack of flour. The boy spins toward me, bare fingers reaching for skin. I catch his wrist and twist his arm as hard as I can.

He groans and punches me in the face with his gloved hand.

I stumble back. For a moment we just regard each other. I see his face up close for the first time and am surprised to notice that his eyebrows are carefully tweezed into perfect arches. His eyes are wide and brown beneath them. He narrows those eyes at me. Then he turns and runs.

I chase after him. It's automatic—instinct—and I'm wondering what I think I'm doing as I race down the sidewalk. I risk a look back at Barron, but he's turned away, bent over the phone, so that all I see is his back.

Figures.

The boy is fast, but I've been running track for the last three years. I know how to pace myself, allowing him to get ahead of me at first when he starts sprinting, but catching up once he's winded. We go down block after block, me getting closer and closer.

This is what I'm supposed to do once I'm a federal agent, right? Chase bad guys.

But that's not why I'm after him. I feel like I am hunting my own shadow. I feel like I can't stop.

He glances back at me, and I guess he sees that I'm gaining on him, because he tries a new strategy. He veers abruptly into an alley.

I take the corner in time to see him reaching for something under his hoodie. I go for the nearest weapon I can find. A plank of wood, lying near a stack of garbage.

Swinging it, I catch him just as he gets out the gun. I feel the burn of my muscles and hear the crack as wood hits metal. I knock the pistol against the brick wall like it's a baseball and I'm in the World Series.

I think I'm as surprised as he is.

Taking slow steps, I hold up the plank, which is split now, a big chunk of the top hanging off by a splinter, the remainder jagged and pointed like a spear. He watches me, every part of him tense. He doesn't look much older than I am. He might even be younger.

"Who the hell are you?" When he speaks, I can see that some of his teeth are gold, flashing in the fading sun. Three on the bottom. One on top. He's breathing hard. We both are.

I bend down and lift the gun in one shaking hand. My thumb flicks off the safety. I drop the plank.

I have no idea who I am right now.

  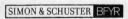